CHASING LOVE

Praise for *In Too Deep*

"*In Too Deep*, by newcomer Ronica Black, is emotional, hot, gripping, raw, and a real turn-on from start to finish, with characters you will fall in love with, root for, and never forget. A truly five star novel, you will not want to miss…"—*Midwest Book Review*

"Ronica Black's debut novel *In Too Deep* has everything from non-stop action and intriguing well-developed characters to steamy erotic love scenes. From the opening scenes where Black plunges the reader headfirst into the story to the explosive unexpected ending, *In Too Deep* has what it takes to rise to the top. Black has a winner with *In Too Deep*, one that will keep the reader turning the pages until the very last one."—*Independent Gay Writer*

"…an exciting, page turning read, full of mystery, sex, and suspense."—*MegaScene*

"…a challenging murder mystery—sections of this mixed-genre novel are hot, hot, hot. Black juggles the assorted elements of her first book with assured pacing and estimable panache."—*Q Syndicate*

"Black's characterization is skillful, and the sexual chemistry surrounding the three major characters is palpable and definitely hot-hot-hot…if you're looking for a solid read with ample amounts of eroticism and a red herring or two you're sure to find *In Too Deep* a satisfying read."—*L Word Literature*

What Reviewers Say About Ronica Black

Wild Abandon

"Black is a master at teasing the reader with her use of domination and desire. Black's first novel, *In Too Deep*, was a finalist for a 2005 Lammy…With *Wild Abandon*, the author continues her winning ways, writing like a seasoned pro. This is one romance I will not soon forget."—*Just About Write*

"The sophomore novel by Ronica Black (*In Too Deep*) is hot, hot, hot."—*Books to Watch Out For*

"If you enjoy complex characters and passionate sex scenes, you'll love *Wild Abandon*."—*MegaScene*

Hearts Aflame

"Sleek storytelling and terrific characters are the backbone of Ronica Black's third and best novel, *Hearts Aflame*. Prepare to hop on for an emotional ride with this thrilling story of love in the outback… Wonderful storytelling and rich characterization make this a high recommendation."—*Lambda Book Report*

"*Hearts Aflame* takes the reader on the rough and tumble ride… The twists and turns of the plot engage the reader all the way to the satisfying conclusion."—*Just About Write*

Deeper

"This sequel to Ronica Black's debut novel, *In Too Deep*, is an electrifying thriller. The author's development as a fine storyteller shines with this tightly written story. ...[The mystery] keeps the story charged—never unraveling or leading us to a predictable conclusion. More than once I gasped in surprise at the dark and twisted paths this book took."—Curve Magazine

Flesh and Bone

"Ronica Black handles a traditional range of lesbian fantasies with gusto and sincerity. The reader wants to know these women as well as they come to know each other. When Black's characters ignore their realistic fears to follow their passion, this reader admires their chutzpah and cheers them on...These stories make good bedtime reading, and could lead to sweet dreams. Read them and see."
—*Erotica Revealed*

The Seeker

"Ronica Black's books just keep getting stronger and stronger... This is such a tightly written plot-driven novel that readers will find themselves glued to the pages and ignoring phone calls. *The Seeker* is a great read, with an exciting plot, great characters, and great sex."—*Just About Write*

Visit us at www.boldstrokesbooks.com

By the Author

CHASING LOVE

by
Ronica Black

2010

CHASING LOVE

ISBN 10: 1-60282-192-5
ISBN 13: 978-1-60282-192-7

This Trade Paperback Original Is Published By
Bold Strokes Books, Inc.
P.O. Box 249
Valley Falls, NY 12185

First Edition: December 2010

Credits
Editors: Cindy Cresap and Stacia Seaman
Production Design: Stacia Seaman
Cover Design by Sheri (graphicartist2020@hotmail.com)

Acknowledgments

This book was quite different for me, and I would love to say it was as easy to execute as I had originally hoped it would be. But I soon found it was quite the contrary. I do hope you, dear reader, will be able to relate to this simple (er, not so simple) tale of a lone woman on the hunt for love. There is humor, there is heartbreak, and there are quite a few harrowing moments of "Oh my God, what is she thinking?"

These are the folks who had to sift through all those harrowing moments: Cindy Cresap, my editor. Thanks for holding the light in that dark dank cave, helping me not to lose my way. Stacia Seaman and the entire Bold Strokes crew. You are all amazing and you continue to bless my life by taking my work and turning it into something incredible.

And finally, for Cait. My one. We've been through hell and back, but we finally learned. You're my weirdo. And I'm yours.

Dedication

For the one who fits me. I love you.

CHAPTER ONE

It was already dark when thunder rocked the sky and the clouds burst open with rain. And Adrian Edwards liked it that way.

There was nothing like sitting in candlelight while a heavy black rain splattered against the windowpanes. It was beautiful, romantic, and a bit gothic.

It set the scene nicely for her task.

She was on the hunt.

For a woman.

Music careened from her stereo. One song, again and again. Annie Lennox, "Cold." She loved the depth, the darkness, the velvety feel that lured her in and held her captive, just like a seeking lover searching and then finding, wrapped in the twisted vines of love.

It was what she played any time she was feeling romantic or restless. Or like tonight…needy. When her blood grew hot and beat with a loud demand beneath her sensitive skin. When it pooled and pulsed behind her clit, causing that sweet, sharp ache in her loins. The music soothed only because it intensified and helped her focus. It fed her hungry blood, lightly caressed her. Drove her to that point just between beautiful ecstasy and sheer madness.

She loved teetering there on that ledge, arms out, searching for balance. But eventually she would have to choose. And ecstasy always seemed to win out.

The wine saturated her taste buds like a warm, tart flood of bliss. She couldn't take much more now. Her body was thrumming.

She opened her eyes and leaned back in her chair as her laptop alerted her to the arrival of the second photo. With a quick click of the mouse the photo opened, showing a very nice young blonde with glam-femme looks and tight-fitting tomboy clothes.

Perfect.

She returned the wineglass to the table and made a steeple with her fingers, pressing them to her lips. Then she hurriedly typed back.

A-game88: Ur pic is nice. U up 4 som fun?

Gotcha4now: Yes. U?

A-game88: Oh yes. Wanna meet? 2nite?

Gotcha4now: Name the place.

A-game88: Core. Eight thirty.

Gotcha4now: Ok. I'll b the young hot 1. ;)

Yes. Literally, just what she needed. Hopefully, this one would be a little more mature than she looked. If she wasn't…well, beggars can't be choosers.

She rose and switched off the music. Reality oozed back in as she stared out at the streetlights, their cones of light swarming with rain. Her cocoon of velvet-lined romance quickly dissipated as if she'd simply closed the book on it and set it aside.

Her usual mantra sped around the circular track of her mind. Tonight was for fun. For the fire. Hopefully, she'd experience both.

Goal in mind, she turned and headed for the shower. Her cats, One and Two, jumped down from their perch on the kitchen table, making little grunts and meows as they followed underfoot. They were hungry again, and frankly, One was getting fat.

"Okay, okay." Sidetracking, she turned into the kitchen and retrieved the bag of Cat Chow from the pantry shelf. One bounded up to the bowl and shoved his face in it as she poured. It was almost as if the food showering down upon him was as pleasurable as the eating itself. He basked in it like an exotic bathing suit model under a cool waterfall, turning his head this way and that, rubbing the bowl with his snout.

Two's skinny little frame wove between her legs. He began to nibble on the scattered bits of kibble while One scarfed directly from the bowl.

"Not now," she said halfheartedly, bending to scratch his head. "Mama's got a date." And a date she needed. The chat room she favored just wasn't cutting it. It was time for some real live human entertainment. Even if she just rubbed up against someone while enjoying a little dancing, her skin, which was screaming for contact, would quiet its howls.

She turned on the bathroom light along with the bath water. Two jumped up on the toilet and made himself comfortable as she stripped. His tail nonchalantly flicked as he watched her.

"What are you looking at?"

He had the nerve to yawn.

"Let's hope I don't put *her* to sleep."

There it was again. The nagging. She tried to force it away, but it came again as she stepped into the shower.

More and more lately, her mind kept returning to the fact that she was all alone. Before, it didn't seem to matter; now it was all she could think about. Something had changed inside and she wasn't sure what. Or even exactly when it had happened. All she knew was that now her conscience was suddenly bombarding her with irritating questions.

Why was she alone?

Why didn't she have a partner?

Was it her?

Did she look okay?

Was she still a catch?

"Why do I care?" she declared while soaping her hair. "Why can't I just forget all this commitment bullshit and go out and get laid?" She peeled back the curtain and eyed Two. "Huh?" He merely stared. She jerked the curtain closed. "You're no help."

There was something that could be causing the sudden concern. But it wasn't a big deal and it really had nothing to do with *her* love life. Tamara, her best friend since Hansel and Gretel, had recently met someone.

It.

That's what Adrian referred to Tamara's new woman as. Because all she ever heard from Tamara lately was "this is it" and "it's for real." Adrian almost expected a little hair-covered person to come walking up to the table when she finally did meet her.

But that hadn't happened yet. Adrian had been putting it off. She didn't want to see Tamara all giddy, glowing, and settled. Not yet. They were still best friends, pals, amigos. Maverick and Goose. Ice Man and Slider.

Tamara had always had great luck with women and she'd always had meaningful relationships. It had never come between them before. But now "it" was creeping in, slowly but surely. Tamara was finding more and more reasons to stay at home and snuggle with her hairy little comrade. What was worse was a few of their other friends had found their "its" as well. Not just Tamara.

"Shit, I forgot to call T." She finished in the shower and dried herself off. After hurrying into her bedroom, she snatched up her cell phone and sent Tamara a text.

Can u meet me at Core at 8 30? Gotta new date.

Per their protocol, Tamara would meet her at the club just in case Adrian needed a quick bail-out.

She was dressing when the answer came through.

2 nite? Ur kidding. I got rocky road thawing and it's Linda Fiorentino nite.

You didn't mess with Linda Fiorentino night. It was sacred.

An image of the lights flickering as she powered up her electric friend came to mind, along with her "screaming for touch" flesh. She was desperate. She couldn't stand another night alone in the apartment. She'd pull her hair out.

Movie night be damned. Or at least put off for a couple of hours.

pleeeeeeze. Come on, Goose. I need u.

<sigh> All right. But only 4 an hour. And I hate that top gun crap u always pull.

Thanks, luv u.

U only say that when u want 2 get laid.

Adrian grinned and pulled on her jeans.

"From your lips to God's ears."

CHAPTER TWO

Tamara was already there, seated at their usual table, one muscular leg crossed over the other, a Seven and Seven at her lips per a tiny red straw.

Adrian nodded a hello to one of the bartenders, noted the familiar scent of vanilla candles mixed with beer, and made her way to the table. Her shoes squeaked on the sticky floor and the jukebox was playing Joan Jett.

"You ruined my night," Tamara said as Adrian slid onto the high-backed chair.

"You can watch it when you get home."

"That's not the point."

"I know, I know. 'It' is waiting."

Tamara narrowed her eyes. "Her name is Harriet."

Adrian couldn't help but laugh. "Harry It."

"Watch it, Edwards."

"I know, I'm sorry. It's just that Harriet sounds so, I don't know, Harry Potter."

"Well, she does manage a bookstore." She said this rather proudly.

"A magic bookstore?"

Again, her eyes narrowed.

"I'm sorry. I'll stop."

"Thank you." She sucked on the straw. "You'd think you'd be nicer to me, interrupting my night."

Adrian flagged down the busty waitress, Bernie, and ordered her usual.

"You're right. I'll be nice." She grinned.

"You're hopeless."

"Don't say that." Adrian turned a little to get a better view of the bar.

It was small. Almost stiflingly small. But she and Tamara preferred it over the larger co-ed clubs. Core was strictly women and it wasn't bad. With its merlot-colored walls, tall, tiny tables, and low lighting, it was almost romantic.

Almost.

But the lingering stench of spilled beer, the loud, deep laughter of the regulars, and the constant play of the same three artists on the jukebox sometimes got to her.

But tonight didn't seem to be so bad.

The main door opened as she watched and a few women walked in, none of them her *Gotcha4now*.

None of them were very interesting. Just the same old, same old at the Core. Thankfully, Bernie returned with her cold Miller Lite and gave her a wink.

Adrian nodded her gratitude and sipped the beer slowly. She couldn't complain. Not really. After all, she was a regular and old news herself.

"So who is it tonight?" Tamara asked.

Adrian turned back to her. "A young one. Blonde."

"She have a name?"

"Not one I know."

"Nice."

"Your sarcasm looks unattractive dripping off your chin like that."

Tamara laughed. "You're never going to change."

"Quit being mean."

Tamara grabbed Adrian's beer bottle and began peeling off the label while Adrian got lost in the flame dancing in the barrel of the candle between them.

"I'm not."

"Yes, you are. You're picking on me."

Tamara placed her hands flat on the table. "Adrian. How long have we known each other?"

"Since Hansel and Gretel."

"That's right. Jack and Jill. Raggedy Ann and Andy. I know you like the back of my hand."

"So? What's your point?"

"My point is—never mind. You're not interested."

"Don't do that."

Tamara looked off in the distance, crossing her arms over her chest.

"Are you going to tell me?"

"No."

"Why?"

"Because you aren't yet ready to hear it. You just don't *get it*."

Adrian sighed. "Fine."

Tamara slowly met her gaze. "I love you, Adrian. You're my best friend and you're better than this."

"Better than what?"

"Than this." She waved her arms at the surrounding room.

"I'm dating."

"No, you're playing. You're screwing. You're not dating."

"Please, don't, T."

"I'm just saying."

"What else am I supposed to do?"

"Stop hooking up online, for starters."

"And what, come here? We know everyone. Six degrees, T. Six degrees."

"Why can't you just relax? Just stop for a while."

"I don't want to. I want a woman."

Tamara stood. "Well, you aren't doing a very good job of finding one. You're so damn picky and then the next minute you're not. You need to forget about women for a while."

"And do what? Join a convent?"

"Focus on yourself."

Adrian leaned back. She felt a bit stricken. "What the hell does that even mean?"

"See, you're not ready to hear this." She rubbed the back of her neck just like she always did when she was frustrated. Three women Adrian didn't recognize walked by, and one looked Tamara completely up and down and then openly ogled her.

"You just got scoped," Adrian said.

"Not interested."

"You didn't even look at her."

"Don't need to."

"How do you know she's not better than 'It'?"

Tamara rolled her eyes. "I'm going to the bathroom. Order me another. I'm going to need it if I have to sit through another hook-up."

She left Adrian and wove between small tables toward the ladies' room. Adrian contemplated her words as she studied her. Tamara had always had a way with the ladies. Her smooth, dark skin always looked luscious and her almond-shaped eyes never failed to lure one in. She also had an easiness about her. A self-knowing and calm. It soothed people, drew them to her. Tamara just knew. Everything. She could handle anything.

Adrian sipped more of her beer. Her own thoughts were giving her enough trouble. She didn't need Tamara adding to it.

It was all just driving another nail into the coffin of loneliness. She was nearly enclosed now in that coffin, with no way out and no rubber tube with which to breathe. But she liked her life. Fuck the norm and expectations.

"Hi."

Adrian nearly swallowed wrong as she swung around to face the voice. "Hi."

The young blonde was smiling at her, a teasing half-grin.

"You're *A-Game,* right?"

"Right." Adrian wiped her lip nervously. *Why am I so nervous? Because she might be my "it"? No way.*

She shook the thought away.

The young woman helped herself to Tamara's seat. "Buy me a drink?"

"Sure." Just as soon as she could tear her eyes away from her, she waved Bernie over. "Another Seven and Seven and whatever the young lady is having."

"Young lady. Sounds so classy." She gave Bernie the same sort of teasing smile. "I'll have a Captain Coke."

Bernie wasn't impressed. "I need to see some I.D., sweetness."

Groaning, she fished out her driver's license. "Satisfied?"

Bernie looked at Adrian and then back to the young woman. "What's your name?"

"Sierra."

"Well, Sierra, you're a smart-ass." Bernie walked away quickly and Sierra's smile fell.

"What a bitch."

Adrian laughed and changed the subject. "Sierra, huh? Interesting."

"Why? And don't even say it's young."

"I—was just about to say that."

"Well, don't. I'm sick of hearing it."

"You are young." And fit and smooth with a tan, nice delicate neckline, kissable lips, slightly exposed midriff... "You should enjoy it."

"No chance." She seemed truly offended. "All I ever hear is how I'm too young to understand anything."

"Like what?" Adrian tugged on her beer and tried to hide her smile as Sierra openly stared at her mouth.

"Like relationships and love and life."

"Sounds like heavy stuff."

"It is. But I can handle it. Just because I'm young, it doesn't mean I don't know what love is."

Adrian took another sip. "I believe you."

Sierra visibly softened. "Thank you."

"So is this the lady in waiting?" Tamara asked as she walked up.

"The what?" Sierra asked.

Tamara sized Sierra up and must've thought she wasn't worth the trouble. "Never mind." To Adrian she said, "I have a headache."

It was code for "Can I go or does she blow?"

"I'm sorry," Adrian said. Code for "Yeah, go. I'm into her."

Tamara eyed Sierra once more in silence. Her face showed nothing, but Adrian knew she didn't approve. Sierra merely smiled, a wordless challenge.

"Why don't you go get some rest?" Adrian asked, placing her hand gently on Tamara's shoulder. "I'm about ready to get out of here myself."

"Yeah, okay." Tamara half hugged her. "Call me tomorrow."

She left quietly, cell phone already to her ear by the time she reached the door.

Sierra seemed happy she was gone. "Who was that?"

"A friend."

"An ex?"

Bernie returned with their drinks and Sierra took hers eagerly.

"T didn't stay long," Bernie said, placing the beer on the table but keeping the Seven and Seven on the tray.

"Headache," Adrian said.

Bernie's eyes widened with recognition. "Ahh. Another one, eh?" She gazed at Sierra from the corner of her eye and smirked. "To each her own."

Sierra watched her return to the bar. She pushed her drink away. "Is T your girlfriend? Because I don't do threesomes."

"What?" Adrian almost choked on her beer. "No. She's my friend."

"Then why's the waitress so concerned? And what was with the headache comment?"

Adrian studied her. She was pretty quick. Paranoid, but quick.

"Tamara is my best friend. She has been for years. Bernie knows her because we've been coming here for a long time. She's *not* an ex."

Sierra seemed to consider her explanation. "And the headache comment?"

Adrian finished off the first beer and started in on the second as she considered her words. Normally, she wouldn't share such information. What went on between her and Tamara was their business. But she had a feeling Sierra wouldn't settle for another vague answer. She decided to be somewhat honest.

"A headache is code for 'Okay, I'm leaving. Have fun with your date.'"

Sierra played with her drink straw. "So she's your wing man?"

"You could say that."

Sierra took a sip and licked her lips in a slow, purposeful manner. "So I get the green light?"

Adrian smiled. "Yes. That okay by you?"

"I think so." She stroked the condensation along the side of her drink glass. "You seem harmless."

Adrian watched as she tugged on her wet fingertips with her lips.

"I wouldn't go that far."

"No?"

"No. I'm not completely harmless."

Sierra lowered her hand to stir her drink some more. In the near distance a new but familiar song crooned. There was a loud clack as someone broke on a new game of pool.

"Should I be afraid?"

Adrian felt that familiar rush of heat. This was it. Her fire.

"Depends."

"On?"

"On what you consider to be scary."

Her expression was coy. "Why don't you take me home and show me and I'll tell you if it scares me?"

Adrian swallowed some more beer. She raised an eyebrow. "I don't think you're really afraid. I think you're intrigued. And interested."

"You'd be right."

Adrian pulled out her wallet and tossed money on the table. "Then let's get out of here."

CHAPTER THREE

The night was cool but not uncomfortably so as Adrian walked with Sierra through the parking lot. The darkness smelled strong, like rain and dirt and metal mixed. The rain had stopped before she'd arrived at Core and the mugginess hung in the air, making it seem thick. The two street lamps appeared to be smothered, weak globes of light trying to penetrate the moisture. She liked it. It made the night all the more interesting. As if one were walking through time as it stood still.

"Do you want to ride with me?" Adrian asked.

"If you don't mind. I was dropped off."

"Ah, so you were expecting to leave with me?"

Sierra shrugged. "I was hoping."

Adrian held the door for her. "So you do this a lot, then?" She rounded the car and climbed in behind the wheel. A tiny twinge started in the base of her chest. She mentally pushed it away. She did this all the time, so why should Sierra doing it cause alarm?

"Probably about as much as you do."

Great. Tamara would have a field day with this info.

She turned toward home and accelerated. Within the confines of her car, Adrian could smell Sierra's perfume. The aroma was light and pleasant with a hint of ginger. It helped settle her lingering trepidation, and she was further comforted when Sierra held her hand after tuning the radio to a pop station.

"This is nice," Adrian said, squeezing her hand.

"I like to hold hands."

"Me too."

Adrian grew more curious. "So what do you do for a living? You in school?"

Sierra crinkled her nose. It was the look twelve-year-olds get when thinking about something gross.

"God, do I look that young?"

Adrian blinked. *Yes.*

"So you're not in school?"

"No."

"Because you're way too old, right?" She gave her a crooked smile.

Sierra didn't appear amused.

"Okay, so what do you do? High-powered attorney, vice president of marketing at a major firm, district judge, trauma surgeon?"

"Very funny."

Adrian thought so.

"So?"

Sierra stared ahead, her bottom lip tucked in her mouth as if she were holding back.

"I have a good job," she finally said. "A great one."

Adrian waited for more but none came.

"Well, that's good."

"It is. I make good money. Really good money." She seemed pleased.

Adrian removed her hand from Sierra's and wrung her hands along the steering wheel as if she were gunning the gas on a motorcycle. She wanted to ask more, but she sensed that she shouldn't press it.

They rode like that for a while, Adrian pushing her Camry through the cushion of the night while Sierra hummed.

"I like you," Sierra suddenly announced.

Adrian glanced at her quickly and then returned her eyes to the road.

"I like you, too." Adrian reached for her hand again.

Deftly, Sierra ran her fingertips up and down the inside of Adrian's wrist and palm.

The sensation caused a stirring just under her skin. It shot up her arms and down her chest to her abdomen and then pulsed with determination between her legs.

"If you keep doing that we won't make it home."

"What about this?" She lifted Adrian's hand and licked the sides of her fingers.

Adrian inhaled sharply. *Holy fuck.* She accelerated and hoped the heavy night would encase her car and keep them safely on the road.

"Or what about this?" She licked each finger up and down and then placed each one in her mouth to suck.

"Jesus." Adrian shoved back against the seat, her toes curling in her shoes. "Stop. Stop. I can't drive like this."

Sierra laughed but kept on, taking her whole finger in and out, sucking with a curled tongue.

"That's it, I'm flooring it." Adrian pressed harder on the accelerator and ran a late yellow light.

"You must really need some TLC," Sierra said with a husky voice.

"You have no idea."

Adrian peeled around a corner and sped down her street. When she reached her apartment, she whipped her car into her parking space and killed the engine.

They hurried up the stairs and Adrian unlocked the door and flung it open. Sierra walked inside slowly and looked over her shoulder in a seductive manner. Her jeans were low rise and her top was fitted and short. The number 9 was on the front in red. A faux football jersey of sorts. She stripped off her light jacket and tossed it onto the couch.

An urge to tackle her came as Adrian closed the door. Instead, she stood there, the rush of confidence gone.

"Can I get you a drink?"

Sierra trailed her fingers over the furniture.

"No."

"Something to eat?"

Her eyes flashed. "Not right now."

Pleasantries were now aside. They both stared.

"Are you a top?" Sierra asked, surprising Adrian.

"I—why do you ask?" No one had asked her that since 1995.

Sierra shrugged. "I thought you older women always wanted to know."

Older women? Ouch.

What a killjoy.

Adrian went into the kitchen where she retrieved a bottle of vodka from the freezer. She was going to need it.

"Did I say something wrong?" Sierra asked, watching her pour.

Adrian sipped some before she answered. "Let's just skip over the top question."

Was she a top? Sometimes. It depended. Why did it matter? Were they going to get in permanent positions? Was someone going to blow a whistle if they left these positions? She pictured a tough-looking dyke with a buzz haircut and a striped referee shirt, blowing the whistle, calling out the positional foul.

The vodka burned a path down her esophagus. She wished it would burn her brain so she'd stop thinking so much.

"The last woman I was with," Sierra said. "She wanted to know."

Adrian held up a hand. "Uh...okay...I don't." The mood was going fast. Just disintegrating and disappearing into the air vent. "I... mean...it doesn't matter."

"It did to her. She had to have it the exact same way every time."

Adrian nearly choked. "Okay. Don't want to hear it."

"Sorry." Sierra stepped up to Adrian and placed her hand on her arm. "I'm glad you're not so uptight." Slowly, she leaned in and touched her neck ever so lightly with her lips. Little kisses, delicate ones. Just enough to tickle and arouse. Adrian felt her eyes flutter close.

"Mmm."

"You like that?" Sierra asked.

"Yes." The glass was removed from her hand.

"Good." She kissed her some more, up and down both sides of her neck. Her fingers skimmed up and down her arms.

Adrian's entire body was awakening. Slowly, but surely, like being gently rocked after a long night's sleep.

"I like you," Sierra whispered. "A lot."

Adrian gripped her waist and pulled her close. "I like you, too." She inhaled her perfume and buried her face in her hair. The smell of cigarette smoke was clinging to the silky strands. Adrian focused instead on her neck. As she nibbled on her, her mind worked overtime.

Was the smoke from the bar? No. It was illegal to smoke in the bar now. Where was it from? She hadn't smoked at all in front of Adrian.

Maybe it was from her friend who'd dropped her off. So was she a smoker? Or was it her friend?

Stop.

Just stop.

She closed her eyes and kissed the warm, soft flesh beneath her lips. Sierra tensed and moaned softly. Her mouth attacked Adrian's with a vengeance, biting and sucking.

Goose flesh erupted along Adrian's skin. The feel of Sierra's slick tongue sent her slow desire into a mad frenzy. Hurriedly, she tugged Sierra closer and then lifted her off the floor. She stumbled forward a bit before they hit the wall and there she growled and kissed her hard on the mouth.

More smoke. Smoke intermingled with rum.

Adrian pushed on, determined not to let it bother her. She didn't care if people smoked, she just didn't like to smell and taste it during intimacy. But this wasn't too bad. Still…Sierra had said she was a nonsmoker on her profile.

"You're a good kisser," Sierra said, breathless. "Mmm, really nice. I like that. I like your place, too."

"Okay." Adrian kissed her again, not wanting to continue the conversation.

"Okay?"

Adrian kissed her neck, bit it, and then flicked with her tongue. "Mmm-hmm."

Laughter echoed in Adrian's ear.

"You don't talk much, do you?"

Adrian set her down. "I just want to—"

Sierra stopped her with the gentle press of her finger. "I know. I know just what you need."

She leaned into Adrian and touched her lips to hers. It was soft yet firm. Thick, supple silk. Again and again. Testing, teasing, seeking. And then she slipped out her tongue. Wanting inside.

Asking and then doing.

Adrian found herself pinned against the wall, Sierra's full tongue exploring her mouth. And then there were hands up under her shirt, massaging and squeezing. First on top of her bra and then swiftly, underneath, pinching her bare nipples.

"Ah, oh God," Adrian let out, her eyes widening and then narrowing with pleasure.

Sierra laughed. "Uh-huh." She kissed her way down Adrian's neck, to the base of her throat to where her hands were working their magic.

Her tongue flicked Adrian's firm nipple. She licked it while squeezing it between her fingers.

Adrian hissed and pressed her legs together, the mounting pressure unbearable. Sierra seemed to sense this and she lowered her hand into Adrian's jeans while her mouth continued to suck.

"Jesus," Adrian whispered.

"Is that good, baby?" Sierra asked, finding Adrian's clit with her fingers. "Like this." She stroked her up and down, first sliding her fingertips into Adrian's opening for her slick arousal.

"Ye-yes. Mmm."

"Good," Sierra purred, moving lower to unfasten her jeans. She looked up at Adrian as she jerked them down, along with her underwear. With a wicked smile she breathed hot air onto her inner thighs, causing Adrian to shudder. Her tongue soon followed, on a determined path to her aching flesh.

"You're—" Sierra started.

Adrian gripped her head. "No—don't talk."

Not now.

"Okay, baby. Whatever you want."

She used her thumbs and opened Adrian up. Flicked her tongue over her sensitive clit.

"Oh, yeah."

She leaned into her, flicked her some more.

Adrian knotted her fingers in her hair. She closed her eyes and felt the slight bobbing of Sierra's head, heard the quick tap of her tongue.

"God. God, yes."

"Mmm. Do you love it?" Sierra asked. "Tell me."

"Yes."

"You want to come?"

Adrian tightened her fingers in her hair. "Ye-yes."

"You want—"

"Yes. Hurry. Please."

Adrian felt the movement of Sierra's jaw as she devoured her further. It only turned her on more.

There was groaning and grunting on her part, licking and kissing on Sierra's. The sensation from the oral assault was powerful and growing hotter and thicker. Right up through her body, until it knotted and surged out from her core and exploded outward, causing her to slam her head back and call out.

Sierra pulsed into her, giving and taking, flicking and then sucking. Adrian rocked into her, her knees growing weak. The kitchen spun. Her ears rang as Sierra began to speak. Something about how it felt and did she like it.

She didn't bother answering. Couldn't have even if she'd wanted to.

With all her strength she straightened and swallowed against a dry throat. Her heart was still going wild as she released Sierra's hair and fell into her as she stood. Silence ensued as they held each other and breathed.

A soft meow came from One as he entered the kitchen to rub up against their legs.

"Who's this?" Sierra asked with a laugh.

"One," Adrian whispered, still struggling for breath.

Sierra bent to pet him. "Oh my God, he's so cute." She nuzzled him. He purred happily, his eyes pleasurable green slits.

"He's huge," Adrian said.

"Aw, I think he's cute. What's his name again?"

"One."

"One? What kind of a name is that?"

Adrian refastened her pants.

"A simple one."

"He should have a big handsome, regal name like Clyde or Winston."

Adrian downed another shot of vodka. Her legs felt like jelly. "If it makes you feel any better, he has numerous nicknames."

One purred and whipped his tail in Sierra's arms. Two then came trotting in with a series of grunts.

Sierra lit up. "Another one? Oh my gosh, he's so cute."

"His name is Two," Adrian said. "Just so there's no confusion."

"They're adorable." She swapped cats, leaving One sitting on the floor looking up at her. "One and Two."

"They're all right." She watched them together for a few more seconds before her thoughts returned to Sierra's talented tongue and exposed midriff. "How about we continue this in the bedroom? They'll still be here when we're finished."

Sierra stopped kissing Two and grinned. "Okay."

Adrian took her hand and led the way. She switched on the bedside lamp and sat on the bed to remove her shoes. Sierra set Two on the floor and held Adrian's gaze as she slipped off her shirt and rubbed her hands over her small, taut breasts.

She was beautiful, youthfully lithe and tan. "You have an incredible body."

"Thank you. I have to work hard for it."

"I doubt that."

Sierra lowered her jeans and stepped out of them. She stood looking at Adrian in her tiny satin panties.

"Come here," Adrian said.

Sierra stepped up to her, her breathing heavy. Adrian touched her, ran her fingers lightly up and down her sides, puckering her nipples. Sierra moved closer, straddling her. Adrian kissed her skin softly, trailing her tongue up to the gentle weight of her breasts. She licked the undersides and then swirled her tongue around the centers. When Sierra arched into her, Adrian took a hard nipple between her teeth and squeezed.

Sierra cried out and ran her nails through Adrian's hair. "You feel good, baby," Sierra said. "But we're going to have to hurry."

"What?" Adrian held tight to her muscular buttocks.

"I'm getting hungry."

Adrian looked up at her. "You're kidding, right?"

Sierra shook her head. "No."

"You're thinking about eating now?"

"I can wait. But we have to hurry."

Adrian blinked, unsure what to say. Sierra kissed her, killing the need to speak. She twirled her tongue inside Adrian's mouth and gyrated against her.

"Touch me, baby. Feel my heat for you."

Adrian could already feel it as she pressed the heel of her hand against her.

"Go inside my panties," Sierra said and then groaned as Adrian did so.

She was incredibly slick inside her panties and she bucked like a madwoman, shoving her clit into the heel of Adrian's hand.

"Yes, yes, yes, yes."

She was going to go over. Adrian tried to stop, but Sierra wouldn't let her, clawing her shoulders and shoving against her hand.

"Yes, yes, yes, yes. Don't stop. Yes, yes, yes, yes, *yes, yes, yes*!" She tensed and pushed hard, slamming herself in a frenzy into Adrian. "Inside me, inside me now."

Adrian winced at the pain in her hand as she shoved two fingers up inside her.

"Ah, ah, yes!" And Sierra straightened, face toward the ceiling. She bounced there on Adrian's lap until the veins in her neck stood out like small snakes, coiling beneath her moist skin. Then she stilled and held her breath as she stared upward.

"Are you okay?" Adrian was worried. She wasn't moving.

There was more silence. And then she exhaled, "And I'm done." She collapsed.

Adrian sat still with her, unable to move. Her hand cramped.

And I'm done?

Who says that?

Eventually, Sierra moved and it was as if nothing at all had happened. She slipped off Adrian, finger-combed her hair, and bent to pick up Two after adjusting her panties. She snuggled with him as Adrian opened and closed her sore hand.

"He's so cute. Mr. Cuddles. That's what I'm going to call him." She rubbed her nose against his. "Mr. Cuddly Wuddly, yes. Let's go eat, okay?" She carried him off toward the kitchen, wearing nothing but her panties. Adrian stared after her, completely numb and oblivious. She heard Sierra opening and closing cabinets in the kitchen. The sound of cereal tumbling into a bowl soon followed.

After washing her hands, Adrian found Sierra sitting lotus-style on the counter, spooning Cap'n Crunch into her mouth. She smiled and a bit of milk ran down her chin.

"Hi." She shoved in another small mountain of cereal.

"Guess you weren't lying about being hungry."

"Nope." One had his face in the bowl, helping himself to some milk. "Want some?" She motioned toward the open box.

Adrian realized she was being offered her own food. "No."

Sierra chewed on. "Why don't you go to bed and I'll come in in a little while and give you more?"

Adrian opened her mouth to argue but then thought better of it. She was tired. And confused. She had to be at work early. The night hadn't turned out like she'd hoped. It seemed they never did. Sierra must've seen her expression because she swallowed and spoke.

"It is okay if I stay here tonight, right? My friend's not getting me till tomorrow morning."

Adrian got herself a glass and poured herself some milk before it was gone. She drank heartily. Hopefully, it would coat the vodka and both would help her sleep.

"That's fine." She put the rest in the fridge. "You can stay."

"Thanks." She chomped happily.

"I'm going to bed." She started to walk away.

"Wait." Sierra lowered her spoon and waved Adrian over. "Give me a kiss."

Adrian hesitated.

"Come on, baby. Give me a good-night kiss."

Adrian, too tired to protest, allowed Sierra to kiss her. Then she walked back to her room and dug Sierra's wallet out of her jeans. She fished out her license and wrote down all the information on a sticky note and hid it in her nightstand drawer. It was a precaution. Just in case she woke up tomorrow morning to find her place cleaned out. At least she would have her name and driver's license number. Her friend on the police force could hopefully find her with that.

Sierra was her real name and she was twenty-one. Well, young enough for school. Her address appeared to be an apartment. So far so good. At least she hadn't lied to her. As she was returning the wallet she noticed a bulge in the front pocket of the jeans. She double-checked the door and reached inside. It was a wad of money. Mostly fives and ones. About a hundred bucks.

Hmm.

This was good. Maybe she wouldn't try to steal anything.

Thankfully, Adrian didn't have anything of much value in the living room and kitchen anyway. Most of her important documents and things were in the safe in her bedroom closet.

Feeling a little relieved, she undressed and climbed into bed. As she extinguished the bedside lamp, she could hear Sierra baby-talking to One and Two.

Adrian fell asleep to a Mr. Cuddly Wuddly lullaby.

CHAPTER FOUR

W akey, wakey, eggs and bakey."
Adrian opened her eyes and focused on Sierra's face. She was lying on Adrian's chest, her chin resting on her hands. Adrian could smell syrup. Maple syrup.

"I made breakfast," Sierra said proudly.

Adrian glanced at the clock. It was set to go off in five minutes. She groaned and Sierra kissed her on the nose.

"I gotta go. My friend's coming. But first..." She hurried from the room.

"This early?" Adrian sat up and gripped her head. It ached like a stubbed toe. She lay back down as memories from the night before came. Sierra had come to bed sometime after midnight. They'd fucked for almost two hours straight.

She lifted her head and stared at her thighs. Purple hickeys marked her flesh, and they stung.

"Here you go, sunshine." Sierra hurried in with a plate of pancakes topped with butter and syrup. She also carried a glass of juice.

Adrian forced herself up. "You didn't have to do this." Her voice was froggy and her lips felt swollen.

"After last night you need a good meal. I know I did." She handed over the plate and shook open a paper napkin. She set it in Adrian's lap.

"Okay, I gotta go." She kissed her. "I'll call you later. Have a good day at work."

Adrian heard the front door open and close. One jumped on the bed and stuck his nose on her plate.

"What just happened here?" she asked.

One ignored her and shook his head as he got a taste of syrup.

"Yeah, you're right. I don't want it either." Slowly, she rose. Her body was stiff and she was sore as she walked into the kitchen. The area was clean and eerily silent. She dumped the pancakes down the disposal and went for her usual Special K. She blinked several times as she opened her cupboard.

Her Special K was missing, along with the Cap'n Crunch and the entire container of pancake mix.

"What the fuck?"

She looked in her garbage. The pancake container was on top, and buried in the bottom she found the cereal boxes.

What was going on?

From her bedroom she heard her alarm going off. She ran her hands through her hair and sighed.

It was time to get ready for work.

She showered and played over everything in her mind as she dressed and then drove to work, hungry.

Sierra was young. She was nice. She was very attractive. But something was off. She was verbally clingy, and what was with the food?

At work, three hours later, Tamara laughed into the phone and voiced her guesses on the situation. "Maybe she's poor."

"Poor?" Adrian sat back and sighed. She'd just relayed the previous night's happenings, and Tamara seemed amused.

"Yeah, maybe she can't afford food. Maybe she's really homeless."

"Oh my God."

"Is she clingy? Already trying to move in?"

Adrian scribbled an *x* with her ballpoint pen. "Kind of. She calls me *baby* and made me breakfast."

"Shit, A. You've got to get rid of her."

"Why do I always get the weird ones?"

"Haven't you figured it out yet? Sweetie, we're *all* weird. You've just got to find a weirdo that complements you."

"I refuse to accept that. Not everyone is weird. They just all seem to find me is all."

"Whatever you say."

"I know. You want to tell me that I'm going about things the wrong way. That I'll never find anyone and I'm doomed to spend all of eternity alone."

"Nah, I'm too tired to go into all that this early."

"That's a change."

"You owe me."

"How was the movie and your date?"

"You really want to know?"

Adrian chewed on her pen and imagined Tamara's night. It was probably way better than hers. Sex included. God, how depressing.

"No. Not really."

Tamara laughed. "We didn't even get to the movie."

"Bitch."

"Gotta go, stud."

"What do I do when she calls?"

"Who?"

"The woman I've been talking about for the past half hour."

"Oh, right. The Cap'n Crunch crook."

"Funny."

"If you don't want to see her again, tell her. You're good at that."

"Hmm." The pen lid softened under her teeth. Did she want to see her again? The sex was great. But everything else…

"Call me later," Tamara said.

They rang off and Adrian sat staring at her ancient metal desk. It was quite drab with a worn desk blotter covered in her drawings, an old phone, and a plastic Iowa Hawkeyes cup full of pens and pencils. She stared at her creations on the blotter and a little flutter warmed in her chest. Drawing was her automatic stress reliever and she'd been doing it since grade school. They always started off simple enough, just absentminded doodles, but soon she'd be immersed in adding the details. And that was what she really loved, creating something intricate from nothing. She sipped some tepid coffee and drew rings around the stain from the mug, creating another beautiful flower. It soothed her as she thought about the tough day ahead.

Thursdays were awful. A long, tortuous process she had to wade through in order to reach Friday. What was worse was the mountain of paperwork she had to get through. Friday afternoon was when they shipped, so Thursday was invoice day.

She groaned.

"Oh, come on. You love it here," said Benny, her coworker of three years, as he breezed into the room.

"You read my mind." She gave him a smile as she leaned back in her squeaky chair. "He in yet?"

"He" was her boss, Jake, an acquaintance of her stepfather, Louis. Accordingly, she referred to him as Uncle Jake. He hated the name; he wasn't very fond of Louis, so she loved it even more. Benny had also started calling him Uncle Jake, along with some of their dealers. It was a running joke and it kept the office lively. There was nothing like a Jake temper tantrum to get your bored blood going.

"Nah, you're safe for another fifteen minutes or so." He plopped down behind his own desk and eyed her stack of invoices. "That's all for me, isn't it?"

"Yep."

He rubbed his face and she could hear the scrape of his five o'clock shadow against his palms.

"I hate Thursdays. Thursday afternoons even more. I hate packing and shipping."

She laughed. "Wanna trade? You enter these and I'll pull parts and box?"

"No." He sighed. "I've just gotta suck it up."

"You're afraid of Uncle Jake."

"Yep." This time he laughed.

Jake didn't like people trading duties. Jake didn't like much of anything.

Despite his constant crankiness and rigidness, she liked him. She'd been working for him since high school. Way back when, she got expelled for getting it on with her girlfriend on school grounds. As punishment, Louis thought she should work, and Jake had given her a job paper pushing. She'd never gone back to high school. Getting her GED had been easy enough.

After a long stretch, she retrieved her laptop from its case. She turned it on and got busy re-listing parts on eBay. It was mindless and easy, a warm-up before the actual run.

"Have I mentioned how much I hate auto parts?" she asked, clicking away.

"Not today you haven't." Benny was reloading shipping labels into the printer.

"Yeah, well, I do. I hate them. Hate this damn place."

"Uh-huh."

"I do. I mean it." She didn't mean it. Not really. Well, not most days. It was just fun to bitch.

"I know."

The phone rang. Benny was still feeding the printer. She answered.

"Jake's."

"Yeah, I'm looking for a set of billet valve covers for a three-fifty small block."

She fought off sighing and readied an invoice and a pencil.

"Flamed, milled, or plain?"

"Oh uh, I'm not sure."

"You can take a look on our website."

"Okay. Can you hold on a second?"

As she replied with a yes, she buried her head in her hand and decided right then and there she would see Sierra again. She needed something to look forward to, weird or not. The sex had been great.

Right?

She tapped the pencil against her forehead and smiled.

Five o'clock couldn't come fast enough.

CHAPTER FIVE

"Hi," Sierra said as Adrian opened the door. She nearly jumped into her arms.

"Hi."

Sierra was glistening with a light mist from the drizzling rain, her threadbare tank and hooded jacket clinging to her. The sight stirred Adrian but the smell of wet, dank cigarette smoke did nothing for her.

Sierra kissed her firmly and held her face. "I missed you, baby."

"I—uh—okay." It was a quarter after midnight and Adrian was just as tired as she was horny.

Sierra entered the apartment almost bouncing with delight as Adrian closed and locked the door. This time she had a duffel bag with her. It looked stuffed full.

"I'm sooo happy!" she said as she twirled around. "Where's my little Cuddly Wuddly?" She immediately started a search for the cats.

Adrian scratched her head and wondered if all this was worth an orgasm or two. Or three.

Probably four.

Yep. It was worth it.

One and Two came trotting into the room, apparently excited to see her. She scooped them both up and rubbed her face against theirs. Adrian could hear the purring from where she stood.

"So you had to work late, huh?" She'd wanted to hook up around seven but Sierra had said she was caught up at work.

Sierra set the cats down and walked toward her. She moved all slinky and seductive. A silly grin on her face.

"Yes, I did."

Adrian fought off drooling. "What do you do again?"

"Customer service rep."

Adrian was surprised at the quick answer.

"Oh."

"I'm ready to service you now." She grabbed Adrian's T-shirt and tugged her closer. "Ma'am."

"Okay."

Sierra pushed her toward the couch and forced her to sit. The stereo came to life and Sierra urged the volume up.

Adrian protested. "It's too loud. My neighbors."

Sierra only giggled. "Trust me, they'll prefer the music."

She began to strip, dancing like a supple, moist temptress. First the jacket and tank came off, and then the jeans. Tonight she wore a burgundy thong, and the muscles of her ass rippled as she turned and swung her hips.

Adrian licked her lips as her heart rate tripled. Sierra's perfect ass continued to seduce her and she wanted so badly to touch it, squeeze it, bite it. But Sierra turned and moved closer. The pale skin of her chest bloomed with red as she moved and excited herself by twisting her nipples.

Adrian wanted her. Right here. Right now.

Sierra seemed to understand and she knelt to dig in her duffle bag. When she straightened she held a pink cock and a bottle of lube. Like she'd done it a hundred times before, she greased up the dildo and put away the bottle. Then she straddled Adrian and unbuttoned her flannel pants.

"I want you to fuck me," she said, careful to rub her tits in Adrian's face as she maneuvered the cock into place just inside the fly of her pants.

Adrian groaned a little and reached for her breasts. Sierra thrust them into her mouth and clung to her hair. "Will you do that for me, Adrian?" She tugged on her hair as she weaved against her. "Will you fuck me?" Her eyes were wild and fierce.

Adrian nodded, nearly breathless.

Sierra kissed her hard. Shoved her tongue in her mouth and twirled it around. Her hands found Adrian's breasts where they pinched and pulled. Adrian groaned again. This time louder.

"That's it, baby. I want you to want me. To fuck me so good." She laughed. The music played on. Insistent.

Adrian stared at her nude body and then down at the cock anchored into her own pants. It was curved and pointing toward Sierra.

"Hold it for me," Sierra said.

Adrian held the base and watched as Sierra turned herself backward. The muscles in her back quivered as she sank down on the cock. A deep grunt escaped her as she did so. Then she arched her back and began to move, her ass pumping. She reached back for Adrian's hands and brought them up to her breasts.

"Make me scream," she demanded, squeezing Adrian's hands. "Do it, baby."

Adrian leaned forward and bit her back as she pinched her nipples.

"Oh yes. Oh God, yes!"

Sierra gyrated some more. Faster and harder.

"Fucking take me, fuck me good." She bounced on Adrian's lap, head back, her center collapsing over the dildo.

Smack, smack, smack.

Adrian bit her and licked her, her lips stunned and tingling at the up-and-down movement of her back. She moaned into her as she continued to work her tits, tugging and pinching.

Up and down she went. Bounce, bounce, bounce.

"Uh. Oh, yeah. Oh, fuck yeah." Her voice grew deeper. "Fuck yes."

The music played.

Adrian grew wet. She could feel it soaking into her panties. The heel of the dildo was just missing her clit, driving her mad.

"I want to come," Sierra said. "I love to come."

The neighbor started banging on the wall behind them. It only drove Sierra harder.

"Do it. Do it. Fucking do it."

And then she stopped and nearly jumped from Adrian's lap. She turned and straddled her again, this time facing her. She eased down on the cock quickly and Adrian swore her pupils dilated.

"Oh God!" she said, gripping Adrian's shoulders. "This is even better. Fucking better." She pumped faster and leaned forward. "Suck my tits, baby. Suck 'em hard."

Adrian took each breast into her mouth nearly completely to suck and hold.

"Oh, fuck. Fuck yes!"

Sierra placed her palms on the wall where the banging was coming from. She pounded back.

"Yes, yes, yes! Make me come. Make me fuck-ing come!"

And then she slammed into Adrian like a woman dying, screaming in a deep, guttural way, pounding on the wall.

There were no words. Just the long, deep scream.

The banging grew worse. Adrian could hear the neighbor hollering.

"Shut the fuck up!"

But she didn't care. She was so close to going over herself. Right there. So good and so close she would've killed for it.

She released Sierra's breast and struggled for air. Sierra went limp in her arms.

"And I'm done."

Adrian laughed. She couldn't help it. "I guess so."

Sierra laughed too.

They held each other for a while.

The neighbor stopped banging but he was still yelling about the music. When Sierra crawled off her and removed the dildo, Adrian rose on stiff legs and switched the music off.

The silence was weird. Heavy. Her ears rang.

Sierra was slipping into a T-shirt she'd pulled from her duffel bag.

"I'm going to the bathroom," Adrian said. She was so wet she could hardly walk.

"Okay, but don't get off. I'll be in after I eat something."

Adrian stared for a moment and thought about saying something. But what would she say? No? Don't eat my damn food?

Instead, she headed for the bathroom where she trembled in near bliss when she peed. She refrained from pleasing herself and after she brushed her teeth, she left the bathroom and collapsed on the bed.

In the kitchen she heard Adrian moving about. The fridge opened and closed. She heard glass clink. Then the microwave.

What the hell was she making?

She clutched her head and forced herself under the covers. She didn't want to think about it.

No.

She turned off the bedside lamp and thumped her pillow. The sex. Think about the sex.

Mind-blowing sex.

Yes.

She fell asleep again to the beep of the microwave and the dramatic meows of happiness from One.

CHAPTER SIX

The alarm went off and Adrian rolled over and growled, silencing it. She snuggled back into the covers and closed her eyes. She opened one as the sounds of snoring came from next to her. And then a long, high-pitched fart followed.

Adrian flung the covers back and hurried to the bathroom. She peed, turned on the shower, and undressed. A hickey marked her neck and two more showed on her chest. The mirror fogged up and she risked a peek back at the bed.

Sierra was under a hump of covers, out cold.

Adrian peeled back the shower curtain and climbed inside. The water was wonderfully hot as it cascaded down her head and over her shoulders. She thought back to the night with Sierra. She'd woken Adrian up around one o'clock with long, firm licks up her inner legs, having taken off Adrian's pants without waking her. And she'd pleased her well into the night, loving her with her mouth and tongue and nimble fingers.

Unbelievable. All of it. The sex. The girl. The smell of cigarette smoke in her hair when she'd come to bed. The food.

Ugh. Adrian wondered what the damage was from last night. She'd felt Sierra climb from bed at least twice. She'd heard movement in the kitchen and in the guest bathroom.

She soaped herself and shuddered as she skimmed over her clit. A warm, tingling feeling spread upward from her center. She knew that feeling and hadn't felt it in a long while. She was sated. At least for the time being.

Sierra had done that.

When she finished, she brushed her teeth and dressed quietly. Sierra snored loudly under the lump and One was strewn across her foot. Two had taken up residence on Adrian's pillow, languishing there like a regal lion, paws spreading and contracting. He flicked his tail at her as she approached Sierra.

Adrian gently shook her shoulder.

"Mmm." Sierra flipped over, looking annoyed.

"Sierra. It's morning. I'm getting ready to leave for work."

She rolled over again and shoved the covers down. Her hair was mussed.

"What?"

"I'm leaving soon."

She opened her eyes slowly. Her hand went to her brow. "Oh." She didn't move.

"I thought you might want some breakfast before you leave." Adrian didn't want to be rude.

Sierra rubbed her eye.

"I'm staying here."

Adrian wasn't sure she heard right. "Sorry?"

"I don't have to work until five."

"Five p.m.?"

"Yes." She sat up. "The night shift."

"And you want to stay here?"

"If that's okay." She offered a sweet smile.

"What about your place?"

She shrugged. "I don't have a ride home."

Adrian sighed. "I could take you."

"Wouldn't it be easier if I stayed here? I'll have dinner ready for you when you come home. Please? I don't want you to have to drive me home right now. You need to go to work."

She climbed up to her knees and tugged Adrian close. She was nude and warm.

"See? Feel my heart." She placed Adrian's hand on her breast. "That's because of you." She kissed her softly.

Adrian caved. "Okay."

Sierra hugged her. "Thanks. I'll have dinner made and ready for you to heat up."

"That's not necessary." She had to get away from her, her warmth tempting.

Sierra smiled. "I know. I want to."

Adrian forced herself to back away. "I better go."

"You want breakfast?" She stood.

"No, no. I eat at work," she fibbed.

"Okay." Sierra walked up and hung off her. "Have a good day, sweetie."

Despite the annoying sweet talk, Adrian wanted to melt into her body. Just crawl back into bed with her. But she couldn't. "Go back to sleep," she said.

They kissed. Sierra gave her a sad pouty look. "Okay."

Adrian closed the door and headed into the kitchen. She didn't want to but she made herself look into the garbage.

A pile of wet paper towels sat on top. They were stained orange.

"What am I doing?" She sighed and then moved the paper towels. "I must be crazy." Beneath them she found an empty box of pasta and an empty container of pasta sauce. There were also several candy bar wrappers. She couldn't bring herself to dig any farther. She knew what this was. Knew it all too well.

She went into the guest bath and found more orange tainted paper towels in the wastebasket. She knelt for a closer look at the toilet. There were orange/red flecks along the base. She lifted the lid. She found two more on the inside of the rim.

"Fuck."

Sierra was throwing up her food. Binging and purging. She'd bet her life on it.

"This is not good."

She closed the lids and sat on the toilet, head in her hands. Her insides clenched as memories came rushing back. Louis slapping her hand at the dinner table, yanking her plate away, calling her fat. Louis laughing at her, pinching her thighs painfully, sometimes leaving bruises. She'd started starving herself but it had made her sick. So sick she'd get dizzy and fall. So she'd started sneaking food. Binging in her room and then throwing it all up in the bathroom.

"Baby?" Sierra called from the bedroom. "You still here? Change your mind about breakfast?"

Adrian jumped up, startled. She scrubbed her hands and face and then stared at her reflection for a few seconds, trying to convince herself that she was grown and no longer harming herself at Louis's hand.

She hurried to the living room, needing to get the hell away. She grabbed her keys and laptop case.

"No, I'm just heading out."

She opened the front door and heard Sierra just before she closed it.

"Good morning, Mr. Cuddly Wuddly Woo. Want some breakfast?"

CHAPTER SEVEN

A re you insane?" Tamara asked over the phone line during
their second conversation of the morning. Adrian hadn't had
the guts to tell her during their first conversation. She sat forward in her
squeaky chair.

"She seems harmless."

"You left her at your house? Alone? For all day?"

Benny looked over at her and wiggled his eyebrows. He knew
something was up. And he loved, absolutely loved, the gossip concerning
her love life.

"It's not that bad. I trust her." *Do I?*

"You don't even know her! You just met her."

"Calm down." Truth was, she was growing concerned. She'd been
so caught up with the bulimia thing she hadn't given much thought to
whether letting her stay was safe. But now Tamara was scaring the shit
out of her.

"I'm fine. You're the one that's screwed. She's probably cleaned
out your place by now."

There was a long silence. Adrian palmed her forehead. "You really
think I should worry?"

"Yes. You don't know anything about her, Adrian. And what you
do know sounds pretty sketchy. A customer service rep? Did you ask
her what company she works for? And if she makes such good money,
where is her car?"

Adrian felt like groaning. *Shit.*

"What should I do?" She hadn't even mentioned her theory on the throwing up yet. Tamara would literally drive to her office and hit her over the head with a hammer to knock some sense into her.

She felt panicked and confused. Her mind completely useless.

"I'd go home."

"Right now?"

"Yes."

"Fuck."

Tamara laughed. "That's the last thing you need to be thinking about right now." There was a brief silence and Benny held up a paper with dark letters written in marker.

More trouble in lesbian land?

She threw a pencil at him. It thumped against his upper arm.

"Ow!"

"She's good in bed, isn't she?" Tamara asked.

"Mmm-hmm." She tossed another pencil as Benny tried to write on another sheet of paper. He yowled when it struck his hand.

"I knew it."

"Come on. I'm not that bad."

"Yes, you are. You and every other red-blooded dyke."

"Not you, T. You would've gotten rid of her, right?"

"Well, I sure wouldn't have left her alone in my house after two days."

Adrian sighed. Benny had given up writing and wadded up the paper. He threw it at her. She caught it with one hand and tossed it back at him.

He laughed.

"Listen, I need to go."

"What are you doing tonight?" Adrian asked.

"I don't know. Hopefully, I won't be taking you furniture shopping."

"Ha ha."

"Call me later?"

"Yep."

"Good luck."

"Thanks." Adrian hung up and perched on the edge of her chair. Benny sat there at his desk grinning at her.

"Don't start," she said.

"I would never." He wheeled his chair over to another desk where the box of doughnuts sat. He grabbed a chocolate éclair and bit into it. Chewing, he wheeled back to his own desk.

Her stomach growled at the sight. She'd yet to eat breakfast. But her head wouldn't let her. She was too nervous. She stood and reached for her car keys. It was pushing eleven o'clock. Her stomach dropped as she imagined opening her front door to find her apartment empty. One and Two gone, along with her possessions.

"Going somewhere?" Benny asked and then took another bite.

"Home. I'll be back shortly." I hope.

"What about Uncle Jake?"

"Cover for me."

He nearly choked. "How?"

"I don't care. Make something up."

"Your period?"

She shot him a look.

He sat looking lost, a crumb on his chin. "What? That's what girls used to say in high school."

She shook her head. "Fine. Whatever."

He snapped his fingers and grew excited. "Cramps. That's it. That's what they used to say. I'll tell him you have cramps."

She stared at him for a long moment. "You're a weird dude, Benny."

He smiled and she headed for the door. "You're welcome."

❖

Adrian approached her apartment carefully, almost as if the door handle would strike out and bite her. Hand on the knob, she pressed her ear to the door and listened. She heard voices. Two of them.

Panic.

Maybe it was the television. She listened closer, willing her heartbeat to slow. There was laughter. A voice. It was a woman's. Then another voice. It was Sierra's.

Adrenaline came. Hot and fast. Adrian shoved open the door. Sierra let out a little screech. The other woman just stared. They were both on the sofa, smoking cigarettes.

Sierra clutched her chest. "Jesus, baby, you scared the shit out of me."

Adrian hurriedly scanned the room. There were boxes with no lids near the kitchen, stuffed full of odds and ends. She noted a standing lamp with a leopard print lampshade. Several feather boas hung off the back of the kitchen chairs. A lazy stack of DVDs stood on the entertainment center.

"What the fuck is all this?" She wanted to scream but her throat was tight with anger.

Sierra laughed nervously. "Sweetie, this is Ginger. My roommate."

Adrian didn't look at her. She didn't want to.

"Former roommate," the girl added.

Adrian did look at them this time. She glared.

Sierra stood, a forced smile on her face. "I wasn't expecting you so soon."

"Apparently."

"Don't get upset. Ginger just brought me some of my things."

"I see that. Why?"

Sierra looked at Ginger and jerked her head toward the door. The girl rose and glided past them, her big blue eyes holding Adrian's gaze. She smiled.

Adrian wanted to smack her.

When the door closed, Sierra tugged on Adrian's hand. She pulled her toward the couch.

"No."

She gave Adrian that pouty look. "You're mad?"

"Mad doesn't even come close."

"It's just for a little while."

"What's just for a little while?"

Sierra spoke softer, almost like a baby. "I don't have anywhere else to go."

So there it was. The truth. Probably just a crumb of the whole pie, but she was grateful for that much.

"Why?"

"Ginger is moving and I haven't had time to get a new roommate or a new place."

"When is she moving?"

Sierra seemed stumped. She fumbled for an answer. "Soon. A few days."

Adrian didn't believe her.

"Look, I promise it won't be for long."

"You're damn right it won't be." The smell of cigarettes was horrible. She felt dizzy and nauseous in her own house. "What about this supposed job you have?"

"What about it?"

"Do you really have one?"

Sierra looked offended. "Yes."

"And you make enough to have your own place?"

She placed her hands on her hips. She was wearing the threadbare tank and Adrian's flannel pants. "Yes."

"Then get dressed." Adrian went for the glass tumbler they'd been using as an ashtray. She took it to the guest bath and flushed the ashes. Then rinsed it and tossed it in the garbage. "And tell your friend to get lost."

"Why?"

Adrian almost expected her to stomp her foot.

"Because we're leaving, that's why."

"Where we going?"

"To find you an apartment." She retrieved a spray bottle of Febreze and saturated her furniture.

"No. You don't need to do that."

"Yes, I do. You can't move in here."

"I'm not! It's just for a few days." Her voice went hoarse and Adrian wondered if it was from smoking or purging. It didn't matter, she didn't want to have to handle either one.

"I don't care. I said no."

A knock came from the door. Adrian opened it to find the smiling young woman.

"What's your name again? Cinnamon?" Adrian asked.

"Whatever you want it to be." She licked her full lips.

"Okay. Well, how about Get?"

She seemed confused. "Get?"

"Yeah. As in get lost." She slammed the door.

"You can't do that!" Sierra struggled to shout, hurrying to open it.

Adrian heard her calling after her friend. They were cussing, voices raised.

The Febreze wasn't strong enough, so she opened the back windows and turned on the ceiling fans. She found two thick scented candles and plugged in the candle warmers. It would take a while for them to heat up, but hopefully they'd do the trick.

Sierra returned looking ashen and angry, her face pinched.

"That was really dick of you," she said.

"So is this." Adrian held out her hands to indicate the room full of foreign objects.

"I didn't do it to make you mad."

Well, no shit.

"I did it because I have no other choice."

"You should've talked to me about it."

Sierra nodded. "You're right. I'm sorry."

"Doing this behind my back—"

"I was going to have it put away before you got home."

"It wouldn't matter, Sierra. It's wrong." She raised her voice and trembled in anger. Not wanting to yell any further, she headed for the bedroom to check the rest of the apartment. The bed was made and everything appeared to be in place on her dresser. She moved farther in and found two garbage bags full of clothes in front of the closet.

Thankfully, all of her own clothes were still hanging in the closet, the safe still on the top shelf.

She breathed deep and walked back to the living room. Sierra was sitting on the couch with her head in her hands crying.

Great.

"I'm sorry. I just—I didn't know what else to do."

Adrian crossed her arms over her chest. *I'm not giving in. I'm not giving in.*

"Ginger totally screwed me on this. She just told me four days ago. Said I had to leave by the end of the week."

"Why?"

"Because she met some guy and she—"

"What about the lease? She can't just walk out on the lease."

"I don't know. She didn't say."

"It's bullshit."

"What?" She looked up at her with watery eyes.

"Her story. Your story."

"I'm telling you the truth!"

"Then why can't you just take over her lease and stay in the apartment?"

"I don't know, okay? I'm just telling you what she told me."

"Well, I don't believe it. So get dressed and we'll go down there and take care of it."

She stood. "No."

"Why not?"

"Because. I don't want to deal with them right now."

"Them?"

Sierra shook her head as if she were confused. "Her—Ginger. She's pissed now."

"We'll talk to the manager."

"No. Not right now." She looked at Adrian. "I'll do it. I promise."

"Today."

"Today."

"Right now."

Sierra sighed. "Okay. But you don't need to come."

"I think I should."

"No, I'm not a baby. I can do it."

Adrian's cell phone vibrated. It was a text from Benny.

Uncle Jake back. Asked how long u wil b gone. We need 2 ship.

"I can do it," Sierra said. "I'll do it right now." She went toward the bedroom. Adrian saw her strip and slip into worn jeans and a light button-down to go over the tank. She finger-combed her hair and wiped her face. Her nipples struggled to poke through the thin tank top.

She looked so fragile. Adrian imagined her bent over the toilet making herself throw up. She remembered how it felt. The horrible burning of the throat, the taste, the smell. She knew what that was like. And she could only wish someone had shown her an ounce of kindness back then.

"Please, just give me a chance. I'll go right now."

"How? You don't have a car."

"I'll take the bus."

"You sure? Why don't you have a car?"

"I do. It's in the shop."

"For how long?"

"I'm not sure. It needs body work."

Adrian wanted to roll her eyes. More bullshit. "I don't believe you."

"Look, I'm telling the truth. It's in bad shape. It's been in the shop for over a week. As soon as I get paid again I should be able to get it."

Another text came. Benny again.

Hello?

Shit.

Sierra hugged her. Trembled against her. Despite the smoky smell, she felt good. And she wasn't trying to take anything. Quite the opposite. She was trying to move in.

"Okay."

Sierra jerked with more sobs.

"Thank you. Thank you so much."

"But you need to go. Right now. I'm not comfortable giving you a key yet. This all kind of scared me."

Sierra pulled away. "Okay. I understand." She wiped her eyes again.

"So take what you need. I'll be home at five fifteen."

"I have to work." She sounded sad. Squeaky.

"Do you have a ride home from work?" *Christ, why am I asking?*

"Uh-huh. Ginger."

"She works with you?"

"Yes."

"But you said she's mad."

"She'll get over it."

Another text came. Adrian didn't even bother to look.

"Okay, I gotta go." She headed for the door. Sierra slipped into her shoes and grabbed a heavy-looking purse. Then she grabbed a duffel Adrian didn't recognize.

They stepped outside and Adrian locked the door.

"One other thing," she said as they walked. "Don't smoke in my house."

"Okay."

"Ever again."

Sierra nodded. "I won't. I swear."

Let's hope you keep your promises, Sierra.

CHAPTER EIGHT

Adrian came home, exhausted, with a six-pack of Corona. The apartment smelled better and she was grateful, collapsing on the couch with a cold bottle of beer. Friday. Thank God. She took a long sip and glanced around.

Sierra's boxes were here and there along with the leopard lamp. She thought about how young she was. How seemingly vulnerable.

One and Two came trotting in as she switched on the television with the remote. They stopped at her feet and looked up at her as if they were disappointed.

"What? I'm not good enough anymore?"

Two yawned. One flopped down and rolled onto his back.

She drank some more beer and settled in for an episode of *The Deadliest Catch*. She wasn't ten minutes into a new episode when the doorbell rang. The cats scattered. Her body tensed as possibilities ran through her mind.

Sierra?

Or was it—what was her name? Ginger?

Groaning, she rose and pulled open the door.

Tamara stood leaning on her arm which was propped up against the wall. She looked like James Dean in *Rebel Without a Cause*. Red jacket and all.

"T." Adrian relaxed. "Thank God."

Tamara followed her inside. "Thank God?"

"Yeah, well, after the day I've had, I'd pay to see you." Adrian returned to the couch and plopped down. "Grab a beer and sit."

Tamara raised her chin. "Smells different in here. Good, but different. What happened, did you burn something and have to cover it or something?"

"Not exactly."

Tamara suddenly stopped and looked around. Her eyes swept over the lamp and the boxes, settling on the feather boas.

"Oh, hell no."

Adrian laughed. What else could she do?

Tamara walked up to the leopard lamp and touched it. "Hell no." She walked to the boxes and dug around a bit, fishing out a stuffed gorilla holding a banana bank. *Beer Money* was written on his tummy. "Hell, hell no."

Adrian laughed again and gulped some more beer. "You don't have to say it. I know. Believe me, I know."

Tamara stared at her. She raised an eyebrow. Adrian held up a palm.

"Really, T. I know. Grab a beer and come sit."

"She's not here?"

"No."

Tamara went to the fridge and grabbed the box containing the remaining three beers. She returned to the couch and sat, twisting open her bottle and setting the rest on the coffee table. She tucked one leg under the other and sipped her beer.

"So what's going on? She's moving in?" Her brown eyes were dancing with curiosity. She still had on her blue denim Steinman's work shirt and her earplugs were dangling from her neck on their necklace. She worked at a small factory and was one of the managers on the assembly line. She'd worked there almost as long as Adrian had been at Jake's.

"No."

"Could've fooled me."

"She needs a place and she brought her stuff over for the time being."

"You let her? Are you nuts? You'll never get rid of her now."

"I didn't let her. I came home and it was here." She finished her beer. Rain splattered the TV screen as one of the boats rode out a storm somewhere near Alaska.

Tamara breathed long and deep. She always did that when she was trying not to get upset.

"I took care of it," Adrian said, reaching for another beer.

"How?"

"I told her she couldn't move in. That she needed to find her own place."

"So what's with her stuff?"

"It was already here. I said she could stay for a few days."

Tamara clicked her tongue like a first grade teacher admonishing a bad student. "You're nuts."

"What am I going to do? Toss it all out on the street?"

"Yes."

"You're cruel."

Tamara smirked. "I've been called worse."

They both drank and sunk farther into the cushions. Tamara kicked off her shoes. Adrian did the same.

"You hungry?"

"Getting there." Adrian yawned.

"Pizza?"

"Sure."

"Half works and half pepperoni?"

"Sounds good."

Tamara found the phone and ordered. Adrian fought closing her eyes. She and Benny had worked nonstop when she'd returned. Her arms hurt from lifting box after box. Jake had walked by and merely grunted at her. She'd sighed with relief.

"So where is she?"

Adrian straightened, more alert. "Work."

"At her mysterious job?"

"I guess. She said she has a car too. It's in the shop."

"Right."

"I'm giving her the benefit of the doubt."

"Obviously."

Adrian smiled. "So where's your hunny bunny?"

"She's probably just getting home."

"Not going to see her tonight?"

"Who said that?" She tugged on her beer. "I'm just making sure you're okay, and then it's home to my sweet mama."

"Ugh. God. Don't talk like that. You're making me sick."

"You're just jealous."

Adrian thought for a moment. "Probably." Not of "It" but of Tamara's assuredness and happiness. Two things she secretly wanted for herself.

"But hey." Tamara slapped her arm playfully. "At least you're having great sex."

Adrian felt herself redden. After all these years Tamara could still get her to blush.

"Don't give me that bashful shit."

"Okay, okay. It's pretty hot. She's, er, energetic."

"She's also twelve."

"Twenty-one."

Tamara laughed. "Close enough."

Adrian saw her face change, saw the far-off look and then the sharpness of her eyes.

"Don't do it."

"Do what?"

"What you always do. Tell me I need to settle down."

Tamara stroked her lips thoughtfully. "But I want to."

"I know."

"This calls for it. It so does. And you know it."

"Yes, I do. But I don't need to hear it."

Tamara started in anyway. "I just don't get why you're doing this. Hooking up online—"

"I haven't done it that much. In fact, Sierra's the first one in…a while."

"The point is you shouldn't be meeting women like that. One after the other. One-night stands, short hook-ups."

"Well, no one interests me beyond a short hook-up."

"That's another thing we need to talk about. The way you find something wrong with everyone."

"Oh come on, T. One woman wanted a threesome with her husband. Another—"

"I'm not talking about the obvious weirdoes. I'm talking about—well, what about Heidi?"

"The clog dancer?"

"It was Irish dancing, and she was totally cute."

"She smelled like ketchup."

Tamara smacked her forehead with her palm. "See what I mean?"

"Well, she did. She always smelled like ketchup. Even her apartment did."

"You're incorrigible."

"Name another one." Adrian set her beer between her thighs and crossed her arms over her chest, determined.

"What about that veterinarian? She was nice."

Adrian fought rolling her eyes.

"She was," Tamara added. "So what was wrong with her?"

Adrian shrugged. "I don't know. She bored me."

"I'm telling you it's not just them, Adrian. It's you. You either go for total psychos or you nitpick the good ones. You always move way too fast. Just give it a rest for a while."

The doorbell rang. Tamara rose and paid the pizza girl. She brought it inside and tossed it haphazardly on the couch between them. They ate right out of the box.

Tamara took a steaming bite and picked up where she left off. "Just chill for a while. Explore yourself. Let love find you."

"Sounds really boring and very Dr. Phil."

"More like Oprah. And you have to do things. Get out more." She paused while they both chewed. "Do things you enjoy."

"Like what?"

"We have that new art class starting tomorrow."

Adrian grumbled. She'd totally forgotten.

"Come on. You'll love it. You're very creative."

Adrian frowned.

"You're not getting out of it. So don't even try."

Adrian continued to eat her pizza as she considered it. She did like art. And she was creative. She'd just never really focused on it before, coming up with most of her ideas and implementing them at work.

"I don't know," she said sipping her beer. "You know how I feel about school." She didn't have fond memories.

"It's not a class class. It's for fun. You don't get graded or anything. You just go to learn and enjoy."

"Are you sure?"

"Positive."

"What if I get bored?"

"We'll leave. You promised me a month ago you would do this with me."

Adrian thought about it some more. It did sound a bit interesting. And she vaguely remembered Tamara selling her on it a while back. They ate in silence for a while with the Discovery Channel playing in the background.

Tamara finally spoke, still trying to convince her.

"I know you like to learn. With all the books you used to read—"

"Okay, okay. I'll go."

"Really?" She took a bite of pizza crust.

"I'll give it a try." It couldn't hurt. Right?

Tamara smiled. "I can't wait. I've been wanting to take an art class. Harriet took one—"

"Harriet." Harriet? Again? God, it had been months of nonstop Harriet.

Tamara stopped. "So?"

She shouldn't have said anything. It had just come out. "Nothing. Sorry."

"What's with it with you? Why don't you like her?"

"I don't not like her."

"Yeah, obviously you do." She finished her beer and sat back with her arms crossed. "And I want to know why. Especially considering you haven't even met her yet."

"I—" She hadn't met her. And she didn't want to.

"I know why." She stood. "Because you're jealous."

"It's not that, T. It's just—"

"Yeah?"

"You're always going on about her."

"So?"

"So it gets tiring."

"I see. I bore you."

"No, come on."

Tamara carried her beer bottles to the trash. Her movements were quick and sharp. She was obviously pissed.

Adrian stood. "I just have to hear about it all the time."

"Well, you won't anymore."

"T, don't be like that."

"I'm not being like anything." She headed for the door. "I'm sorry I bore you with talk of my girlfriend."

"You don't bore me. It's just constant is all."

"That's because she's special. I think she's the one and I happen to be excited about it." She pulled open the door. "And I really wish I could share that with my best friend."

"T, come on."

She turned and slipped into her jacket. "I'll call you tomorrow about the class."

"Forget about the class."

"Hell, no. You're going. Consider it punishment for being an ass."

Adrian laughed. Typical Tamara. She couldn't leave mad.

"Now, give me a kiss so I can go." She offered Adrian her cheek. Adrian kissed it. "I'll call you. Good luck with Cap'n Crunch."

"Thanks." Adrian watched her go and then closed the door. She put away the leftover pizza and then settled back down on the couch. She turned off the lamp and stretched out to watch more TV.

A half a hour later, when sleep came, she let it.

CHAPTER NINE

A drian stirred as she heard the front door open and close. Someone was humming. She opened her eyes and saw it was Sierra.

"Hey, baby," Sierra said.

Suddenly she was at Adrian's level, a huge grin on her face. The smell of beer and cigarettes permeated from her.

Adrian sat up. "Hi."

"You fell asleep waiting for me? How sweet."

Adrian didn't argue. "I guess. Was watching some TV."

Sierra sat on her lap. "Poor baby. So tired. I think you deserve a prize."

She blinked her heavily made-up eyes and she looked almost like a woman of the sixties with thick eyeliner and mascara.

"Where have you been?"

Sierra stroked Adrian's hair and hugged her. "Hmm? I've been at work."

"What's with the makeup?"

Sierra stiffened, then stood. To Adrian's surprise, she went straight into the bedroom and closed the door. Water ran and soon, the shower.

Seeing an opportunity, Adrian knelt next to Sierra's bag. She dug through it carefully and immediately found two rubber-banded stacks of money. Fanning them, she saw they were mostly ones and fives and a few twenties. She returned the money and continued to dig. She felt more paper. Wads of it. Looking farther, she saw they were fast food wrappers. A dozen or so. There was also a small red book full of names and phone numbers. She flipped through it and found that most of the names were men and most included a symbol. Some had hearts, some had stars, some had dollar signs. A few had skull-and-crossbones designs.

Adrian's heart went into panic mode. The book and its meaning made her feel sick inside. She closed it and dug farther. She found a pack of cigarettes, a can of pepper spray, and several pairs of thong underwear.

What the hell is all this?

She held up the underwear, knowing the answer somewhere down deep.

"Fuck."

She shoved everything back into the bag. Sierra wasn't telling her everything. In fact, she probably wasn't telling her *near* everything.

She walked slowly into to the bedroom and sat on the bed, staring straight ahead. She could hear Sierra singing in the shower. It was a popular song about trust. How ironic.

Adrian stripped out of her clothes and pulled back the covers to climb into bed. It was after two and she was beat. Her mind, though, couldn't relax. Sierra was trouble. She just knew it.

The light from the bathroom soon extinguished and Sierra emerged naked. She smelled of shampoo and sweet pea–scented soap or lotion. Her skin felt warm and slightly moist as she crawled under the covers and snuggled next to Adrian.

"Hi."

Adrian considered pretending she was asleep. But she decided against it, too worked up to sleep anyhow. "Hi."

"I'm surprised you're still awake." Sierra clung to her. "You ready for your prize?"

"No, not really."

"Not in the mood?" She sounded pouty.

"No."

"Ah, that's too bad."

Sierra stroked her face. Her breath smelled like toothpaste with a hint of beer. Maybe she was a bit inebriated.

"Are you okay?" Sierra asked.

Adrian didn't answer right away.

"Baby?"

"I don't think so."

The room was dark and silent. The only light a dim nightlight from the kitchen.

"Why?"

What to say?

"I don't know."

Ask her. Ask her. Ask her.

Ask her what?

Are you a stripper?

A bulimic?

A house hopper?

Adrian rolled over. She just wanted to sleep. To wake up and find Sierra gone, off living her life happily somewhere. Anywhere. Just not here.

It wasn't that she didn't like her. She did. She just didn't want her living in her home. They weren't girlfriends. They weren't anything. She didn't even know her last name. She knew it, but Sierra hadn't shared it with her.

"I bet I can make you feel better." Sierra slipped her hand around Adrian's waist and tried to place it between her legs. Adrian stopped her by grabbing her wrist.

"No. Not tonight."

"How come?"

"I'm tired."

"Too tired for me?"

"Yes."

She felt Sierra move away from her. Heard her huff and felt her climb from the bed.

"Where are you going?"

"I'm leaving you alone."

Adrian turned. Sierra was rummaging through a pile of clothes in a box. For a brief moment, Adrian thought she might dress and leave the apartment.

But that thought was stymied as Sierra slid into some panties and a sleeveless shirt.

"You're getting up?"

"I'm hungry."

Of course you are.

One and Two seemed to understand and they came out from under the bed and followed her into the kitchen.

Adrian listened for a while, wondering what was left in there to eat other than pizza. She heard the fridge open and close, then the microwave and then Sierra talking to the cats. After a while, it was silent and Adrian closed her eyes.

She recalled the two years she'd suffered with bulimia. The binging until she was stuffed and then the purging into the toilet. She remembered the fear, the total loss of control. How it had made her so sick she could hardly swallow or hold anything down.

It was bad.

The stench.

The taste.

The retching.

Awful.

Humiliating.

And now she was living it again.

Through Sierra.

CHAPTER TEN

Saturday morning burst through the bedroom windows in cheery, bright rays of yellow and orange. Adrian blinked against it and rolled over, expecting to find Sierra. The bed was empty and she strained to see if she could hear her moving about the kitchen or talking to the cats. But there was nothing.

Sighing with relief, she stretched and groaned and languished in her sheets. The alarm clock on the nightstand read 10:15. She'd slept late and her body seemed to be thanking her for it, her muscles wonderfully relaxed and warm from her stretch.

Saturday was always her favorite day. No obligations, no Uncle Jake— Wait. She sat up.

"Shit. The damn class." It started at eleven. She hurried into the bathroom and turned on the shower. Sierra's toothbrush sat staring at her along with a kid's tube of bubble gum–flavored toothpaste. A good-sized makeup bag was snug against the mirror, covered in a thin layer of facial powder. Sierra's name was written in marker across the front. *Is she afraid I'm going to use her make up or mistake it for my own? Good grief.*

Where was Sierra? Why did she care? She wasn't there, and that was all that mattered. She jumped in the shower and tried not to think about her as she bathed, but the task was difficult with Sierra's shampoos and conditioners huddled in every corner of the tub. She was like a virus. Her toiletries, her germs, spreading and growing and occupying her world. Pretty soon she'd be breathing her in, carrying her presence into every cell in her body.

She had to do something or she was going to go insane. She

climbed from the shower and dressed quickly, running a cream pomade through her hair and hurriedly going back to brush her teeth. When she entered the kitchen she found a note from Sierra on the counter.

I'm gone for the day and I have to work very late. S.

Adrian crumpled up the message and threw it away. She was probably afraid she was going to bug her again about finding her own place. And she was right, because that was exactly what she'd planned on doing. Taking her apartment hunting.

But it was just as well. She had class and she preferred to have her place to herself. She searched through her cabinets and scowled, unable to find much of anything left she felt like eating. So she downed a glass of juice and slipped on her coat, leaving the cats asleep against one another on the couch.

She enjoyed the drive to the community college, loving the feel of a bright fall day. Tamara was waiting for her outside one of the main buildings. Her face showed pleasant surprise as Adrian approached.

"What? You really didn't think I'd show, did you?"

"Nope."

"Thanks."

"You came to get away from her, didn't you?" Tamara looked freshly scrubbed and wide-awake, wearing her trademark red jacket and carrying a large tote that was probably full of supplies.

"No. She wasn't there when I woke. Said she would be gone all day and wouldn't be back until late."

"Really?"

"Mmm-hmm."

"She must be afraid to stick around while you're home."

"That's what I figured."

"Try not to worry about it right now. Don't let her ruin this class."

They entered the building and Adrian felt snug in its warmth. She powered off her phone and let it sink in her pocket. Tamara was right. It was time to focus on this, even if it wasn't something she was totally excited about.

They wound their way through a peppering of people and turned the corner into a second hallway. The smell of paint and clay and graphite struck her nose and Adrian found herself smiling in sudden anticipation. She eyed one open classroom and then another as they passed by. And then Tamara led them into theirs.

"Welcome," a smooth female voice said as they entered. Adrian searched for the source and found it standing off to the side wearing a knee-length free-flowing dark green dress with black leggings and fur-lined black boots. Adrian bumped into Tamara, caught up in the woman's sun and sand–colored hair and green eyes. Her smile could've melted Antarctica.

"Let's sit here." Tamara led her to the far back table where they made themselves comfortable on stools. The room smelled like paint and clay just like the hallway did, only with the faint scent of chai. Adrian ran her palms over the soft, thick wood of the table, trying not to stare at the woman who had greeted them. Tamara took their coats and hung them on a rack along the wall. She was all smiles as she returned to sit next to Adrian.

"This is gonna be so much fun."

"Is that our teacher?" Adrian asked.

"Probably."

"She's really...pretty."

"Pretty?"

"Yeah. You know."

"She is pretty. And probably married. Way off-limits."

"I'm not interested. I was just..." *Noticing.* She stole another glance. The boots weren't high heeled. They were flat and looked very warm. And the small beads wrapping her wrists looked modest and pleasant. Her earrings dangled and matched. But she wore no necklace. More importantly, she wore no ring.

The woman greeted another student and closed the door. She crossed to the front of the class and clasped her hands together as she smiled. Her gaze drifted to Adrian, where it lingered oh so briefly.

"Can I have everyone's attention?"

The people around them, all of them women, quieted down.

"Thank you. I'm Morresay Morgan. And I will be your instructor for this class. Art Expression for Women."

Adrian shot a look to Tamara. "A women's class?" she whispered.

"I thought we'd be more comfortable here."

"You surround me with women but you don't want me worrying about one ruining class?"

"Shut up and listen."

Up front, the woman had stopped talking. She was looking at Adrian, who blushed profusely. Thankfully, the woman continued.

"Please call me Morresay."

Morresay. Adrian grew more curious. What an unusual name. Who was she?

"I teach art at one of our local schools along with a beginning art class here at the college. I created this one for the general public to help connect women with expression through art. I find there's nothing more therapeutic or stimulating."

She crossed to a side table full of supplies and lifted a stack of off-white art paper and began passing it out.

"Use the pencils on your tables to write down your name and telephone number and an e-mail address if you have it. After that, I want you to tell me about any art experience you have, such as classes you've taken or books you've read, et cetera. Then tell me why you're taking the class."

When she reached Adrian's table she didn't look up, just slid over the papers. Tamara passed around the pencils from a basket in the center and Adrian got busy doing as instructed. She finished quickly, having no previous art experience and no real reason for taking the class. She simply wrote "my friend wanted to."

Everyone passed their papers forward and Morresay started in on expression and how to use art to express oneself with the upcoming art media, and how the class wasn't about perfection but about individuality.

"We're going to start with pencils today. I want you each to just start drawing. Let your mind go and see where it takes you. Don't be afraid. Draw whatever is there. Use the pencil, use shading, use the colored pencils. Just let it all out."

The class mumbled and stirred as Morresay handed out larger pieces of paper. This time she smiled at Adrian when she reached their table.

"Do you have a question?"

Adrian shook her head.

"Don't hesitate to ask." She touched her shoulder and Adrian's body reacted at once to the heat she felt coming from her hand. In a flash, it was gone and she was patting the middle-aged woman next to Adrian on the back as she walked away.

"You may begin," she said, once again glancing at Adrian. "You have until the end of class."

There was more rustling and soft whispers as everyone focused. Soon the class was silent, save for the scratches of their pencils across paper. Adrian started in with a new pencil Tamara handed over from her bag. She'd brought plenty of supplies for the both of them. Adrian stared at the paper and started drawing a large oval shape, completely unsure where she was going. To her surprise, a face developed. Then eyes, cheeks, chin…and an *X* where the mouth should be. Something within her churned and she pulled the paper closer, knowing what she must draw. It was just suddenly in her mind's eye and she couldn't get it out fast enough or dark enough. She worked furiously, going over and over her lines. Then she started with the shading, laying her pencil down to use her fingertips. She pressed and smeared and pressed and smeared. Her heart thumped pleasantly and her whole body seemed to hum, powering her hand.

Before she knew it, time was up and Morresay was speaking.

"Please place your papers on my desk on your way out. I'll e-mail you with some notes about the next class, so please check your mail. If you need a hard copy you can take one from my desk. Thanks, everyone. See you Wednesday."

"You ready?" Tamara was standing next to her. "Whoa, Adrian. That's incredible. Look at mine." She held up a colorful drawing of a peacock.

"That's good."

"It's remedial. Yours is…Jesus. What is it?"

"Nothing." She stood and they made their way to Morresay's desk. Adrian's heart rate slowed when she saw a framed photo of a man sitting on the desk. He looked to be laughing and the light seemed to be dancing in his eyes. He must be her boyfriend. Or lover or something intimate. She was too attractive to be single. Still, Adrian knew she'd enjoy looking at her. She read the wooden nameplate next to the photo. It read *Morresay* in cursive. Adrian placed her paper face down and breathed deeply as they stepped into the noon air. She felt refreshed and at ease, as if the class had been a pleasant rush of adrenaline.

"So you're going to come back with me Wednesday?" Tamara asked, fishing out her car keys.

"Yes." It was out before she knew it. "It was fun."

WTF? Fun?

Tamara seemed surprised as well. "I wasn't expecting that good a reaction. But great."

Adrian found herself smiling again. The smile lasted all the way home but diminished as soon as she entered her apartment. The virus that was Sierra was everywhere still, staring at her from the numerous boxes. She sighed and sank down on the couch next to the cats. The reality of her day slowly eased in followed by the all-too-familiar restlessness. The class had cleansed her somehow and she wanted nothing more than to retain that feeling and just relax the rest of the day. But Sierra's things, her presence, reminded Adrian of what she didn't have, of what she wanted and always was after. Passion. Romance. That rush of fire you feel just as you kiss a new lover. It was a high that leveled everything else in her life. Loneliness, bad thoughts, bad memories. All of it was just obliterated when she had that fire.

She rose and went into the bedroom closet to retrieve her laptop. She'd hidden it from Sierra under a loose stack of folded sweaters on the shelf. With it in tow, she sat at the kitchen table and switched it on. It didn't take long for her to log in to her favorite chat room, and once she had, she turned on her stereo and found "Cold" by Annie Lennox and powered up the volume.

With a quick rub of her hands, she started up conversation with a few regulars and settled in for the hunt for someone new to play with. Even if she couldn't meet them in person, she could still obtain her high through words. And with it being Saturday, the chat room was hopping and she knew it would only be a matter of time.

❖

The alarm on Monday morning came way too early. Adrian rolled over and smacked the snooze button, hoping she was dreaming. But the loud snoring next to her confirmed reality. She grabbed her head and stared up at the ceiling. Normally, her heavy eyelids would threaten to close, to take her back to sweet slumber land, but she was too upset to fall back to sleep. The weekend had been long and strange. Sierra had worked for most of it, claiming she'd had no time to look for a place of her own. Adrian had sat at home, staring at her laptop, chatting with numerous women, wishing like hell she had her place to herself. She'd moved the boxes, trying to shove them all to one corner and then searched through the newspaper herself, trying to find Sierra a place. When she'd shown the ads to Sierra last night when she'd returned home, she'd seemed uninterested. But she'd promised Adrian she would go and look at the places today.

Adrian hoped so. Prayed, even. Because her life was being intruded upon by someone she hardly knew.

The snoring grew louder and there were long pauses between snorts. Adrian elbowed her and it shook up the pattern of her breathing a bit, but the snoring continued. Giving up, Adrian rose and showered, standing beneath the hot water for a good ten minutes after she'd washed herself.

I'll give her the day, and if she doesn't find a place, I will take tomorrow off and take her myself.

She climbed from the shower and dried herself. When she entered the bedroom, she was surprised to find the bed empty. She heard rustling in the kitchen as she dressed, the smell of maple syrup strong.

"Good morning, sunshine," Sierra said from behind her.

Adrian turned and found her standing in the doorway, a plate of pancakes in her hand. She was nude. And stunning.

"Hi."

"I made you breakfast."

"I see that."

"Aren't you hungry?"

"Not really. Where'd you get the food?" The pantry was empty. Adrian had lived off peanut butter sandwiches all weekend, refusing to buy groceries, preferring to wallow in her sad, precarious state of "no food thanks to crazy house guest" instead. She'd even refused to go out with Tamara for drinks Saturday night. Another reason to avoid meeting Harriet.

"I stopped at the store on my way home last night."

"I didn't see any grocery bags." She grabbed her keys and wallet off the dresser and slid both into her jeans pockets.

Sierra's brow furrowed. "I didn't buy much, and I stuck what I did buy in my duffel bag. Why does that matter anyway?"

She shouldered past her. "It doesn't."

Sierra followed. "What's wrong with you?"

"Nothing." She opened the fridge, searching for juice, but found nothing.

"Don't you want this? I made it just for you."

"I told you I don't do breakfast."

She closed the fridge, pissed. Maybe she should have at least bought herself some more juice.

"Can't you just this once? Since I did it for you?" She sounded hurt and her eyes looked sad.

Adrian leaned back against the counter. "Sierra—"

"Please? Just a bite? Just to be nice?"

"I—"

"Don't tell me you don't eat breakfast." Her voice had lowered and suddenly her words were razor sharp. "I saw the cereal boxes, I know—"

Adrian stepped up to her quickly and took the plate. "Okay. I'm eating it. Thank you." She took two big bites and chewed, hoping it would settle her down.

Sierra still didn't look happy. "You know, when people do nice things for you, you should be nice and grateful and you should be thankful. Didn't anyone ever teach you that?"

She swallowed. "Yes." No, not when Louis came along. That wasn't Louis's way.

"Then why won't you accept things from me?"

"Like this?"

"Like anything. I've made you meals, tried to give you massages, cleaned the apartment, tried to give you money…"

She set down the plate, unable to force any more down. She had done those things, but mostly at around three a.m. when Adrian was dead to the world.

"I don't want those things, Sierra."

"Why?"

"Because I didn't ask for them."

"So you can't accept something you didn't ask for?"

"No." Not in this case. It would mean giving up what tiny bit of control she had left, and the thought terrified her.

Sierra crossed her arms over her breasts.

"Look, Sierra—"

But she'd turned and headed toward the bedroom. "Just forget it, Adrian."

Adrian followed and found her standing by the bed, head down. Her shoulders shook as she cried.

"Sierra—" But she didn't know what to say. She just wanted her out. No amount of do-gooding on Sierra's part was going to change that.

"Don't. I don't want to hear your crap, Adrian. You just don't like me and you're not woman enough to say it." She flopped onto the bed and yanked the covers up over her head.

Adrian didn't know what to do. She felt like shit, like some ogre who'd attacked an innocent villager. Fuck. Why did Sierra make her feel this way?

She walked to the bed and touched her shoulder. Sierra jerked.

"Sierra, I'm sorry. I just—"

Sierra pulled down the covers. "Just what? Can't force yourself to eat my pancakes?"

"I don't eat that kind of stuff for breakfast. I eat cereal."

"And you can't eat pancakes? Ever?"

"I—" She sighed.

"Face it, Adrian. You hate me and you want me out." She wiped away her tears and scowled at her. "Ginger is right. You're a self-centered, stuck-up—"

"Ginger? Your friend?" She shook her head. "She doesn't know me. She shouldn't have even been in my house…"

"See? You're mean and you hate me."

"I don't hate you, Sierra. I'm just—mad." She turned and paced. Her skin felt hot with anger. She couldn't seem to find the words to explain anything to her. She felt helpless and trapped.

Sierra sat up. "Why? What did I do? Other than fuck your brains out, which I might add, you loved every damn second of, I've done nothing to you."

"You moved in here! Without even asking me!"

Sierra clamped her mouth shut. "So that's it, then. I'm not wanted."

"I can't do this, Sierra. No, it's not that I can't—it's that I won't. I just won't. Not after you just moved in like that. It scared the shit out of me." She had done enough arguing with her for one lifetime. She couldn't do it anymore. She turned to leave. "You need to find your own place today."

"I don't have a car yet."

"Too bad."

"I need another four hundred to get mine out of the shop."

"So get it."

In the living room, she slipped her arms into her jacket and zipped it up. Sierra came out after her, tears streaming down her face. Her chest was red and splotchy from emotion. Her perfect little breasts bounced slightly as she walked. Adrian had to force herself to look away.

"I will," Sierra said. "I will get it. Just let me stay until then. Please." She touched Adrian's chin, tilted her face to meet her gaze. "Please? And then I will have a car and I can go. Please tell me you like me at least that much."

Adrian felt her stomach clench with guilt. What if she was telling the truth? Could she really kick someone out to the street? She stared into her beautiful eyes and cleared her throat.

"I'll be home at five thirty."

Sierra hugged her, squeezing her tight. "Thank you. Thank you."

She stood there for a moment with Sierra clinging to her. She wasn't sure what to do with her hands, so she tapped her shoulder blade a few times.

"Don't smoke in the house."

Sierra pulled away. "I won't. I swear it." She smiled.

Adrian tried to return it but couldn't. Her face felt like stone.

"Have a great day at work," Sierra said.

Adrian took one last look at her living room, then turned and walked out the door.

It was exceptionally loud as she slammed it closed behind her.

CHAPTER ELEVEN

Y ou are the most gullible woman on the planet," Tamara said just before she bit into a crunchy-sounding taco. Red sauce dribbled down her chin and she wiped it away quickly with a brown paper napkin.

"I'm not gullible. I'm not even being nice. I told her to get out."

"Yeah, when she gets the money for her car. When's that gonna be?"

Adrian paused, taco held in midair. "She has money. I've seen it in her duffel bag." She bit in and chewed.

"She keeps money in her duffel bag? How much?"

"I don't know. A few hundred at least. Small bills."

Tamara dropped her taco. Her eyes hardened.

Lunch was quickly becoming strained and it was short enough already. They only had forty minutes to eat after the driving time from work. And today Chicken and Tacos was packed, taking away another five minutes to wait in line.

Adrian tried to steer away from the subject of Sierra by refilling their sodas, but Tamara was determined, biting into her instead of her taco as she sat once again.

"Please tell me you've got a clue."

Adrian grew annoyed. "A clue about what? Can't we just enjoy lunch?"

"Forget lunch. I'm talking about your Cap'n Crunch crook here." Her eyes widened and she got that look that always came over her just before she said something deadly serious. "Your girl's a stripper, Adrian."

"Wha—?" Adrian felt the blood rush to her face. She'd tried not to think about it, tried to ignore all the signs. But now Tamara was forcing it in front of her face, making her look. And suddenly she was sick from the sight. "Shit."

She slapped down her napkin and felt truly embarrassed. Why had she ignored it? Because facing it would've meant many different things. Namely, that Sierra had way more skeletons in her closet than bulimia.

"You really didn't know?" Tamara was studying her.

She forced herself to swallow. "I—I had my suspicions."

"And you're okay with that?"

"Of course I'm not okay with it. I just didn't—know what to think." She stared at her plate as shame and anger collided with the embarrassment.

Tamara touched her hand. "Do you think I'm wrong?"

"No." She said it softly, her gaze still fixed on the wasted taco.

"Are you okay?"

"I'm not sure what I feel."

Tamara leaned back in her chair. "Well, I'd be pissed. I wouldn't want some chick like that all up in my place and all over me."

"Why didn't she tell me?"

Tamara laughed. "I wouldn't tell, either. It probably scares people away. Which is why she has no place to stay."

"No, her friend, the one that was at my place…she's a stripper too. I'm pretty sure." She recalled Ginger's outfit and the way she'd looked at her like she was trying to bait her, like she *knew* how to bait people. "It all makes sense."

"Aren't you mad?"

"I don't know. I think I'm—I feel stupid. I knew something was off."

"Maybe you refused to accept it."

"Maybe." Everything else about Sierra had bothered her. Why hadn't she delved further into this aspect?

"What are you going to do?"

Adrian balled up her trash. "Right now I'm going to go back to work and let this all sink in. Then I'm going to call Smith and see if she'll check into her for me." Smith was a mutual friend and a cop.

Tamara rose to throw their trash away, then returned and threaded her fingers together on the table. Around them people chatted and laughed, slurping on drinks.

Adrian wished she could rewind her life to two weeks before. She and Tamara would be sitting there shooting the shit without a care in the world.

"What do you know about her?" Tamara asked, eyeing her watch.

Adrian considered the question. "I know her full name and address and her birthday. I secretly looked at her driver's license."

"Well, that's good. At least you got that." She seemed to think for a moment. "But it could be a fake."

"Ugh. God, don't go there."

Tamara flipped open her phone.

"She's refused to tell you what her job is, right? I mean, you've asked her?"

"Yeah. A few times."

"So she's hiding it. Lying."

"I guess."

Tamara began to type with her thumbs.

"What are you doing?"

"Texting Smith."

"I'll do that—"

"I'm doing it for you. Something's weird about this chick, Adrian."

She sat back and scoffed, upset. "I hate it when you do this shit."

"I know."

"No, I mean I really hate it. I said I would do it."

Tamara finished and closed her phone. "I know. You don't like not having control."

"What?" She squinted at her. "It's not about that..." Was it?

Tamara's phone rang. "Hello?" She smiled. "What's up, Officer Smith?" She laughed and made small talk for a few seconds. Then she caught Adrian's scowl.

"Oh, yeah, listen, can you look someone up for Adrian?" She laughed again. "Yes, she's still fine as hell but very angry." She winked at her. "Okay, here she is."

She handed the phone over.

"Hey, Smith."

"Hey there, Adrian. How's life?"

"Not too good at the moment."

"Need some help?"

"Yeah, if you can. Can you tell me anything about a Sierra Ann Franklin? Age twenty-one, birthday December third."

There was a pause and she could hear Smith mumbling the information and typing.

"I got a Sierra Ann Franklin here, but she's not twenty-one. She's nineteen."

Adrian cursed under her breath.

"December third."

"That's probably her."

"Five-six, blond hair, blue eyes. One twenty."

"That's her."

"I see. Give me a sec. Yep, she's got a record and…yep, there's an arrest warrant out on her right now."

Oh, fuck.

"What for?" Panic beat in her brain.

"Indecent exposure, underage drinking, and resisting arrest."

Adrian gripped the phone so tight her fingers hurt. She felt sick and betrayed, like an invisible hand had just slapped her hard across the face.

"You know her?" Smith asked. "Listen, Adrian if you do, my advice is to stay away. Her rap sheet's a mile long and that's not counting her juvenile record—"

"Thanks, Smith. I owe you big time." She couldn't take hearing anymore. She handed the phone back to Tamara and stood.

Tamara stood as well and told Smith she'd call her back.

"Are you okay?"

Adrian started walking to her car, her legs on autopilot. "No."

"What are you going to do?"

"I'm going to kill her."

"What?" Tamara fell into step next to her. "No, you're not."

"Yes, I am. I'm going to go home and I'm going to kill her. Then I'm going to throw her out."

Tamara took her keys from her.

"Hey—"

"I'm driving," she said, rounding Adrian's car.

"You're coming with?"

"Oh, hell yeah. I wouldn't miss this for the world."

She unlocked the doors and Adrian slid into the passenger seat.

Tamara scooted in behind the wheel and started the engine.

"I'm also keeping your ass out of jail."

"What about work? I don't want you to get in trouble." Adrian knew she damn near ran the place and her boss adored her. But still... Tamara didn't have to do this.

"I'll call in. Tell them it's my period."

"You're kidding."

Tamara smiled as she put the car in reverse. "It works every time."

CHAPTER TWELVE

O kay," Tamara said as they sat looking up at Adrian's apartment. "Smith said two units are on the way. So you've got two minutes to go in and scream at her. Do you think she'll put up a fight?"

"Probably. Until I tell her the cops are coming."

"All right."

They climbed from the car and headed for the stairs.

"I got you," Tamara said as they reached the door.

"I know. Thanks." She got out her key and hesitated. She was suddenly bombarded with images of Sierra's sad face with tears in her eyes. "I don't know. What if she really is trying—"

Tamara took the key. "Let me do it." She turned the lock and shoved open the door.

Adrian blinked with shock as she caught sight of Sierra. She was on her knees in front of the couch, her head bobbing back and forth over a man's lap. Her small tits swayed, resting on top of the cups of her bra.

"What the fuck?" Adrian let out, startling the man and Sierra both.

The man jumped up, terror on his face, wet cock in his hand. Sierra turned and leapt to her feet. Her tits were red and hard.

"What the *fuck* is this?" Adrian couldn't believe what she was seeing. She was so disgusted and shocked her guts fell to the floor and throbbed.

"Babe, babe," Sierra started, palms toward Adrian, ring of saliva on her mouth.

Rage rose from Adrian's chest and words came, seemingly from nowhere.

"Get out, *now!*" She shook, teeth clenched, hair on end.

Sierra halted and the man, who was pudgy and bald and very obviously scared out of his mind, yanked up his pants and fumbled to secure them. He started mumbling prayers, something about *God* and *get me out of here* and *I knew I shouldn't have done this especially after last time.*

Sierra started coming at her again, tucking her breasts back into her bra.

"Babe, it's not what you think." She tried to touch Adrian but Tamara pushed her back. She kept talking. "It's nothing. I swear it's nothing. Babe…"

"Get away from her," Tamara said. "And don't you even think about touching her."

Sierra glared at her. "Who the fuck are you?"

"Her best friend and now your worst nightmare."

"I'm supposed to be afraid of you?"

"If you're smart. But oh wait, that's impossible."

Sierra looked at Adrian and Adrian couldn't stand to look back at her. The pleading eyes, the pleading mouth, the sad, "pitiful me" look. She hated it. Hated every last little detail.

"Adrian, please."

"I said get *out!*" she screamed at her again.

Sierra tried to touch her again.

This time Adrian got right in her face.

"Out!"

Then she stalked toward the man and threw her keys at him as hard as she could. He cowered, shielding his face with his arms.

"I don't want no trouble. I don't want no trouble," he mumbled.

"Then get the hell out of my house."

He whimpered in fear as she marched up to him, grabbed him by the shirt, and shoved him out the door. He stumbled and fell into the stairwell. He prayed some more as he got to his feet and then nearly tumbled as he ran down the stairs.

Adrian turned, facing Sierra. "And as for you…you better get out of here before I do something I regret."

"But babe, I—it's not what you think."

"You were sucking some guy's dick," Tamara said. "What is it about that she's not getting?"

Sierra kept staring at Adrian. "I was trying to make money for my car. Remember, you told me to get it? The money? He meant nothing to me. Only you do. Babe, please."

Tamara laughed.

Sierra snapped at her. "It's not funny!"

"What? Prostitution isn't funny?"

"I'm not a prostitute."

"A prostitute in denial? Even funnier."

Sierra looked at Adrian again. Adrian stared right through her. She had nothing more in her as far as Sierra went. She was done.

"Get out, Sierra."

"I don't have anywhere to go."

"Yes, you do. The cops are on their way. I'm sure a jail cell will be nice and comfortable tonight."

Sierra fell silent. Looked from Adrian to Tamara. "You're lying."

"I'm not lying. I called the cops. You have an arrest warrant. I suggest you leave. Now."

A look of panic came over her. She took a step and then stopped. Then she did it again. In the distance, a siren wailed.

Sierra looked out the door and her young face went slack. Then, without looking back, she took off down the stairs and ran through the parking lot wearing nothing but a pair of baggy jeans and a bra.

Adrian and Tamara watched as the cop cars pulled in and caught her trying to run into the surrounding woods. There was yelling and cursing.

When one of the cops gave chase and finally tackled her, Adrian and Tamara closed the door.

"You okay?" Tamara asked.

Adrian stood in the center of her living room. She felt like a zombie. "No."

Tamara looked around, scowled at all of Sierra's things, and opened her cell phone. "You will be as soon as we get this shit out of here."

CHAPTER THIRTEEN

I really don't feel like being here," Adrian said as she and Tamara neared the building of their art class. It was Wednesday evening and all she'd wanted to do after work was go straight to her online chat room and talk up a few chicks for some mindless cyber fun. Anything to keep her mind off the Sierra fiasco. The sooner she replaced that nightmare, the better. A new fire was just what she needed.

"Trust me, this is just what you need. Besides, you even had fun last class."

They headed inside and began the weave through the mass of students, making a perfect zigzag stitch by the time they reached the appropriate door.

Adrian had checked her e-mail before she'd left work and read over the notes Morresay had sent on their upcoming class and the use of charcoals.

Morresay had also said to choose something meaningful to draw and to bring it with them. Adrian had the photo of the Native American woman she kept on her bookshelf at home. She had first seen it with her nieces in a *National Geographic*. She'd said she would love to draw her someday so her nieces had framed it for her and given it to her for Christmas.

"Adrian?" Morresay was looking at her with hopeful eyes.

Adrian's heart skipped a beat before any kind of rational thought even processed in her mind. "Yes?"

"Can I talk to you for a moment?"

Adrian looked to Tamara who shrugged. "Sure." She followed her to her desk, taking in her thick purple sweater and dark pants. Today she had three rings on, all of them large turquoise. A matching necklace hung from her neck. Her thick sun and sand–colored hair was tugged back into a loose ponytail. Her earrings were simple silver hoops.

Adrian stared at the fine blond hairs along her upper jaw. She wondered briefly what it would feel like to kiss her right there, to whisper words of desire there so close to her ear as she inhaled her scent.

"I wanted to talk to you about your drawing from Saturday night."

Adrian blinked back to reality and struggled to recall what she'd just said. Morresay cocked her head and Adrian knew she was doomed.

"Sorry?" *Please don't think I'm an idiot.*

"It's very good. Very good." She opened a manila folder and pulled it out. "But I noticed you said you didn't have any prior art experience?"

"That's right." They were on safe ground and she relaxed a little. Her blood still thrummed though, making her skin feel alive.

"Well, I must tell you you've got some talent. Has anyone ever told you that before?"

"My friend."

"No art teachers in school?"

"No."

She paused and studied Adrian for a moment. "Are you interested in art?"

Women were milling in around them, excited about class.

"Yes."

"Good." Her eyes sparkled and a crooked smile came. "I really think you should develop your talent."

Adrian wasn't sure what to say. She wasn't used to compliments like this.

"Do you mind if I use your drawing as an example in class today? Are you okay with that?"

"Sure." Was she? Too late now.

Morresay nodded. "Great."

Adrian headed back to her table and tried to clear her mind.

"She likes your drawing, doesn't she?" Tamara asked. "I knew she would."

Adrian glanced back at the photo of the man on Morresay's desk before focusing in on Morresay once again. She stood at the head of the class and began talking. Adrian liked the way she moved her hands as she spoke. Liked her laugh. She seemed so sincere and extremely passionate about art.

Passion.

Adrian sighed. She would never have that with a woman like Morresay. She was too…taken. And her tastes seemed to be unlike any woman Adrian had ever dated. She was…eccentric. Yes, that was it.

Morresay started in on the drawings as Adrian went over and over in her mind as to why she shouldn't be having physical reactions to her. It calmed her mind, but her body was still surging with energy. It must be the room. The art of creation. It stirred her in powerful and unusual ways.

Morresay held up a few drawings in front of the class and asked their artists a few questions. Adrian began to grow more nervous, knowing her turn was coming.

"I have one last drawing I'd like to show you." She held up Adrian's for all to see. There was a collective gasp. Adrian's drawing was unlike any of the others. It was completely void of color and very dark in content. It showed a face with an X where the mouth should be, wicked-looking trees and vines behind it, and the word *MUTE* written along the bottom.

"This one was done by Adrian Edwards. Adrian, can you tell us what this represents?"

Her face was aflame. Just a raging fire on her shoulders. But she had to speak. For once in her life someone was actually wanting her to confess her feelings.

"She can't speak," she said. "The woman. She can't speak."

"But she wants to," Morresay replied. "You can see it in the eyes."

"Yes." Adrian cleared her tight throat. Morresay seemed to understand. "She wants to but can't."

"Tell us about the vines."

Adrian looked into her eyes, saw the depth and the encouragement.

She felt safe suddenly, lost in her warm gaze. "The vines keep growing because she can't speak. So they keep growing and twisting around her. Same with the trees. There's all this mess and growth and she can't do anything about it because she can't speak."

There were some mumbles and Morresay held her eyes for a few long seconds and then smiled. "Thank you, Adrian. Very good work."

She felt odd and incredibly hot. Tamara touched her hand and she nearly jumped out of her skin.

"I'm glad you're here."

Adrian went to speak, but her voice had run off. Something was happening. Something was coming up from deep inside. She nodded at Tamara's sentiment and suddenly she felt like crying. She covered her mouth, overcome with an overflow of emotion.

"Are you okay?" Tamara asked, looking concerned.

Adrian darted for the door, heard her stool tumble somewhere behind her. A hush fell over the class as she pushed out into the hall. She made it two doors down before she doubled over with pain. Her ribs screamed and her throat ached as she leaned against the wall. Aching attempts at sobbing came. Wave after wave, and she felt like the face in the drawing, the vines twisting and cinching around her, insisting she stifle her cries. It hurt. God, did it hurt.

"Adrian?" A hand came to rest on her shoulder.

She straightened, expecting to see Tamara. But it was Morresay. Adrian wiped her eyes, more than embarrassed.

"I'm okay."

"No, you're not." She moved her hand up and down on her arm. It still felt so warm. "And I'm so sorry. I should've never had you do that in front of everyone like that."

"I'm fine." She breathed deep. "Really. I don't know where that came from."

"It came from in here." Morresay placed her hand on Adrian's heart.

Adrian straightened, panicked she could feel just how hard her heart was beating.

"That's what this class is about." She gave her another soft smile, one that offered understanding, and removed her hand. "If you ever want to talk about it…I'm here."

"Thank you." Adrian wiped her face again and smoothed down

her jeans. She wanted to bolt. To say to hell with this and just leave it all behind. But she remained. And Morresay could somehow see it all.

"Can you continue with class?" she asked.

"Yes." It was over now. The pain had dissipated almost as quickly as it had come. She trembled a bit, knowing the emotion could return, the path already cleared. But she held fast to hope and tried to focus on Morresay and her soothing voice and understanding eyes. She fell into step next to her and nearly closed her eyes as Morresay opened the door and smoothed her hand over her back.

"It will be okay," she whispered, encouraging her to reenter.

To Adrian's relief, everyone was already hard at work, drawing their item from home. Nobody paid her much mind, and those who did offered nods and kind smiles of understanding. Tamara stood to hug her but Adrian couldn't, afraid she'd be overcome again.

"I'm okay. I just need to forget about it."

"Okay." They both sat and Tamara handed Adrian her framed photo. Morresay was walking around the class, instructing on charcoal use. Adrian kept her calm voice in the back of her mind as she started to work. Each of them had a small table easel today and a supply of charcoal pencils. Adrian focused on her photo of the Native American woman and drew her face quickly, outlining the contours and shape first. Then she started in on the detail and the shading. She moved her drawing to the flat table and liked the feel of it better. Tamara worked next to her, humming a popular song. She had brought an old teddy bear to draw.

Before Adrian knew it, Morresay was winding down class and Adrian's fingers were covered in black.

The drawing looked good. Incredibly real. But it needed more work.

"Okay, everyone. Please return your charcoals to the baskets."

Adrian groaned, feeling like she'd run out of time on an important test.

"Please turn your drawings in. You can work on them some more on Saturday. If anyone wants to wash up, there's a sink in the back."

A few women stopped to look at Adrian's work as they walked by. All of them were impressed. Adrian thanked them, feeling somewhat shy. She couldn't believe class was already over. The hour and a half had flown by. She'd been lost in her own little world.

She stood and stretched, surprised at how stiff she was. She must've been really hunched over while she worked on the drawing.

Morresay smiled at her again as she and Tamara turned in their work. She stared at Adrian's for a long moment but didn't say anything.

"Have a nice rest of the week, ladies."

"Thanks, you too," Tamara said.

They stepped out into the night and Adrian felt lighter. Like a weight had been lifted. She closed up her jacket as they headed for their cars. They walked slowly, winding through campus, making note of the main student union. Tamara suggested they eat dinner there before class one Wednesday.

By the time they reached the parking lot, Adrian was feeling so relaxed she was ready to go home and go to bed. Tamara was telling her good-bye when she caught sight of Morresay in the near distance. A man emerged from a sedan and enveloped her in a tight hug. He looked a lot like the man in the photo. Adrian forced herself to look away, feeling like she was intruding on a private moment.

Tamara followed her gaze. "She's really nice."

"Yeah."

"That her man?"

"Probably."

"All right, well, call me tomorrow." She gave her a half hug and set off toward her car. Adrian did the same, sitting behind her steering wheel watching Morresay and the man follow one another out of the parking lot. As she started her car and headed toward home, she thought of the lonely night ahead, and that old restless feeling came once again. Sleep would not be easy in coming.

❖

"Thank God for Bobbie," Adrian said as she and Tamara climbed the ancient brick steps to their friend's place.

"I can't believe I'm here," Tamara said as she knocked on the door of the old two-story farmhouse. The stereo was booming, shaking the windows. A huge rainbow sticker was pressed against the window on the end. Sort of like those big red E's stay-at-home moms used to put in their windows to let the neighborhood kids know their house was a safe haven should they ever need it, should a stranger be after them. Adrian imagined dozens of queer kids sprinting toward Bobbie's house, backpacks trailing behind them, faces red with exertion as bullies and parents who refused to understand chased them. Bobbie would welcome them with strong arms and a firm pat to the back.

Laughter came from inside the house. "A party is the last thing either of us needs," Tamara added.

"I know." She was lying through her teeth. She wanted this. Needed it. "I think I hate parties."

"Since when?" Tamara smoothed down her own shirt. She looked good in her red jacket, jeans, and a pale button-down. Her two necklaces, both thin suede with attractive crosses, led down to a hint of cleavage. Sexy but tasteful.

Adrian didn't feel near as suave, wearing worn jeans and an old sweater she favored. Her peacoat had seen better days as well, but she didn't care. Not tonight anyway. She was there to occupy her restless spirit and to scope for women. She couldn't care less if someone was scoping her.

"You've been down in the dumps since See—whatever her name was."

"Sierra."

"Right, Sierra. The hooker."

"Did I tell you she actually had the gall to call me and tell me she was a go-go dancer?"

"You did."

"Can you believe that? She's in jail and she uses her phone privilege to call me and try to explain everything. Said she wasn't a stripper but a go-go dancer. As if that would make it all better."

"What was the blow job, then? A new dance move?" Tamara wrapped an arm around her. She squeezed. "Hopefully, you'll have some fun tonight."

"One can hope."

"You've even been quiet in class. Did Morresay piss you off or something?"

"No."

"She tried to talk to you this morning and it was like you were zoning her out or something."

"Everything is fine." Everything was as it always was, but

she knew Tamara wouldn't consider that fine. Other than work and Morresay's class, she hadn't gone anywhere, preferring to stay home to wallow in isolation, fearing all things young and attractive for the time being.

The sad thing was she'd actually enjoyed her isolation, becoming a bit of a slug, trudging slowly around the apartment, leaving a trail of ooze behind her. The time alone had been safe, padded in silence and peace. Cocooning her in her little apartment, in a nice warm place where a sensitive slug could move about without fear of being punctured or prodded.

The gears in her head had slowed during her time alone and even the meows of One and Two had seemed drawn out and eerie. And now she felt a bit dizzy as her eyes and head tried desperately to take in the real world at real speed once again.

Tamara knocked harder on the door and it was eventually answered by three very attractive, very young gay men. Adrian recognized one as Bradley, Bobbie's nephew. He'd lived with his aunt for the last ten years, and together they ran the small farm. Bobbie had taken him in, taught him all she knew, and playfully referred to them as "the two fags with a farm" ever since.

"More lesbians!" the shortest one yelled.

Skinny arms pulled them inside and they were welcomed enthusiastically with half hugs and cheek kisses. Bradley wore his usual ear-to-ear grin along with a tight-fitting long-sleeved shirt tucked into a pair of jeans that would've cost Adrian a week's salary. Despite his blue-collar earnings, Bradley had very expensive taste and loved to show off his costly accumulations whenever he could. One would never guess he shoveled pig shit for a living.

"Good to see you, Adrian," he said, giving her a wink.

"You, too."

She and Tamara moved farther inside and found the house thick with women, cigar smoke, and heavy music. She recognized the CD playing at once. Nine Inch Nails. From there, more heavy, throbbing bands would ensue. Anything that was good to fuck to. That was always Bobbie's motto when she chose music for her parties.

The music, the smoke, the press of sweaty bodies against her as they walked, it all seeped into her senses and reminded Adrian of better times.

She breathed deeply.

Ah, yes. A party at Bobbie's.

There were at least two a year and they were always heavily populated and wild with every lesbian within the county lines attending. Adrian mused that the rainbow sticker in the window drew them in.

She started to relax a little, the familiarity comforting. Tamara seemed to notice, slapping her arm around her again and hugging her close.

"There you go," she said, happy. Her eyes danced. She took a beer from a young, offering butch and pointed. "Go forth, my friend. Go forth and find happiness."

Adrian looked around, thinking she just might do that. "Where will you be?"

"In here, waiting for Harriet."

"Right. Harriet." Why hadn't she just ridden out with them? Oh yeah. She'd had to work and wanted to get ready. Why did she have to come at all?

"So we'll be around."

We'll be around? She hated the sound of that.

"Until you want to leave," Adrian sniped. "Guess that means I'm driving myself home?" She cringed as soon as the words escaped her. When did she start sounding like a whiny bitch? "Never mind. God, I'm sorry. I'll be fine."

Tamara seemed a little surprised as well. She tugged her closer. "Hey, I'm not going to leave you here. Why do you think I insisted on riding with you? I came because of you."

"Thanks. I'm just so—"

"Depressed."

"Yeah, I guess I am."

"It's okay. This'll be fun. You'll talk to friends, make new ones…"

"I thought you wanted me to focus on myself more?" She smiled, teasing.

"I do. Notice I didn't say go forth and find a woman. I said go forth and find happiness."

"I see. Distinction noted." But there were women everywhere. If Tamara wanted to cheer her up while focusing on herself, then she should've taken her to a straight shindig.

Tamara handed over the beer. "Forget about what's-her-name and go have fun."

Adrian took several big sips and nodded. "Will do." She tipped the beer at Tamara and wound her way through to the kitchen. Bobbie was sitting at the round table holding playing cards, a thick, dark cigar hanging from her mouth. She looked the same. Short dyke do, winter weathered face, thick fleece shirt. Four other women sat with her, all of them concentrating on their hands.

"Hiya, kiddo," Bobbie said to her, not holding her gaze for long. "Want in?"

"Nah, thanks though."

She anteed up. "Drinks are outside in the cooler, along with the keg. Brad made cookies and other goodies. They're on the counter. You know the drill."

Adrian looked to her right and saw four huge plates of cookies and brownies along the counter. Several women lingered, laughing and touching one another in casual conversation as they nibbled.

"Thanks," she said to Bobbie, who had already refocused on the game.

After nodding a few more hellos, Adrian grabbed two big chocolate chip cookies and headed out the back door.

The night air was cold and welcoming. Large gas lights tried to penetrate the winter fog and a few standing heaters did their best against the cold. Not many women were out there, preferring to huddle in the warm house instead. A few shouldered past her, heading back to the door, plastic cups full of beer.

She walked to the edge of the large redwood deck, turned and leaned on the railing, and ate her cookies. Even with the heaters, the night was crisp enough to see her breath, but she didn't mind. It felt refreshing, and it seemed to help penetrate her body and mind. She stared up at the country sky. It was pitch black with millions of tiny, piercing stars.

Beautiful.

She inhaled the cold and caught the scent of weed over the frozen but ever-present stench of manure. The mingling scents further relaxed her. She took in the stars and ate her cookies. They were "magic" cookies, baked with weed but still damn good. Bradley was the master of baked goods.

With two in her belly she realized it might just be a good night after all. More women emerged from inside, most looking for the keg. An image of Morresay came and Adrian imagined her breezing through the door with a soft smile on her face, her hair loose and bouncing thickly on her shoulders. She imagined her wearing a heavy oatmeal-colored sweater and worn jeans with silver rings on all of her fingers. Her fingertips were dark, smudged with graphite or charcoal. Her eyes were alive and glinting at her. Burning. And they were looking directly at her as if they'd finally found what they'd been looking for.

"Yes," Adrian whispered, almost closing her eyes, wanting to get lost in that fantasy.

A small group of women approached and interrupted her thoughts. They came to a stop near her, huddled to light a hefty-looking joint, then passed it around. Her gaze fell on a fit woman near the center waving the joint away. She wasn't Morresay, but she was attractive… and maybe even actually obtainable. She was a light blonde with a creamy white, beautiful face. Dark, deep looking eyes matched the surrounding blackness, pulling in all things dark and nightlike. The woman looked up and caught her stare. Adrian looked away, pretending to sip her empty beer. She waited a few seconds, then carefully moved her eyes over to her again. The woman was laughing. Happy. She had a nice smile. Not a big smile but a nice one.

"You want in on this?" one of the other women asked Adrian, holding the joint out to her.

"Uh, no. Thanks." Normally she would've said yes. But the smoke always burned her chest and made her cough. And she wasn't about to do that in front of the blonde. The magic cookies would have to do. And the beer. Speaking of which, she needed another. She crossed the patio, tossed her empty bottle in the trash, and looked in the open cooler. There was no ice, just a pile of various bottles.

She groaned and dug through the Bacardi and Mike's Hard Lemonade, preferring not to drink the light beer in the keg. Finally, she managed to rummage out a bottle of Killian's Irish Red. The taste was worth the trouble and she sipped it as she worked her way back to the far edge of the deck.

The blonde was still there, looking fine in nice-fitting jeans and a leather jacket. Her boots had heels. Very high, thin heels. The sight sped up Adrian's adrenaline a bit, causing her to become even more curious.

She stared at her body and noted that her bosom appeared as full and as ample as her ass and her legs looked thick with muscle. She either lived on a stair climber or she walked straight up mountains every day.

Nice.

But wait. Adrian wasn't supposed to be there for a woman. She was there to relax and have fun. So why wasn't she inside with Tamara and some of her other friends?

She should return inside.

But her feet remained anchored. This was the game. The lure. The spark that lead to the fire.

She drank some more.

Then…

"I can't do it either." The blonde was next to her, talking to her. Smiling.

"Sorry?" She turned with her, putting the house behind them.

"The pot," she said. "I can't do it either."

"Oh."

"Because of work. They drug test."

"Right."

She liked her, found her very attractive. The night was good. Great even. The fire was coming, she could almost *feel* it. She was a heroin junkie slapping her arm for a vein, the goods already cooked and ready, loaded in the syringe.

The blonde didn't seem to notice her inner turmoil. "I'm Joanne." She held out her hand and Adrian hurriedly pulled the beer from her lips and shook it.

"Adrian." She tried to sound suave, smooth, ambivalent. Instead it came out deep and quick.

"Yeah, I've seen you once before, I think. You're friends with Tamara, right?"

"Yes."

Joanne nodded. "I thought so. I saw you here at the Christmas party last year."

"You were here?"

Joanne's face fell a little. Adrian struggled to explain. "I would've noticed you."

That seemed to do the trick.

"I wasn't here long. My friend got sick and I had to take her home."

"It wasn't Bradley's infamous cookies, was it?"

Joanne laughed. "I don't know what it was, but it was pretty scary. I didn't eat for two days after witnessing that. I think it might've been the eggnog."

Adrian laughed and leaned more on the railing. She was at ease with Joanne and she tingled with the kind of warmth that came after a deep laugh. She felt good.

"So what do you do that requires such drug testing? Fly commercial airliners?"

"Right." Joanne grimaced playfully. "I hate flying, and believe me, everyone on the plane would know it." She took a sip of her Bacardi. "I'm a mail carrier."

"Ohhhh," Adrian let out, long and slow.

Joanne cocked an eyebrow.

Adrian blushed as she explained. "I…you look strong…I figured you—" She stopped, feeling ridiculous.

Joanne studied her for a long moment, her dark eyes penetrating. The irises were so dark they reflected the light, like black, mirroring disks. When she spoke, her voice was smooth and low.

"I lift weights. Several days a week. And I walk a lot. Several hours a day. Six days a week."

"I figured." Adrian couldn't help but sweep her eyes over her once again. Joanne caught her.

"You like my legs?"

The air between them grew dangerously hot. Adrian swallowed, the junkie finally isolating a good vein. "Yes."

"Really? Even with the jeans?"

"Yes."

Joanne moved closer. Adrian could smell her cologne. It was slightly masculine, contradicting the high heels, fueling her awakening libido even more.

"I like yours, too. In fact…" She touched Adrian's hand with the tips of her fingers. They were cold with rings on every finger. "I like everything about you."

Adrian felt herself grow light-headed with pleasure.

"And these I really like." Joanne reached out and touched her lips. "Can I—?" Joanne licked her lips. "Kiss them?"

A short, hot breath escaped Adrian. Joanne moved closer, inhaled it. They stood very still, breathing in one another.

Adrian closed her eyes and allowed the tingling feeling to move up through her body and into her chest. She wanted to kiss her, wanted to touch her. The junkie was flicking the syringe, giving it a quick squirt.

"Yes."

She wanted to shout it into the night, then laugh deeply as it echoed back to her.

She felt good. Damn good. And she felt even better when Joanne's lips touched hers. They pressed and then parted, the insides warm. Joanne slipped out her tongue, asking. Adrian met it with her own and the night around them spun.

The heroin plunged into her vein and was surging up through her.

Around and around it went inside her. Just like the night surrounding them. Lights, music, stars. All of it spinning.

Adrian clung to her as if Joanne were an anchor, never wanting it to end.

This was it. This was the fire. Her drug.

She blinked with surprise and wonderment as Joanne pulled away and spoke.

"Bathroom, now."

"What?"

"Now."

Joanne took her by the hand and led her quickly into the house. They maneuvered through the mass of women and tunneled through the wall of smoke. Adrian heard a couple of people call her name, but she was in a zone, in her own little world of Joanne and the humming pleasure stroking her insides. She knew she was smiling but she didn't remember thinking about doing so. It was just there, plastered on her face, stinging her cheeks. They reached the bathroom just as a woman emerged. Joanne tugged Adrian inside quickly, closed and locked the door, and then slinked up to her.

"You're even sexier in the light." The corner of her mouth lifted in a seductive grin. She moved into Adrian, pinning her against the wall between an ancient standing sink and a hanging towel. The scent of mouthwash and cigars was powerfully strong.

"You look pretty good, too." The tiny room threatened to spin just as the stars outside had moments before.

"Just pretty good?" She flipped back her long mane of hair. "I think I better do something to change that." Holding Adrian's face, she leaned in and kissed her.

Her lips were warmer than before, almost hot. But her tongue felt cool as if it weren't connected to her body. Adrian's mind fought to make sense of it.

"What's wrong?" Joanne asked.

"Huh? Nothing."

Joanne appeared concerned but then her attention went to their surroundings. She seemed unnerved. Adrian pressed her head back and stared at the mauve ceiling. Matching roses trailed down the white walls. She had the urge to reach out and touch one. Instead, she reached for Joanne and nuzzled her hair. It smelled like flowers. Not roses but better.

"Smells so good."

"My hair?"

"Mmm. Hmm."

"It's clean."

"I know. I can tell." Oh, she just wanted to get lost in it. She wanted to get lost in everything, just take it all in and examine the microscopic beauty of it.

Joanne glanced around again. "That sink looks scary. Look at that drain."

"Huh?" Adrian pushed off the wall and looked. The drain was a dark hole with no guard but it wasn't dirty. It was just an old sink.

"That's terrible," Joanne said. "And God only knows how old that toilet is."

"Old." Adrian laughed, amused at herself. "This house is very old, Jo—" Oh fuck, what was her name? It was Joanne right? Yeah. Right? She laughed again.

Joanne smiled and came at her again. "You can call me Jo. Or whatever you like." She pressed her hips into Adrian. Their lips met again. Warm and soft. No tongue, just powerful tugs that made Adrian's legs tremble with desire.

But then Joanne was looking around the bathroom again. She turned on the sink and scrubbed her hands, rubbing them together furiously. "You better wash yours, too. No telling how many people have been in here. And who knows when it was last cleaned."

Adrian tried to comprehend but it was difficult. The roses on the wall were jumping at her. The bathroom seemed soft and alluring. She wanted to stroke the fuzzy pink rugs, rub her face in the pink towels. She started laughing. Joanne grew impatient.

"Can we get out of here?" She was drying her hands on her jeans.

Didn't you just want to come in?

Adrian nodded, though she was confused.

Joanne motioned for Adrian to open the door. She didn't seem to want to touch the doorknob. Adrian found it cool and perfectly round in her palm. Smooth.

She opened the door and they emerged into a surreal haze of women and smoke.

By the time they reached the living room, Joanne's hand was on her ass. "I wanna take you home," she said into Adrian's ear.

Adrian liked the sound of it, the strum of her syrupy voice, the feel of her breath near her ear.

Turning in to her, Adrian slid her own hand down Joanne's backside. She squeezed and was thrilled at how thick and firm it was. She wondered what it felt like without the jeans. She yearned to be completely nude with her, slipping and sliding beneath white cotton sheets.

"Okay," Adrian said and then kissed her, this time urging her tongue into her mouth. Joanne groaned and kissed her back, grabbing her head and twisting her own tongue around Adrian's. Somebody whooped.

Adrian kept kissing her, eyes closed, posture relaxed, loving that she didn't have to worry who Joanne had been possibly kissing hours before. Or where her hands had been and on whom. She didn't have to worry about who had touched her, put their mouth on her, used her, ogled her. All the things she now thought about when she thought of Sierra.

The freedom from worry was exhilarating.

Applause echoed throughout the living room, intertwining with the music like some strange cacophony of percussion that didn't quite fall into rhythm. It sounded eerie, like the musical score of a bad B-movie full of psychotic human hunters.

For a brief second, it scared her.

Adrian pulled away and saw Bradley's friends, grinning and clapping like children egging on a first kiss. They protested at the cease of action.

"We need more privacy," Joanne said. Waving them off, Joanne took her hand and led her to the front door. More people spoke to them, spoke to Joanne. They were her friends, giving her hugs. She seemed to be rather popular and it made Adrian feel a little special.

Adrian looked past them, and was just about to step outside with Joanne when she caught sight of Tamara sitting on the couch next to a beautiful redhead.

"Hang on a sec," she said to Joanne, kissing her quickly before making her way to Tamara.

"What in the world are you doing?" Tamara asked, standing. "Who's that?"

Adrian smiled. "That's Joanne."

"Uh-huh, yeah, I know who she is. Tell me you aren't leaving with her."

"I was thinking about it." She bobbed on the balls of her feet and felt her eyes widen. "I'm having fun, T."

Tamara held her face. "Your pupils are huge."

"They *feel* huge. Like cat's eyes or something." She felt like she could see anything, even in the dark. Everything was intensified and the detail was amazing.

"Adrian." She stared into her eyes. "You're tripping. You need to sit down and drink some water. I knew I should've made you eat something before we came." She grimaced over at Bradley. "What did you put in those cookies?"

"Just the usual. With a little something extra, just for fun." His friends laughed and several women made a beeline for the kitchen, apparently anxious to get their own.

Tamara urged her toward the couch. "Sit down."

"No, I'm okay. I'm going to go with Joanne. She's really amazing. And her hair smells sooo good."

"Uh-huh. Okay." Adrian looked to the redhead who stood

alongside them. "Adrian, this is Harriet. Harriet, this is my best and very high friend, Adrian."

Harriet smiled and stuck out her hand. Adrian shook it, moved by her soft beauty.

"It's very nice to meet you, Adrian. Tamara adores you."

"Wow." This was Harriet? She was so pretty.

"I hope that's a good wow?" Harriet looked a bit worried but her eyes sparkled with humor. Her posture was self-assured but open, almost soft, as if anyone could hug her if they so desired. Adrian wanted to, curious about the scent of her appealing white V-neck sweater. Would it smell like warm cotton? Fresh laundry detergent? Maybe fabric softener?

Adrian forced her odd curiosity from her mind, and noticed instead how nicely the sweater went with her khakis and how her oversized watch and brown boots were the only thing giving away her otherwise well-hidden tomboyish tendencies.

"Yeah." Wait, what was she saying yes to? Never mind. She was nice, yes, that's it. And…what was the word? Sincere. Tamara's other girlfriends had been so obviously fake, so jealous of her relationship with Tamara. But this woman seemed really cool. And grown up. And… Adrian could just sense everything about her. She just knew. As if she suddenly had this antenna with the ability to really read into people. "You're really…" She couldn't explain herself. Had no idea how to even begin. "Thanks for being real."

She knew she sounded weird. But she couldn't help it. How could she explain the suddenly rational and incredibly clear realizations racing through her head?

Tamara shrugged as if she had no idea if Adrian was really the one inside her body or not. She could've been an alien after all. It would certainly explain her strange behavior.

But Harriet wasn't bothered, double clasping Adrian's hand in response. "Thank you, too, for being real."

Tamara spoke and Adrian could hear the concern in her voice. It seemed to be dripping from her mouth. She even looked at her, ready to wipe it away.

"We were just getting ready to leave, Adrian. So why don't you come with us?"

Harriet released her hand. Adrian touched Tamara's chin, surprised to find it dry and smooth. Tamara grasped her hand, forcing Adrian to focus.

"Well, let's all leave, then," Adrian said.

Tamara seemed pleased. Relieved.

"Wait." She reached in Adrian's pocket and retrieved her car keys. "I'll drive."

"Yeah, good idea. You take my car. I'm going to ride with Joanne."

"Wait, what? You're not seriously going with her, Adrian. We haven't even been here an hour."

"So?"

"So you don't even know her." She pulled her close. "This is what you're trying to avoid, remember? The one-night stands, the getting in way over your head too soon."

Adrian hugged her, so moved by her concern. She loved her so much and she squeezed her until she pulled away.

"I know, T, but this is different. And she smells good and she's an adult. She's a mail carrier. Do you know how incredibly *normal* and *amazing* that is?"

Tamara's eyes grew wider. "What did I tell you about normal?"

"I have no idea."

Tamara closed her eyes as if offended and impatient. "No one's normal, Adrian. Not even you. We all have issues and anyone who says they don't or pretends not to—"

"Joanne is normal. I can *feel* it."

"You're high, Adrian."

Adrian laughed. Just the way Tamara had said it, seriously cracked her up.

"I love you, T. I love it when your eyes open real wide like that." She looked at Harriet. "Don't you love it when her eyes do that?"

Harriet nodded and gave a half-shrug as if she didn't want to agree with her but she had to, the truth demanding it of her. "You know…I do. It's adorable."

"Yes! Directly from the mouth of babes."

"I can't argue with her," Harriet said to Tamara.

Adrian was pleased. "See, Harriet's a good woman, T. She knows her stuff."

Tamara shook her head. "The both of you?"

Harriet shoved her hands in her pockets. "Can you blame us? We love you."

Tamara sighed long and slow and led Adrian by the elbow. "Yeah, yeah. Come on, let's go." They slipped into their jackets as Adrian waited and then headed for the door.

Joanne was waiting outside, hands stuffed in the pockets of her leather jacket. A striped scarf was wound around her neck.

"Hey, you ready?" she asked Adrian as they approached.

"I think Adrian better ride with me," Tamara said. "I think she better go home."

Joanne glanced at Tamara, and for an instant she appeared offended and even defiant. Adrian thought she was going to lash out. But when she spoke, her voice was light, almost airy.

"Oh, well, okay. But I really don't mind taking her. And she wants to go."

Images shot through Adrian's mind. She did want to go with her, wanted to run her fingers through her long mane as Joanne gyrated atop her, her ass flexing as she moved.

"Really, T. It's okay. I'm going with her." She walked with Joanne toward a small pickup truck. "I'll get my car from you tomorrow." She smiled and gave Tamara a thumbs up.

Tamara didn't look happy but she gave in, helpless. "Okay. But you call if you need me. I don't care what time it is."

"I will. Bye, Harriet."

Harriet held Tamara close, as if comforting her. "Bye, Adrian. It was nice to meet you."

"You, too." Why did Tamara seem so sad?

"Have a good time. And be careful."

Adrian smiled. "I will." She turned and walked with Joanne to her truck. By the time she climbed inside, buckled her seat belt, and looked out the window, Tamara and Harriet were gone.

❖

Joanne's place was on the opposite end of town from Adrian's. They didn't say much on the ride over, Adrian pleasantly buzzed and grinning, Joanne humming and tapping her thumbs on the steering wheel. When she did speak she talked about her house and all the work she'd done on it, even making some of her own furniture. It sounded impressive and Adrian was very impressed and more than a bit excited at the prospect of possibly having found someone she could really sink her teeth into. So to speak.

Joanne seemed well spoken, well taken care of, and very creative. Adrian rested her head on the cool window and considered adding the phrase "in bed" after each of those statements.

"Something funny?" Joanne asked, looking over.

"Oh, no." Had she laughed aloud? "I'm just happy is all."

"Me, too."

Her house was small but cute and looked, as best she could tell in the dark, to be painted a pale yellow with white trim. A short chain link fence surrounded the quaint front lawn. There was no garage so they exited the truck in the driveway and Joanne opened the gate to lead the way to the front door. On the front stoop she smiled, bent to adjust a ceramic statue of a gnome, and then unlocked the door.

Adrian watched her wipe her feet on the welcome rug and step inside. Lights came on. Adrian followed quickly only to see Joanne removing her shoes and placing them on a wooden rack next to the door.

"I don't wear shoes in the house."

"Oh."

Adrian closed the door and removed her own shoes. Joanne took them and set them next to hers on the rack.

"It helps keep the floor clean."

Adrian took in the tiny but impeccably neat home. It smelled lemony. "Makes sense."

"It upsets some people."

Joanne was watching her closely, apparently waiting for her to say something.

"Nah, it's good. I understand." The wood floor was gleaming and the carpet in the living room was pale and looked new. She totally understood. She wouldn't want it messed up either.

Joanne still looked anxious. She was clenching her hands together, tugging on her fingers, standing there in her thin socks. She was quite a bit shorter without her boots on. But still over five foot five.

"Did you do all this yourself?"

Joanne released a breath and her body relaxed. "Yes. All of it."

"Very impressive."

"Thank you."

Her eyes shined.

"It really is. I wouldn't have a clue how to do—"

Joanne moved quickly, silencing her with a kiss. Adrian felt herself being pressed against the wall. She moaned softly and went limp, allowing Joanne to take the lead.

Hands tangled in her hair as Joanne's tongue came. It didn't tease. Didn't ask permission. It just came, all slick and smooth and knowing. Cool and soft with womanly wine like lips, kissing her, tugging on her, awakening her, wanting her.

Adrian pulled her closer and kissed back, their tongues dancing, a blooming desire spreading between her legs. The room didn't spin this time but she didn't need it to. Joanne was enough.

She could feel her large breasts pressing into her, soft and heavy and so beautifully woman. Joanne seemed to understand as she pulled away and held Adrian's gaze, her fingers trailing down her own shirt only to tear it open. She held it open while panting, chest heaving and elevated. It was an offering. Like sweet, soft, pale flesh to a bloodthirsty vampire.

Adrian attacked, face buried in her cleavage, leading her back to a nearby couch. They fell upon it with grunts and groans and Joanne held fast to Adrian's head, begging her take more.

Adrian bit her billowing flesh while sneaking her hands around her back to unlatch her bra. When it fell from her hands, Joanne sat up and stripped out of both her shirt and bra, throwing them quickly to the floor. Then, with a dangerous look, she pulled Adrian back down atop her.

"Take them. Ah, please, take them."

She was pushing her breasts inward and upward, holding them for Adrian, nearly breathless.

Dark chocolate nipples stared up at Adrian, surrounded by large fudge-colored areolas. Her mouth watered as she thought about the taste of chocolate and flesh mixed. Maybe if she kissed her hard enough, swirled her tongue thoroughly, sucked all the flavor to the tips, maybe she could actually find out. She dipped her head and took one completely, causing Joanne to cry out in ecstasy.

It was fervent and loud, throaty and smoky like the esophageal burn of a shot of whiskey.

It shot inside Adrian's ears and widened her eyes with lust, squeezed her heart with a gnarled fist of desire. She took her harder, devouring her breasts like they were fruits of the earth, the last remaining nourishment for humankind. She fed until they were slick, swollen and rimmed in red, puckered and reaching for her, screaming for more.

Joanne cried for more for them, lifting her head to look at her with needful irises and rich merlot lips.

She was beautiful in a desperate, hungrily vulnerable kind of way at that moment. Her thoughts and physicality were controlled by desire, ruled by lust, her breasts slimy with ache, her lips plump with heated blood.

Adrian watched her chest rise and fall with hurried, passionate breaths. Watched her lips twitch, her tongue sneak out to moisten them, her eyes focus and flash. Then she crawled off her and unbuttoned her jeans, yanked them down forcefully along with her panties. She threw them to the side, removed her socks, and stood looking down at her.

Joanne didn't speak. She just stared back.

Adrian dropped to her knees and pulled her to the end of the couch, swinging her feet around to touch the floor, her back resting against the cushions. With their eyes locked on one another, Adrian pushed her legs open and kissed her way up her inner thighs. She felt her jerking and hissing and when she reached her clit and flicked her tongue over it, Joanne sank her nails into Adrian's scalp and shouted.

"Yes!"

She thrust her hips, shoving herself into Adrian as if unable to stop. Small noises came from her, little pushes of air escaping her lips as she rocked into her.

Adrian gave to her, used her tongue to press against her clit, flicking and licking, Adrian fucking her clit, Joanne fucking her face. Again and again and again until Joanne's cries grew louder and louder, until her voice eventually gave out, and Adrian wrapped her hands around her thighs and took her clit between her teeth and shoved with her tongue while shaking her head.

Joanne went hoarse, her body went rigid, and when she threw her head back the muscles in her neck stood out and climbed alongside the column of her throat.

She held Adrian to her, milking her orgasm, desperately trying to get every last molecule of pleasure from Adrian's tongue. Her breasts swayed a little and Adrian could feel her heels digging into her back. Darkness began to creep in on Adrian just as Joanne went limp and fell back into the confines of the couch. Adrian breathed deeply and collapsed onto the floor, staring up at the ceiling, watching in a mindless state of numb awareness at the floating dark flecks moving in her line of sight.

With the free flow of oxygen to her lungs, the flecks began to disappear one tiny speckle at a time.

Joanne was saying something from the couch. She couldn't hear her. She sounded too far away.

Soon she was standing over her and lifting her by the hands.

"Come on."

Adrian sat up and focused. Joanne was moist with sweat and her breasts looked pleasantly bruised. The thick muscles in her legs slinked up and then down as she pulled Adrian into a stand. Her ample ass cheeks took turns boxing themselves as she walked ahead of her, leading into the bedroom.

"Go ahead and undress," she said with a naughty grin. "Take off everything."

She disappeared into the bathroom and Adrian heard water running. As she undressed she took in the room. Like the rest of the house, it was small but neat with pale carpet, a queen-sized bed, and matching furniture. The only thing odd about the room was its color. It was orange. Bright orange.

The blanket on the bed matched, cream with orange trim. The throw pillows looked like orange slices. The room even smelled a little…tangy. Adrian went to pull back the covers and was startled by a framed photograph lying just below one of the pillows. Curious, she picked it up. It was a photo of a ferret.

"So you're okay with him sleeping in the bed?" Joanne had emerged from the bathroom, toothbrush dangling from her mouth.

"Who?"

She nodded toward the photo. "Freddie. He was my boy. I lost him two weeks ago."

"And you sleep with the photo?"

"He always slept with me. Lay right here." She pointed to her bosom.

She shrugged. "I guess." Her weird alert started to ping like a deep-dwelling submarine searching for others.

"Good." She seemed really relieved. "You want to go get ready for bed?"

Adrian wasn't sure what she meant. To sleep or to fuck.

"There's a toothbrush and a washcloth laid out for you."

"A toothbrush?"

"I always have extras."

Did that mean she did this a lot? The thought immediately linked to her initial trepidations about Sierra. She mentally battled as she made her way to the bathroom. *Joanne is not Sierra. Joanne is not Sierra.* She just had extra toothbrushes. She probably bought them in bulk at Costco or something. Nothing to worry about. Still…Tamara hadn't seemed happy about her leaving with her. And then there was the photo of her dead ferret she slept with.

"You can use my toothpaste," Joanne called out. "Just be sure to squeeze from the bottom not the middle. Oh and rinse out the sink when you're done."

Adrian leaned on the sink and forced herself to breathe out long and slow. She turned on the faucet and splashed cold water on her face. For a second she thought it might sizzle right off her skin. She splashed some more and ran it through her hair and along the back of her neck. She allowed her skin to air-dry as she brushed her teeth. It wasn't until she finished that she realized she'd squeezed from the middle.

"Shit." Hurriedly, she squeezed from the bottom and placed it alongside the toothbrush. Then she dried her face and entered the bedroom.

Joanne was under the covers. Carefully, Adrian rounded the bed and pulled back the covers on her side. She stretched her legs and lay down. The sheets felt cool against her bare skin.

"Mmm, this is nice," Joanne said, inching closer to her. She kissed Adrian's shoulder, then moved down her arm to her chest where she teased her nipple. Adrian hissed with rising pleasure. It felt nice and Joanne felt warm and smooth, lulling her deeper into sensual bliss.

"Roll over," Joanne whispered.

Adrian considered asking why, but Joanne's tongue convinced her, trailing up and down along the sides of her torso, back up to her breasts, where she flicked at her nipples.

Groaning softly, Adrian turned and settled on her stomach. Joanne straddled her quickly, pressing her hands into Adrian's back as she rocked against the flesh of her buttocks. Adrian could feel the cool slickness of her as she gyrated and began to pant.

"You feel so good," Joanne said. "Your ass, ah, yeah."

She leaned forward, raking her nails down Adrian's sides, and kissed her ear.

"Are you ready?" She kissed her neck and shoulders and began to move her mouth downward over her back. When she reached her buttocks she devoured the remnants of her own slickness. "Mmm, you better be ready."

Adrian's heart thumped wildly and she muffled her moans in the pillow. She felt Joanne lower herself farther, felt her ease apart her thighs, felt her eager tongue lick its way up to her nucleus.

"Ah," Adrian let out, lifting her face from the pillow.

Joanne made a wicked noise and buried her mouth in Adrian, her tongue rubbing over and around her clit and then sneaking into her hole.

Adrian clenched the pillow and lifted herself to Joanne, unable not to.

"There we go," Joanne said between forceful swipes of her tongue. "Get on your knees."

Trembling, Adrian rose to her knees and elbows. She nearly came out of her skin when Joanne teased her hole with her fingertips and then shoved her fingers up deep inside.

Her throat seemed to tighten as Joanne pumped quickly and firmly, holding Adrian's hip with her other hand.

"Take it," Joanne said, again and again, in tune with her powerful thrusts. "Take it. Take it full and hard."

Mouth hanging open, muscles taut, body rocking back and forth, Adrian clenched her eyes and took it, her vaginal walls clinging to

Joanne's fingers, wanting to hold them captive, wanting them to stroke and pump and fuck for all eternity.

She couldn't speak, couldn't think, couldn't do anything but hold herself up and offer herself for the taking.

Her body thrummed with the hot pleasure as it stabbed, forced, filled.

Louder smacking sounds ensued and she knew she was slick with wet. She was heavy with it, felt it encasing the swordlike fingers, felt it dripping onto her clit and inner thighs.

She pushed back farther, needing more of Joanne.

Oh God, how she needed it.

"Fuck me," she managed to say through a sandpaper throat. *Oh God, just fuck me. Fuck me hard. Harder. Oh God, harder. Until your fingers come out my mouth.*

But then suddenly the fucking stopped. Adrian nearly collapsed at the shock. Her head fell and she gasped for breath with her forehead pressed to the pillow as she trembled, still on all fours.

"What—what's going on?"

She heard and felt Joanne moving. Soft pillows were put between her knees. Then Joanne was gripping her thighs and sliding beneath her, resting her head on the pillows so that her head was just beneath her saturated flesh.

Wet fingers found her again, sliding in quickly to pump.

Adrian started feeding into the thrusts, unable to control herself.

Joanne groaned, pleased yet hungry. "Bring yourself to me," she said, her voice coated with seduction. "Rest on my face."

A warm hand pressed against her buttocks, encouraging her to lower herself. She struggled for breath and shook as she relaxed her legs and brought her center to Joanne's wet and waiting mouth.

"Oh!" It felt good. Hot and slippery, devouring her clit and surrounding engorged tissue. And then the pumping started again. In and out. In and out. First two fingers, then more, stretching her, filling her, stroking her walls like hot, knowing lances.

She clenched her eyes and then opened them, desperately wishing Joanne's flesh was beneath her so she could lower her mouth and feed. "I want you," she managed. "Beneath me."

Joanne pulled her mouth away to speak. "No. This is just you."

She reattached and ate more of her, sucking and licking, holding firmly with her teeth.

Adrian cried out, her body now completely out of her control. It was its own being, starving and feeding.

She stared at the orange wall as her hips flexed and pushed into Joanne.

She was going to come. Now. Right now.

Oh God. The pumping of the hot fingers. The sucking of the fevered mouth.

Oh God.

The weight of her on Joanne's mouth. Hinged there. Rocking.

Fuck.

She clenched her jaw, her eyes and her hands.

And she came.

Her body went into a frenzy as the orgasm rushed through her. She bit into an orange slice pillow and squeezed the bedding so hard her fingers hurt, with Joanne laughing wickedly beneath her all the while.

When she finally stilled, Joanne crawled out from under her and came to rest up on the neighboring pillow. She fixed the blankets and covered them both up after Adrian settled down onto her back.

She felt like rubber, easily pliable. Her heart still pumped thick and heavy behind her rib cage. It felt nice. Like her blood was rich with heat and pleasure and all things wild.

"That was fabulous," Joanne said, tugging Adrian close to rest her cheek on her balloon-like breast. "You're really responsive."

She was exhausted. Couldn't keep her eyes open.

Joanne stroked her back and Adrian got lost in the warmth of her breast, the sound of her muffled heartbeat soothing.

"Shh, that's it. Go to sleep."

Adrian closed her eyes and Joanne extinguished the light. They lay there in the darkness and Adrian drifted off to sleep.

CHAPTER FOURTEEN

It was barely light when Adrian woke. She was snuggled under light blankets, shivering profusely as gray light drifted in through the windows. The orange walls looked dull and suddenly she remembered where she was.

She turned and shifted onto an elbow. Joanne was asleep on her back, resting on two pillows with something strange on her chest.

Blinking for focus, Adrian eased down the covers to get a better look. The photo of Freddie was resting on her breasts.

Adrian stared for a long moment, unsure what to think, if anything, before she turned away. As she relaxed and looked at the ceiling, she recalled the love making the night before. Her muscles felt stiff as she stretched and her center felt warm and tight, reminiscent of a recent fucking.

She'd never let anyone take her like that before. Not from behind. And never in a way that was so forceful and raw and animalistic.

And she wasn't sure how she felt about it.

The chill of the early morning air seeped in through the covers. Joanne pushed out puffs of air next to her, the photo of Freddie rising and falling with each breath.

She glanced around for more blankets but didn't see any. The bedroom was extremely tidy, with nothing on the dresser or night tables save for lamps and an alarm clock.

Why wasn't the heat on? She sat up and searched for her clothes. She found them in the bathroom folded neatly on top of the clothes hamper. After she relieved herself and dressed she walked silently around the small house. She stopped in the hallway and studied the thermostat. The heat was on auto but it was set at fifty-eight. She hugged herself as she continued into the kitchen.

After rubbing the sleep from her eyes, she sank into a chair at the table and glanced around. Everything was new. From the cabinets to the countertops to the sink to the stove. All of it had been replaced, and probably recently, based on the modern look to it. The floor gleamed and she ventured she could probably see her reflection if she tried.

She tugged open the stainless steel fridge and peered inside. Juice bottles were lined up neatly along with stacks of already made food stored in plastic containers. She helped herself to a small water bottle and sipped as she headed back toward the bedroom.

There were no photos of family on the wall or anything that suggested Joanne had a past at all. The tiny house was just neat and full of new things. Even the sofa they'd screwed on the night before looked new. And the television across from it looked modern, staring at her from an IKEA entertainment center.

It was a very nice home. Anyone would be proud of it. So why did she feel strange in it?

She peeked in on Joanne and found her still fast asleep. She looked kind of sweet as she slept, her long mane cascading around her head, her hands resting on the photo.

Adrian shook the thought away, convinced she was still half asleep or still a bit high from the night before. She left the doorway and headed down the hall. She found her shoes on the rack by the door. After slipping them on, she found her peacoat nearby on a wall hook and slid into it, buttoning it up all the way. She unlocked the front door and stepped outside, pushing in the lock on the doorknob to secure the house behind her.

The air was cold, stinging her face and lungs. She looked around and reality sank in.

Shit. Tamara had her car.

She searched in her jeans and found her cell phone. There was a text from Tamara sent at two a.m.

Text when ur ready 2 leave.

Adrian smiled and began typing. Tamara replied quickly, informing her that Harriet lived nearby. She was there within fifteen minutes with Harriet in a car behind her.

Adrian met them at the end of the driveway.

"That was fast."

Tamara crawled from Adrian's car, leaving it running. "I was expecting you to call."

"You're that smart, huh?"

Adrian waved at Harriet, who quickly waved back.

"I just know you."

"Yeah, well, it wasn't *that* bad." She stared back at the house. Right? In fact, it was kind of…powerful.

"No? Hmm. You must like getting it from behind."

Adrian whipped her head around. "What?"

Tamara laughed. "Go home and get some sleep, Adrian."

"Wait, no, how, what do you mean?"

"Nothing. I don't mean anything." She stood by the passenger door of Harriet's car. "Call me later."

"Wait, T." What had she meant? Did she know something about Joanne? Who else knew?

"We're tired," Tamara said opening the door. "We haven't even slept yet." She grinned.

Adrian scowled at her and gave up. "Yeah, yeah. Whatever." She waved. "Thanks."

"Don't mention it."

Adrian slid into her car and closed the door. As she drove home she thought of Joanne, knowing she'd have to call her later to explain. It wasn't something she was looking forward to. She hated trying to explain her sudden early departures to women she hardly knew.

When she entered her apartment, she set the heat to seventy, dodged the noisy cats, kicked off her shoes, and collapsed onto her bed. Snuggling into a soft, white pillow, she drifted back off to sleep.

❖

The ringing phone interrupted her trance, causing her to jerk. A wild mark streaked across the page and she tossed her charcoal onto the table and crossed the room. She managed to grab the phone by the seventh ring. The dial tone greeted her rudely.

"Great." She pushed the Off button and returned to her drawing.

The sketch had started off simply enough, just her sitting down to draw freely. A few long, easy strokes had soon turned into long, thick, wavy hair. Those had soon led to a face. A beautiful face. Morresay's face. And as she drew her she fantasized about her, wondering what her cheekbones would feel like to the back of her fingers. What her hair smelled like when it blew in the breeze. What her voice sounded like first thing in the morning after a long night of clawing and crying out to the moon in passion.

She sat and stared at the drawing, ran her finger over the developing flesh of Morresay's soft breast. Traced another finger over the delicate swoop of her bottom lip. She tried to get back there to that place where Morresay moved and spoke freely, encouraging her onward. But the fantasy was gone. Killed by the ringing phone.

"Damn." She sat back and gave up. It had been wonderful while it lasted. Seeing his opportunity, One quickly jumped up and pressed his paws to her chest. She scratched him behind the ears, set him down, and rose to stretch. Her muscles were still a bit stiff and her center ached but in a good way. She took a quick shower, dressed, and settled on the couch with a Diet Pepsi and a big soft pretzel she'd nuked in the microwave.

There wasn't much on television, so she decided to call Tamara.

"Hey, you up?" Adrian asked when Tamara answered sounding groggy.

"Not quite. What time is it?"

"After one."

"I need to get up."

Adrian heard her rustling.

"I can call you back later."

"No, no. Talk now. How was last night?"

Adrian extended her legs and crossed her sock-covered feet on the coffee table.

"It was okay."

"Just okay?"

"Yeah. Why? I haven't forgotten your little comment, you know."

"I bet."

"What exactly did you mean by that?"

There was a brief silence and Adrian grew a bit nervous. Her palms actually started to sweat as she recalled the way Joanne had fucked her the night before.

"Joanne likes to give it from behind," Tamara finally said.

Adrian felt herself flush. "And how do you know this?"

"Everybody knows."

Adrian sat up and placed her feet on the floor. "Everybody?"

"Well, obviously not you."

She didn't know what to say. She was beyond embarrassed. "Why didn't you tell me?"

"You mean last night? Why would I? Besides, it wouldn't have stopped you."

"It might've. Had I known the entire town would know what we would be doing."

Tamara laughed softly. "It's no big deal, Adrian. You enjoyed yourself, didn't you?"

"I'm not going to answer that."

"You did. I heard she's good."

Adrian stood. "Oh my God." Could she be any more embarrassed? Was every lesbian in the county discussing her and Joanne and their sexual positions?

"I gotta go."

Tamara ignored her. "Are you going to see her again?"

"I don't know." She paced the living room, worked up. "Not if the world is going to speculate and discuss our sex life."

"Oh, come on. You know how lesbians talk. That's all it is. Mindless gossip."

"I don't know." She still didn't like it. Allowing herself to be fucked like that left her feeling vulnerable enough. She didn't need the world knowing about it.

"What about everything else? Did you like Joanne?"

She opened the front door and leaned against the jamb to stare out at the parking lot and trees beyond. The air still felt cool but the sunshine was bright and kissed her face gently. "She was okay."

"Just okay?"

She squinted up at the sky. "Yeah. Why?"

"I've just heard some things."

"You mean other than the taking from behind?" She cringed, upset at the mental image of herself on all fours, taking it, *loving* it.

"Yeah." There was more rustling and Adrian could hear Tamara talking to someone else. "Listen, I gotta go. Harriet's up and we need to get ready to go eat."

They ended the call and Adrian lay back on the couch, phone resting on her chest. She shifted for comfort and her thighs tightened like a taut bow, reminding her again of the night before.

Joanne. *Shit.* She'd forgotten to ask Tamara for her number.

Oh, well. She'd get it later. Frankly, she wasn't all that excited about seeing her again. Yes, the sex had been interesting, but she was left feeling awkward and exposed. And Joanne was just...

What?

She couldn't put her finger on it. Not right now anyway. She stretched and snuggled into the cushions, tugging down the throw blanket resting along the back of the couch. Two meowed from the coffee table and joined her by jumping on her stomach. He tucked his front paws under his chest and relaxed like a hen sitting on her eggs. His body felt weighty and warm. His wicked gold eyes stared back at her, blinking longer and slower. Soon they were both asleep.

The ringing phone woke her sometime later, entering her strange dream about work where she was hurrying to pack boxes. There was a loud alarm going off at her tardiness.

She blinked and clawed her way from the dream, fumbling with the phone, realizing it had been the sounding alarm.

"Hello?" she croaked.

What time was it?

"Well, hello."

The voice was familiar, yet she wasn't confident enough to say her name.

"Hi."

"You owe me an apology."

"I do?" She shooed Two off her and sat up, causing One to grunt and jump from her feet as well.

"Yes. For leaving without saying good-bye."

It was Joanne.

"You're right. I do. I'm sorry." She rubbed her eyes. "I was going to call but—"

"But you didn't get my number."

Adrian cleared her throat. It felt scratchy from sleep but tight with sudden nerves. Was Joanne really pissed? She couldn't tell.

"Right." She rose and stretched. "I'm sorry about that too. But wait. How did you get mine?"

"I had to be resourceful." There was a throaty chuckle. "I tried to call you earlier but you must've been out."

"Oh. Yeah." She would've said she'd been asleep, but for some reason she didn't want to say that to her, feeling like she was the type to judge her for such a thing.

"I'm glad I caught you now."

Adrian wasn't sure what to say. Was she glad Joanne had called?

"Are you busy?" Joanne asked, filling in the silence.

"Me? Uh, well, you know. Just the usual." She searched for something to do, to grab, to busy herself with as if Joanne could see her. Why did she make her feel this way?

"Good. Then open the door."

Adrian stiffened. "Sorry?"

"Open your door."

She cleared her throat again, this time fighting against the clinching quickly moving up her windpipe. She crossed to the door and looked out the peephole. Joanne was waving.

Shit.

The dead bolt made a loud metal on wood thud as she disengaged it and pulled open the door. A rush of cold air slammed against her a split second before Joanne's perfume. Today it was more feminine and strong.

"Hi." The wind was playing with her long mane and her smile was made up with heavy lipstick. Her tits were nearly directly beneath her chin, cinched up tight and high and bountiful. The black turtleneck hugging them looked very thick and snug fitting under her open leather jacket.

"Hi."

Her dark eyes moved quickly over Adrian's body and settled on her hair. "Were you sleeping?"

"What? No. Of course not."

She forced a smile. "Good. I didn't want to disturb you."

Adrian nervously smoothed down her jeans. She didn't like being caught off guard like this. Didn't like it at all. It brought up those feelings she'd experienced with Sierra and her moving in without permission.

"Actually, I was just—"

"Aren't you going to invite me in?" Her deep red lips peeled back to show more of her teeth. She didn't have a large smile to begin with, so the made-up lips seemed overbearing and contradictory.

"Sure." She stepped back and allowed her in, closing the door after her. Her high-heeled boots clicked on the concrete and then fell silent as they hit her carpet. Adrian stared at her ass for a moment wondering how she got in her dark, tight jeans. Did she cinch up her thick ass like she did her breasts? It appeared so, but she looked like she was well balanced. Full breasts in the front and full ass in the back.

She was definitely something to look at. Men and women both probably stumbled when walking by.

Adrian moved past her to stand in front of the coffee table. She fidgeted and then shoved her hands into her pockets.

"Would you like a drink?"

Joanne was busy taking in the apartment, her eyes sliding over every last inch.

"This just a one-bedroom?"

"Uh, yes."

She nodded. "Thought so." She eyed the coffee table and crossed to sit on the sofa. When she saw the blanket an eyebrow shot up on her forehead. "You sure you weren't sleeping?"

Adrian could feel her blood catch aflame beneath her skin. "Did you want something to drink?" She leaned over and snatched the blanket, folding it to return to the back of the couch.

Joanne crossed her leg over her knee and sat back. "What do you have?"

"Water, juice, soda."

"Diet soda?"

Adrian nodded and headed for the fridge.

"That's fine," Joanne said.

"So how did you find my place?" She grabbed a can of Diet Pepsi and returned to the couch.

"I told you. I'm resourceful." Joanne studied the soda. "Do you have a glass?"

Adrian fought off a groan and hurried back to the kitchen where she found a glass and then opened the freezer.

"No ice," Joanne said.

Of course not.

Adrian closed the freezer and brought her both the glass and the can. Joanne took them with a smile and poured herself some soda. She sipped casually as Adrian perched on the end of the sofa feeling uncomfortable in her own home.

"So," Joanne finally said. "I thought we could go to dinner."

"Oh?"

"Yes. I thought that would be nice."

Adrian didn't want to go to dinner. But she didn't want to stay there with Joanne either. "Okay, sure."

"Great." She blinked long grateful eyelashes at her. "Why don't you go get ready?"

What the hell was wrong with what she was wearing?

"I don't feel like going anywhere really nice."

"I don't either."

Okaaay.

She forced herself to be nice. "I'll be right back."

Just go change, have dinner, and get rid of her.

She entered her bedroom and closed the door. One and Two peeked out at her from under the bed.

"Sure, throw me to the lions."

She scraped her clothes hangers over the wooden rod as she searched for a nicer shirt, shoving one after another aside. She liked the worn look. The soft, faded yet stylish look. It was a statement. A "you may think I don't care, but this was actually carefully planned" look.

After some more internal deliberation, she decided on a wine-colored blouse and a pair of dark blue jeans with worn creases.

She dressed quickly and spent a few minutes on her hair before stepping into a dark brown pair of thick-soled, below-the-ankle boots. She laced them up, straightened, and slapped on her watch. When she entered the living room she saw Joanne moving about. She stopped short when she saw Adrian.

"Oh good, you're ready." She looked like she'd been caught with her hand in the cookie jar.

Adrian looked around, curious. The coffee table was completely clean with the soda cans and paper plate from her pretzel gone, along with her magazines.

"I just tidied up a bit," Joanne said.

"Where are my magazines? And the remote?"

"In the drawer."

"What drawer?"

"Here." She crossed to the end table next to the couch and pointed. "And I redid your books."

Adrian looked to the bookcase. Every book and every knickknack had been rearranged.

"Why?"

"Well, it looks better that way, don't you think? I grouped them by author so they'd be easier to find."

Great. Wonderful. Life changing. Truly. Thank you.

"Why did you move my statues?"

Joanne seemed at a loss, like she didn't know what to say, as if it should be entirely obvious. When she finally spoke she almost sounded like a child. "They just didn't seem happy where they were."

"Happy?"

WTF?

"Yes. You know, they seemed lost." She took a big breath. "I believe everything has a soul. Even statues. Especially statues. Especially ones of fairies and gnomes."

Adrian was dumbfounded. She stared at her for a long moment waiting to see if she'd correct her statement or bust into laughter at the joke. She did neither, and now Adrian was at a loss.

"I—" Though it bothered her, her books didn't look bad that way. But still, the unannounced visit, the uninvited phone calls, the unwelcome rearranging of her things. It wasn't cool. "Let's just go."

CHAPTER FIFTEEN

They went to a local dive with sawdust on the floor and peanuts in small buckets on the tables. It peeved Adrian a bit knowing she could've worn the faded navy thermal and soft jeans she'd had on before. But she tried to forget about it, realizing it was a control issue. She would've dressed nicer for a date, yes. But she didn't consider this a date, and she didn't like being strong-armed into doing anything.

"You gotta try the Firefly," Joanne said, tossing the menu aside. "It's a drink. You look like you could use one."

"Do I?" *Should I be offended? Can you tell I'm upset?*

One side of Joanne's mouth pulled into a smirk. "Yes." She lifted her finger and got the waiter's attention.

"Two Fireflies with water and a lemon twist."

Adrian thought about protesting, but Joanne was right. She was in desperate need of a drink.

"What's good here?" she asked, studying the menu nearly dripping in red meat. Country music blared from the overhead speakers. The smoky scent of sizzling steaks was in the air along with the freshly baked smell of buttered rolls. Nearby, people laughed and slammed back mugs of heady beer. If she'd been in a better mood, she would have somewhat liked the place.

"Anything. And it's on me. So get what you want."

On you? She fought against arguing, knowing somehow that it would be useless. The waiter returned with their drinks and Joanne ordered a slab of red meat with a baked potato. Adrian decided on a grilled chicken sandwich with avocado. She sipped her drink tentatively and was pleasantly surprised by the nice flavor. Joanne was watching her closely.

"It's Firefly sweet tea vodka. Doesn't taste like alcohol, does it?"

"No, not really." She drank more, pleased. "It's good."

"I love it."

"I can see why." She sat back and tried to relax. Joanne picked at the complimentary bread in the red plastic basket. She looked nice in her dark turtleneck, and once again Adrian was mesmerized by the light reflecting off her irises.

"So tell me about yourself, Adrian. But first tell me why you left."

"No reason really. I woke up very early and I didn't want to disturb you."

"You should've wakened me. I would've made coffee, breakfast. We could've spent the morning doing what we did last night." Her eyes flashed playfully.

"I needed to get home."

"How did you get home?"

"My friend."

"Tamara?"

"Yes." Adrian wasn't sure but she thought she heard a hint of jealousy.

"She came and got you that early? She must think I'm so rude."

"Why would she think that? I told her you were asleep."

They both sipped their drinks and Adrian began to feel the effects of the vodka. It warmed her from the inside out and smeared the edges of her reality just a little bit.

"So." Joanne leaned on her elbows. "Do you have any family? I noticed some photos on your shelves."

Thank God they weren't on the bookshelves. You would've moved them.

"I have a sister."

"She live around here?"

"No." She moved her thumb up and down, making a condensation trail along her glass. "She married into the Air Force. They move frequently."

"And those were your nieces in the photo?"

"Yes." She wasn't keen on talking about her family. She loved her sister Ava and the two girls, but she didn't get to see them very much. When she did she was happy for a while but then overwhelmed with loneliness and sadness, reminded that she was alone.

"What about your folks?"

Adrian snapped her gaze up from the glass to Joanne's face. "What about them?"

"Are you close?"

This was going too far. She didn't even know this woman. She wasn't about to slit open her skin and show her insides.

"It doesn't matter." She finished her drink and motioned toward the waiter for another. Joanne could sit and stare at her all she wanted, but she wasn't going to get any more from her. Her mother and Louis were hard enough to deal with, much less think about.

"That's an off subject, I see." Joanne pushed the small bucket toward her. "Peanut?"

Adrian shook her head. If she hadn't been buzzing already she would've gotten up to leave. She would've called a cab and left Joanne where she sat. She hadn't wanted anything to do with this dinner, Joanne's visit, or even Joanne herself. And now she was being probed about her personal life?

"Can I ask about the safari hat I saw on your entertainment center? Or the old looking glass next to it?" She linked her hands and leaned forward, resting her chin on them, waiting patiently for answer.

She's lucky she's beautiful.

"They were a gift."

"Do you hunt or something?"

"No. Not in the traditional sense."

"Are you going to elaborate?"

Adrian considered this for a moment. Should she? It was obviously a game. Joanne was thoroughly enjoying it. She wasn't the least bit deterred by Adrian's attitude or lack of disclosure.

"Tamara gave them to me." The Firefly was running under her skin fully now, helping to ease her resentment. She felt hot and free and decided to be honest and a bit facetious. "To help me find a woman."

Joanne was obviously surprised and even sat back in her chair. "Well. I wasn't expecting that."

"Sorry you asked?"

"No. I'm glad I did." She sipped her drink slowly. "You have trouble finding women, Adrian? I don't see why you would."

"I don't have trouble finding women. I have trouble finding a good woman."

"You mean one to settle down with?"

"Yes."

"And your friend Tamara finds humor in that."

"Most do." She didn't add that Tamara no longer found it so humorous.

"It can be a complicated thing. I know I've had trouble."

"And why is that?" *Because you're pushy?*

A new country song came on. This one a slow twang of sorts. The mood in the restaurant immediately changed, growing quiet and calm. When Joanne spoke, her tone had softened along with her face.

"Because I'm a romantic."

"A romantic?"

"Yes. I'm waiting for the love of my dreams."

"A prince on a white stallion?"

"So to speak."

"Sort of like your fairies and gnomes?"

Joanne froze for a moment, then flicked her eyes down over the table. She rearranged her silverware. "I guess you could say so."

They sat in silence for a while and Adrian watched her closely, too buzzed to care about being rude or playing coy. Joanne was beautiful. Her creamy skin, her large dark eyes, her long blond hair...not to mention her full chest and ass. But there was something there, just under her skin, just under the surface of those eyes. She didn't know what it was. Couldn't tell. But she knew it was stark and unlike the rest. Something was brewing there, something that ran along with the current at the same speed and temperature, but it was different, noticeable, like blood in water. It made her uneasy, like she should watch her every move. The feeling wasn't pleasant.

Nothing much else was said when the food came and Adrian was grateful, enjoying her chicken sandwich in peace. She didn't like being upset when she ate. It brought back memories of Louis slapping her hands away from her plate, calling her fat. She'd sit in her chair and fight tears, wanting to shove the plate away, but he'd make her sit there and eat a certain number of bites. Not too much and not too little. It had to be his perfect amount.

She shoved the memories away, glad she was free of him. She would be free of her too, soon.

She had more Firefly with her meal and by the time she was finished she was flying high…or low…maybe both. Louis Shmouis. And Joanne Shmoanne. She grinned, her trepidations and memories buried in a shallow grave in her mind, easy to dig up, but for now, out of sight.

"How was your meal?" Joanne asked, lifting a coffee mug to her faded red lips.

"Good."

"You look happy."

"Happiness is relative."

"Meaning?"

Adrian shrugged. "Nothing. Are you ready to go?" Joanne had already paid the bill with cash. She'd grabbed the waiter's wrist as soon as he'd handed over the check, making him wait as she dug in her purse.

Joanne's after dinner coffee mug clinked slightly as she set it down. After a long look Adrian couldn't place, Joanne patted her mouth with the napkin and rose. The speakers were back to playing loud country music as they wove through tables. Joanne held the door for her and when they reached the parking lot, she took Adrian's hand.

Inwardly, Adrian knew she should pull away, but she didn't seem to have the strength or the stamina to keep allowing the warning signals to fire off inside her head.

"You had quite a bit to drink," Joanne said as she opened the truck door and motioned for Adrian to get inside.

"Not really." She'd had four full glasses. She was surprised she was walking upright, actually.

Joanne crawled in next to her and started the engine. Adrian closed her eyes and melted into the seat. When she opened them she was surprised to see they were headed to the other side of town.

"Where are we going?"

"I thought we'd go to my place."

She straightened. "Why?"

"I just thought it would be nice."

Then you should've asked. Adrian leaned back again, her frustration quickly dissipating. They pulled into Joanne's and Adrian struggled to walk without feeling dizzy. She wasn't totally blasted but she knew she was close.

"Here, let me help you," Joanne said as they stepped inside the door. She knelt to untie Adrian's shoes. "Hold on to my shoulders."

Adrian did and Joanne slipped off her boots. Then she quickly unzipped and pulled off her own before crossing into the kitchen. She removed a cold bottle of water and two glasses.

"Let's go sit." She handed Adrian her glass and led the way to the couch. "Come here," she said to Adrian as she patted the cushion next to her. Adrian hesitated.

"Maybe I should just go."

"No, don't be silly. You just got here." She tugged on Adrian's hand and faced her as she finally sat. "How are you feeling?"

"Fine." That wasn't a lie. She did feel good. She just wished she was at home feeling good.

Joanne touched her face, traced the outline of her forehead down to her jaw.

"I like the way you look, Adrian. So sexy."

Adrian's eyes fluttered, Joanne's touch so luring and seductive.

"And I love the way you respond to me in bed." She leaned in and kissed Adrian, following the path of her fingertips, delicate lips skimming across Adrian's forehead, temple, and jawline.

The light, repetitive caresses brought gooseflesh to life along Adrian's skin. She inhaled sharply and trembled as Joanne's hair tickled her along with her lips.

"I want to worship you, Adrian."

"But—"

Joanne hushed her with a kiss, taking Adrian's lips in her own to pull and tease. When she pushed in with her tongue Adrian couldn't help but moan and nearly crumbled beneath her.

"Yes, Adrian. Just let me," Joanne whispered just before kissing her deeply once again. Soon Adrian was being led down the hall and into the bedroom. A large ball was in her throat, bobbing in tune with the beat of her heart. Her clit ached and she knew she was wet. Her knees went weak when Joanne turned and slinked up to her, dropping to her knees to remove Adrian's jeans and panties and then standing to unbutton and remove her shirt and bra.

"There," she purred, eyes glinting with obvious lust and approval. "This is what I like."

Soft fingers ran up and down Adrian's sides. Then the press of firm nails did the same. It awakened her, causing Adrian to grip Joanne's arms.

"Yes," Joanne said, dipping her head to sink her teeth into Adrian's shoulder. "Are you liking this, baby?" She bit again and Adrian gasped.

Joanne pulled away and tugged Adrian over to the bed. Nearly panting she said, "Lie down. On your stomach."

When Adrian tried to think, Joanne helped her along, easing her onto the bed. And then there was no time for thought as Joanne mounted her like she'd done the night before, this time bending to assault Adrian's back with long licks and powerful sucks.

Adrian was up on her elbows quickly, moaning, struggling for rational thought and bits of oxygen. She couldn't speak, Joanne moving too quickly, ravishing her back with her mouth and hands, trailing down to her center where she parted her with expert hands.

Hot breathing beat against Adrian's flesh as Joanne teased her, blowing on her.

"You're so ready. So wet and glistening." She laughed wickedly and rimmed Adrian's opening with knowing fingers.

"Come up for me, Adrian." She lifted Adrian's hips. "That's it."

Adrian's fog-laden mind fizzled with electricity, but the thoughts weren't connecting, weren't forming a clear picture. And then the mouth was on her again, this time biting and sucking her cheeks as Joanne's fingers went around and around inside Adrian's opening.

"Yes! Here I come, Adrian. Here I come."

Hot, long fingers shot up inside Adrian, seemingly slamming right into her spine, shooting ecstasy right up her back and into her brain. She cried out just before her voice left her. The covers were bunched in her hands and she slid back and forth as Joanne pumped her harder and harder.

"Take it. Take it all. Fucking take it."

Adrian grunted, the pleasure consuming her entire body, the sounds being forced from her with every thrust.

"God, Adrian. Yes. You feel so good."

Adrian clung to the bed covers, got lost in the oblivion of the orange wall. She could hear herself against Joanne's fingers, the smacking intensifying her pleasure.

All reality blurred and she was rocking on the planes of heaven where nothing could ever come close to feeling better. In the distance she heard Joanne talking. Telling her to come. Telling her to take more. Telling her she was turning her hand inside her.

Adrian felt that. Felt the full hand. Felt it pressing and shoving against her G-spot. Hot, fiery, heavenly hand.

"Come, Adrian. Come so I can flip you over and eat you out."

Hot. Slamming. Pleasure. Forcing. Filling.

Yeeees.

Adrian clenched her eyes and shoved herself back into Joanne and came.

She managed to call out, to rock furiously, to spasm in a fit of sheer ecstasy. Joanne called out, too, as if she were there on that plane with her, feeling every saturated firing nerve ending.

Adrian rocked and grunted, slowed and stilled. The orange came back into focus and she collapsed on the bed, her vagina pulsing around Joanne's entrapped fingers.

Aftershocks shot through her as Joanne slowly removed her hand. A mouth, somehow hotter than before, began to suck on her cheeks again. It moved lower, tongue extending to line the crease of her ass. Adrian shuddered and groaned and then strong hands lifted and turned her and she rolled onto her back. She tried to speak, to raise her head and look, but Joanne was already there, taking all of Adrian's slick flesh into her mouth like a crazed half starved creature.

A heat wave of pleasure burst up through her and Adrian tensed, her back arching, her hips bucking into Joanne's face. Blond hair twisted around her fingers as she grabbed Joanne and held tight to her head, loving the rapid back-and-forth movement of her, the smacking sounds of her mouth as she fed.

Adrian came quickly as Joanne's tongue followed the powerful suction of her lips, stroking and flicking and bathing her sensitive clit again and again. Adrian dug her nails into Joanne's scalp as her entire body very nearly came up off the bed. She tensed and grunted, unable to make any other noise. She could feel the pleasure pushing against her skin, filling the strained veins on her temples and neck. She was going to explode with it. Just completely explode.

Joanne shoved fingers into her again at the last second and Adrian did indeed explode.

She let out a throaty animalistic cry and then fell like a slowly drifting feather back onto the bed. She imagined more feathers falling down around her as she lay there with her heart beating in her ears. They turned from white to gray then from gray to black as she felt Joanne rise and cover her with the sheets. There was a gentle kiss to her forehead and the soft command that she sleep.

And then there was nothing.

CHAPTER SIXTEEN

Something was there. Adrian sat straight up and searched the darkness. She felt around with panicked hands, felt covers and a pillow. Her heart eased as her eyes adjusted to the darkness.

Joanne's. She was at Joanne's. She reached for the bedside lamp and gold light seeped into the room. Next to her, on Joanne's pillow, was Freddie, staring up at her from the photograph.

Where was his mommy?

The bathroom light was bright and it penetrated her eyes. Another photo of Freddie she'd never noticed before stared at her from the top of the toilet tank.

"I can't pee with you looking at me."

She backed out of the bathroom and found her clothes folded neatly on the dresser. After yanking them on, she hurried to the spare bathroom down the hall. She could hear Joanne somewhere nearby, moving around.

In the bathroom she sat to pee and then washed her hands and face. A throat-tingling nausea was present, along with an emerging headache.

"Wonderful." And what time was it?

She glanced at her watch. It was after nine p.m. Already dark. How long had she been asleep?

She recalled the fucking. It blew into her mind like a careless breeze. Joanne had taken her again. And she had loved it.

She'd also been drunk.

Damn it, how did this all happen today?

She killed the light and made her way down the hallway to the living room. Soft music could be heard. It seemed to be coming from the television. One of those music channels.

When she caught sight of Joanne in the kitchen she had to blink to be sure she was seeing correctly. Humming along with the music, Joanne stood at the sink facing her. She was nude, save for a pair of rubber yellow cleaning gloves. Adrian stared in disbelief, unsure if she was wearing anything below the waist. Adrian took a step back and peeked around the corner, watching as Joanne dipped a scrub brush into a nearby bucket and then scoured the sink with it. Her tits swung as she worked and she worked hard, giving the sink a thorough cleaning. Then she turned on the faucet and rinsed it out, then dried it with a soft towel.

Adrian waited a moment longer, thinking she might be finished and ready to dress. But as soon as she set down the towel, she dug in the bucket for her brush and started in on the counters, breasts swinging and mouth humming. Blushing, Adrian stepped into view and cleared her throat.

Joanne looked up and stared.

"Sorry to interrupt," Adrian said, careful not to look at her breasts.

"You're up." She sounded stunned.

"Yeah. I uh,—"

"I thought you'd sleep through the night."

"Oh. Well, I have work tomorrow—"

"I know. I was going to wake you in plenty of time."

Adrian wasn't sure what to say. "Well, I'm up now."

Joanne tossed the brush into the bucket and peeled off her gloves. When she walked Adrian heard clicking. And when she rounded the counter Adrian was shocked to see her bare legs and thick black stilettos. She couldn't help but stare.

"You like what you see?" Joanne asked.

What? "You're wearing heels."

"Yes."

"To clean in."

"Yes."

Adrian rubbed her forehead.

"I always do."

"Why?"

"I like heels."

This was weird. Way fucking weird. How much had she had to drink? Was it still in her system? No. This was real. And too strange feeling to be imagined.

"I think I should go."

"Why?"

Was she serious?

"Because I have things to do and, well, you do too. I don't want to impose."

"You're not imposing." She clicked her way over to the fridge and opened the door. "You thirsty?"

Adrian moved a little, following her so she could keep her in her line of sight.

"No, thanks."

Joanne closed the fridge. Her chocolate nipples were hard. She was unscrewing a bottle of water. "You really should hydrate after that vodka."

"I will, thanks. At home."

"Why don't you stay while I finish cleaning?"

"Why would I want to do that?"

Joanne retrieved a glass and poured. "I don't know. You could relax and watch TV."

"No thanks."

Joanne walked over with the water. The way she moved was sensual, ass shaking, legs slinking with thick muscle. She smirked. "I think you do like what you see."

Maybe. But you're crazy.

Adrian took the glass but didn't drink.

"I gotta go."

She handed Joanne the glass.

Joanne wasn't fazed. "I have cleaning to do."

"You can take me home first."

"No."

Adrian was growing angry. "I want to go home."

"Then you'll have to wait until I'm done. It's Sunday night and I have to clean."

"You want me to stay. While you clean."

"I want you to stay all night." She smiled and tried to touch her, but Adrian headed for the door.

"I said no thanks. Now take me home. Please."

Joanne's face hardened and suddenly that something that had been hidden just below the surface came to a rise. "I said no. I have things to do. You'll have to wait."

"You have to do them now? Right this second?"

"Yes."

"Or what? The world will end?"

Joanne clenched her jaw and her eyes deadened, like somebody blew out the flame to her candle.

Adrian dug in her pockets for her cell phone. She had to get out of there.

"I thought you liked me." Her voice was deep and dangerous.

Adrian reached for the door. Joanne came closer.

"It's Freddie, isn't it? Because I miss him and still sleep with him."

"No, it's not Freddie."

"I knew it." She threw her hands up and then buried her face in them and began to cry. "It's always Freddie. Nobody has ever liked him. Now he's dead and you still don't like him."

Adrian watched her sob, her body shaking in the high heels.

She tried to calm her down. "It's not that."

"Then it's me."

Adrian dropped her hands in defeat. "I like you just fine, Joanne."

"No, you don't."

"Yes, I do."

"You always leave."

"I have things to do. I have a life. And you're…busy. I don't want to sit here while you clean. How is that fun?"

She looked up. "It's something I have to do. Life isn't always fun."

Oh my God. Adrian was at a loss. "You obviously don't get it. Which is why I need to go. I'm not going to argue with you. I just need to go home and do my 'not so fun stuff' while you do yours. Okay?"

"And you'll see me again?"

"Sure. Yes."

"Tomorrow?"

"I have plans."

"See. I knew it! You're brushing me off."

"No, I'm not. I'm truly busy."

"I want to see you. I thought maybe I could make dinner."

"Okay. Yes. Fine. Later in the week."

"Tuesday?"

"Can't."

"Wednesday?"

Adrian didn't have the nerve to say no. "Wednesday's fine. I have a class but I'll come over when I'm done."

"Really?"

"Really."

Joanne seemed to think long and hard, studying Adrian as she did so.

"And you want to go now?"

"That would be nice."

Joanne left the room without another word and for a while Adrian wondered if she was coming back. She debated texting Tamara. What would she say? *Joanne fucked me good again but then refused to take me home?* But she'd had to swallow her pride many times before. Why should tonight be any different?

Because I'm tired of being a fuckup when it comes to women.

Joanne returned wearing a pair of sweats. To Adrian's continued surprise she knelt and pulled on her high-heeled boots, zipping them up quickly before rising to pull on her coat. She was a sight to see.

"You really like heels don't you?" Adrian asked as they backed out of the driveway.

"Yes. Most people find them sexy."

With sweats?

Adrian nodded but said nothing.

"So what are you going to do at home?" Joanne asked.

Eat something, throw in a load of laundry, sip a Diet Pepsi, and watch TV.

"Clean, mostly. Scrub. Really get down on my knees and fucking work that kitchen floor."

"Really?"

"Sure." She did like a clean floor.

"I still have a lot to do too. The kitchen, the bathrooms."

"The floors." She was just throwing out random things now.

Joanne looked at her. "No, not the floors. Floors are Wednesday."

"Oh. Right."

"Then the living room, the bedrooms, and the hallway."

"And you can't alter that any."

"No, you can't. Then everything gets screwed up and I lose my mind. I'm going to have to really hustle it when I get back home."

Adrian patted her leg. "You should've cleaned instead of coming after me today."

"Oh no, I don't start until seven. I like to do it at night."

And nude and in heels.

Adrian stared straight ahead and kept quiet the rest of the ride home. When they reached her apartment she hopped out quickly and poked her head in the door to say good-bye.

"Don't forget to come Wednesday. I'll have dinner ready."

"I'll call you as soon as I get out of class." She smiled and closed the door. She felt Joanne's eyes on her as she walked up the stairs. As she slid her key into her lock she turned and saw her sitting in her car, looking up at her.

With a wave she pushed open her door, stepped inside, and closed and locked it behind her.

❖

Work was mind-numbing and blissfully mundane that week and Adrian thanked her lucky stars. She sat slumped at her desk on Wednesday going over the eBay sales and printing out invoices while sipping some tepid coffee. Her eyes often threatened to close but she battled them open, forcing herself to focus.

"You must've had a wild night," Benny said, shoving the rest of a sprinkled doughnut in his mouth. He chewed loudly as his sausage-like fingers stabbed at the keyboard.

"Mmm" was her reply. "More like weekend."

He swallowed and it sounded like he'd forced down a billiard ball. "Know what I did?"

"You're going to tell me, aren't you?"

"I went to my buddy Jack's Saturday night and got a lap dance from a former Playboy Playmate."

She rolled her eyes and continued working. She could see him looking at her, waiting for a response.

"Did you hear me?"

"Uh-huh."

"A fucking Playboy bunny."

"That's nice."

"Nice? That's fucking insane! She was so hot."

"I bet."

"Woulda been better if she'd a given me a hummer." He cracked open a Dr Pepper and slurped. "So what did you do?"

"Oh, you know. I got fucked from behind by an obsessive compulsive with great big tits and a killer ass."

"Fuuuck you." He waved her off. "I don't even know why I ask. You always lie."

She rolled back in her squeaky chair and stretched. "Toss me that other soda. I need more caffeine."

He did so and she let it settle for a while before opening it. It was pushing noon and she was working through lunch wishing she could leave to go meet Tamara. But they'd canceled lunch since they were meeting up later in the evening for class.

She still wasn't crazy about going. And she was even less thrilled at the idea of going to Joanne's afterward. She didn't know what to do about that situation. She'd thought about it as she'd tossed and turned all night. After Sierra she'd hoped to find a serious woman. A responsible woman. A woman over twenty-five with a somewhat normal life. Joanne fit those to a T. So she was a bit obsessive. And a bit of a controller. There were worse things, and Sierra had been proof of that. Maybe she was being too picky like she had before. Maybe she should give her another chance. But her gut was saying no. Her gut was saying run, run, run. Besides, how could she ever have fun with someone so damn uptight?

She slurped her drink as Benny interrupted her thoughts.

"When are you gonna come over to my place for my barbecue ribs?" he asked. "And don't say soon. You always say soon."

"I don't know."

"There's always trouble in Lesbian Land or something and you never come."

"Well, there's—"

"Always something going on. I know."

He punched angrily at his keyboard and she wondered for a brief second if he was hurt over her putting him off.

"I'll come soon. I promise."

He kept typing and she felt bad. She scooted back up to her computer and got busy working on the website. "So what was her name?"

"Huh?"

"Your bunny."

"Oh. You really want to know?"

She looked over at him and saw his huge hopeful eyes.

"Sure. Give me all the details."

He smiled and rubbed his hands together. "You're not going to believe this."

❖

Five hours later she was stretching in front of her computer while Benny vacuumed. Uncle Jake had been in and out all afternoon, cranking up a storm about everything from the price of gas to the weather in Timbuktu. She and Benny had been on edge, walking on eggshells, careful to look busy even when things slowed down. So she'd worked on the website, taken more photos of parts to put up and answered the phones. Benny liked doing physical work, so he'd pulled parts, organized the stockroom, and cleaned.

It had been a long day and she was itching to text Tamara to cancel the class. But just as she set foot in her car a text came through.

Don't u dare cancel. Get ur ass here.

Sighing, Adrian started her car and headed for the community college.

Tamara was waiting outside at a picnic table, hands stuffed in pockets, wearing her red jacket. She still had on her blue denim work shirt and khaki pants. She looked beautiful regardless.

"Hey," Adrian said as they embraced for a quick hug.

"You came. That's how many classes in a row? I'm impressed."

She laughed and they walked to a nearby building that said Student Union.

When the door opened, a warm rush of cafeteria smells assaulted them. They made their way through a small cluster of students and stood in line at a small food service area.

"So how was your day?" Tamara asked.

"Slow."

"Mine too. But I'm excited for class."

"I wish I was."

They ordered two turkey sandwiches and moved to the checkout line.

"I don't know what your problem is. I thought you were enjoying it? You just need to tap into it a little bit and give this class more of a chance."

After they paid and filled their soda cups, they sat at an empty round table. She did like the class, but the truth was it scared her a little bit. Every time she went she felt like she was scratching at the surface of a barely healed wound. One that once opened would never heal. How could she explain that to Tamara? To anyone?

Morresay would understand.

The thought came from out of nowhere and she nearly choked on her drink. Yes, Morresay would probably understand, but she felt additionally anxious around her. She wasn't sure if it was because she was attracted to her or because she seemed so safe and sincere. Maybe it was all of it. Bottom line was she needed to tread lightly. If she could.

As she took a large bite from her sandwich, her phone rang. She checked the display as she chewed. She decided not to answer.

"Who is it?" Tamara asked, after swallowing some soda.

"Joanne."

"You don't want to talk to her?"

"Not right now. I told her I'd call her tonight when I was finished."

The ringing stopped and Adrian waited for a voice mail alert. A text came in instead.

Haven't heard from u. Where r u?

"She's so pushy." She shoved the phone away, upset.

"Things aren't going well?"

"No."

"Because she's pushy."

"Yes. Among other things."

"Mmm-hmm. So I've heard."

Another text came through.

Hello? I've started dinner. Can u tell me when ur coming?

Adrian scoffed. "I wish you would've warned me."

"I tried to." She took another bite, her sandwich almost gone. "Did she fuck you wearing high-heeled boots?"

Adrian nearly choked. "No."

Tamara laughed. "Really? That's her signature fuck. Naked with high heeled boots, giving it to the woman from behind. She loves it."

Adrian flushed. "There were lots of high heels. But not while we were fucking. At least I don't think."

"I heard she won't fuck a woman any other way than from behind."

Adrian chewed but didn't 'fess up.

Tamara seemed to understand. "I take it the rumors are true, then. Wow." She shook her head. "That is one intense woman."

"You have no idea."

"I don't want to either. Why do you think I never went out with her? The shit I've heard…"

"She's asked you?"

"Yep. A few times."

"I really need to listen to you more often."

Laughter echoed from Tamara as she threw back her head. "That's the understatement of the century."

"I thought maybe I was being too picky again."

"I don't think so. Not from what I've heard."

"I told you I get the weird ones."

"You get people who are weird for you, yes. Because you don't take the time to get to know a woman before you screw her."

"Yes, I do."

"No, you don't."

She tried to think back to her previous lovers and how long she'd spent with them before going to bed. She was stymied.

Tamara shook her head. "Mmm-hmm."

"I think I waited a day or two days with some."

"Not near long enough."

"But I was attracted to them and they to me."

"Adrian." She pushed away her drink. "This isn't rocket science. Your biggest problem is you. You rush into things and think just because you had good sex and you were attracted to them that everything else will fall into place. I know you know this. You aren't stupid."

"Thanks."

"You aren't. You just aren't really ready."

"And now I am?"

"Are you? I think after Sierra you damn well better be getting there."

She cringed. "Yeah. I am. Getting there. I think."

"Be sure and then quit this bullshit."

Adrian sucked on her straw, finishing off her soda. Several students looked at them as they passed by. One woman smiled at Adrian and caught her eye. She was dressed in jeans and a thigh-length leather coat; her afro was short and bleached at the tips. She disappeared through the door, still smiling, her hands in her pockets.

Tamara followed Adrian's line of sight, curious. "What?"

"Nothing."

Her phone alerted to another text.

Dinner will be ready very soon. Call me.

"You better answer her," Tamara said looking at the phone. "Or she'll be up your ass all through class. Speaking of class, we gotta go."

They threw away their garbage and headed back out the way they'd came. The sun had set and the night felt crisp and fresh as they meandered through the well-lit campus. Adrian followed Tamara while making a quick call to Joanne.

"Adrian," Joanne said, answering on the second ring.

"Yes."

"What the hell. You said you were going to call."

"I am calling. I said I had plans and I would call you after."

"So you're finished now?"

"No. I'm calling because you won't stop calling."

"I'm making dinner!"

"Well, I'm not done here. I haven't even started."

"But we have to eat. Dinner—"

"We can eat when I'm finished."

"No, no, no, no, no!"

"Why not?"

Tamara stopped at the entrance to their building. She turned and waited for Adrian to finish. Adrian began to pace, finger plugging her other ear.

"Joanne?"

"Just never mind. Come when you damn well please."

There was muffled noise and then silence.

"Hello?" Adrian pulled the phone from her ear and looked to Tamara, incredulous. "She hung up on me."

"Good. We have a class to focus on. And this is supposed to be fun." She held open the door.

The familiar scents of clay and paint stirred Adrian as she entered, as they did each time she walked in. Her palms began to sweat, anxious to create, and she was careful to head directly to her table without stealing a glance at Morresay. She sat on her stool and placed the ceramic cherub she'd brought in front of her.

It was chalk pastel night and the class was buzzing in anticipation. Morresay closed the door and started class. Adrian finally looked at her and found that she was looking at her as well. She gave Adrian the familiar soft smile and then set in on instruction, gliding about the classroom, touching shoulders, giving hints on pastels. Her black blouse was thigh length and loose, bunched a bit at the waist with a gold coin and chain belt that reminded Adrian of belly dancers. It jingled and clinked as Morresay moved about the class explaining the importance of color and blending. *Pastels are forgiving, you don't have to be precise. So go with the flow of your mind, do your best and rub, rub, rub those colors together.*

When she reached Adrian, she lifted her hand to touch her shoulder but then stopped awkwardly and crossed her arms over her chest. "How's it going over here, ladies?" Her smile was broad but it seemed almost forced.

"Good," Tamara said, returning the smile.

Morresay studied their items from home and nodded her approval. Adrian could feel her energy as she stood next to her. A silence fell over the table as Tamara and the others started in on their drawings. When Adrian didn't speak or look up at her, Morresay finally spoke.

"How are you, Adrian?"

Adrian angled her head and caught sight of her face. She looked different. Guarded. And almost…sad.

"I'm fine, thanks."

There was another brief silence and Adrian chose to study her cherub rather than look into Morresay's eyes. She was afraid she could see right through her. That her attraction and mixed emotions would be more than obvious.

"Okay, well, I'm glad you're all right. Let me know if you need anything."

She left her before Adrian could respond, leaving behind a cool whoosh of her chai scent. Adrian was both relieved and disappointed. She propped her elbow on the table and rested her cheek in her hand.

God, she just wanted to run. She didn't want to deal with any of it. Not the art and the way it peeled back her layers, not Joanne and her pushiness, and definitely not Morresay and her kind and stirring ways.

She could do it. She could bolt. But Tamara would chase her. Guilt would chase her. For whatever reason, she didn't want to hurt or offend Morresay.

Upset at her rising tide of emotions, she slid over her piece of thick paper and plucked out a piece of pastel chalk.

Fuck it. Just fuck it all. She was going to draw.

She started in with a light pink and created the plump face and body, shading in quickly and forcefully. Then she chucked the pink chalk and grabbed the orange. She was going to have to create her own color of skin tone.

"What's wrong with you?" Tamara asked long and slow, placing the pink chalk back in its slot carefully as if Adrian had abused it.

"Nothing." She didn't want to talk about it. She wasn't in the mood for Tamara's opinions.

"It's Joanne, isn't it? Don't let her ruin this for you. No woman—"

"Just stop, okay?" She didn't look up at her, but Tamara paused at her tone. "I'm fine." She kept coloring in with the orange and then dropped it to smear it all together with her fingertips. The colors blended nicely, but she needed a bit of white for the reflection of light. She dug with her dirty fingers and picked out the white. Tamara was watching her and she let her. Adrian didn't say a word. Neither did Tamara. Eventually, Tamara got to work on the photo she'd brought from home and Adrian was grateful. She needed to get lost in her own work.

They concentrated and drew in silence for the next hour. Adrian was immersed in her cherub, so intense she felt like she was in the image itself, spreading out the colors, rubbing hard here, blending lightly there. She could hear her nieces laughing, recall the way their eyes danced when they gave her the cherub. They had painted it themselves, and its wings were multicolored and in stark contrast to the peach skin. Tamara and the woman next to them made small talk and Adrian mumbled one-word replies from time to time, blocking out most of the conversation.

"Tell me about this, Adrian," Morresay said softly, startling her. Her slender fingers gently touched the page and she was so close Adrian could feel the gentle brush of her blouse as she breathed.

Adrian cleared her throat as her body rushed with heat.

"It's a cherub."

"It means something to you, doesn't it?" Her eyes met Adrian's. Adrian again caught the scent of chai, and it brought images along with it. She saw an old-fashioned room with a high-backed chair next to a roaring fireplace. Thick candles were lit on the mantel. Soft music came from a source unknown. She imagined standing there by the fire, holding her. Holding on for dear life, Morresay a tether in a blinding storm, a buoy on a raging sea. The embrace would last forever and never waver.

Adrian trembled as the thought passed through her.

Morresay seemed to notice and her hand moved from the page to Adrian's shoulder. Its warmth and strength only encouraged her longing and she suddenly thought of her mother, knowing the person in the old-fashioned room could never be her. She'd accepted that a long time ago. The hurricane was hers to bob in alone.

"Adrian?" Morresay whispered. For an instant she looked concerned, like Adrian had broken down again.

"My nieces made it for me," she said, eager to get control of herself. She shifted a little, her body nearly raging with heat at Morresay's close proximity. She thought about the fire she always craved and how this felt different. This was all consuming, uncontrollable, and…effortless.

"You made a great choice." She dropped her hand and slowly moved toward Tamara. Adrian could sense her disappointment, could feel her sadness. Was it because of her? She had been distant in class lately. Uneager to talk or engage with her. But why would Morresay care?

Adrian watched as she spoke to Tamara, who was busy drawing a boat on the water from the photo she'd found in a magazine. Morresay gave her praise and encouraged her to relax some more and use more color. The drawing didn't have to be perfect. It could look however Tamara wanted it to. Adrian thought it looked pretty good. Very Monet.

Tamara visibly softened at Morresay's praise and Adrian found herself moved by Morresay's sincerity. She even asked Tamara to stay after class so she could help her. Tamara agreed, much to Adrian's dismay, and Morresay walked away to speak to some other students and officially end class.

"You ready?" Adrian asked Tamara, hoping she would change her mind.

"You in a hurry?"

"Yeah."

"Why?"

"I'm just ready to get out of here is all."

"It's not because of Joanne?"

"No. Believe me, she's the last thing I want to deal with right now."

"So stick around."

"Can't."

She quickly returned Tamara's pastels and left her drawing next to Tamara's. She retrieved her coat and cherub and fished out her car keys.

Her hands were dry and chalky but she didn't want to take the time to wash them. Morresay was already heading back to their table.

"I'll see you later." She shoved her arms into her coat and darted from the room, rushing by a surprised-looking Morresay, who she heard call after her. But she didn't look back, didn't dare look back.

She'd stayed and done the assignment. Her obligation was taken care of. Anything else would have to wait. She hurried to her car, sucking in big gulps of cold air as she did so. She powered up her phone and saw that she had several new texts. All of them were from Joanne, telling her not to come over.

"Shit. I have to end it." The decision just flowed right out of her mouth, as calm and as natural as an exhale of air. The class, as always, had cleared her mind a bit, despite all the brimming feelings.

She climbed in behind the wheel and called her but there was no answer. She had to go over there. She had to do this tonight and do it right. She drove in silence thinking about what she was going to say. She felt she was doing the right thing by talking to Joanne face-to-face. Besides, Joanne was already pissed. A "get lost" phone call would probably only add to the fury.

A slight drizzle welcomed her as she turned onto Joanne's street. She eased up in front of her house and saw light illuminated in the front window. After closing her door softly, she hurried up to the gate, opened it, and crossed the path to the front porch. She nearly kicked over the gnome next to the post.

"Sorry."

If he had thoughts, like Joanne believed, he was probably cursing her out.

She held up her hand to knock but stopped when she saw movement in the long window next to the door. She leaned over for a better look and saw Joanne on her hands and knees bare ass naked, body swaying madly. Her black heels were pushing back on the carpet and soon she was backing up and Adrian could see that she was scrubbing the edge on the kitchen floor.

Fearing she'd be seen, Adrian stood and put her back against the door. Her pulse raced and suddenly she remembered that this was the day for floors. Seven o' clock. This was why she'd wanted to have dinner right after work.

Adrian stood still trying to slow her heart rate. She felt like a peeping tom. *Joanne should really hang curtains or wear clothes. Fuck.*

At a loss, she leaned over again and sneaked a peek. Would she be finished? Would it be okay to knock? Suddenly there was a loud thump and a click and the door was pulled open. Adrian stumbled, trying to back away from the window.

Joanne stood there naked in her high heels, anger set like stone on her face. Sweat coated her neck and her long hair clung to it.

"What are you, some kind of pervert?" she said.

"What, no! I came—" Adrian stepped away and into the drizzle.

"I told you not to come." Her eyes had that dead look again. Whatever lay dormant inside her had settled into her bones now and soon it would overtake her completely.

"We need to talk," Adrian said.

"No, we don't."

"I'm sorry about dinner. I told you—"

"Dinner is over. And so are we."

Adrian opened her mouth. "We are?" She blinked in surprise.

"Yes. Now get the fuck off my lawn."

"I—" She backpedaled and tripped over something. A gnome. She struggled to get to her feet. Joanne's eyes went wide and she came out after her, tits swaying, heels clacking. Adrian thought about fighting back. Thought about standing up and squaring off with her. She'd done it with Louis more times than she could count. But Joanne was crazed, with the dark eyes of a wild animal, angry enough for the both of them.

"I said get the fuck out of here!" She reached her just as Adrian gained her footing and Joanne shoved her, sending her back down on the slick lawn. "You fucking pervert!"

Adrian scrambled to her feet again and ran to her car. The bitch was insane and still coming after her. Her hands shook as she fumbled with the remote to unlock the door. Joanne kept coming, throwing fistfuls of dead grass.

"Go away! I hate you! I hate you!"

Adrian yanked her door closed and started the car. Then she took off with squealing tires, leaving a nude and screaming Joanne in the street behind her.

"Holy shit," she breathed. "Holy, holy shit." She wound her way out of the neighborhood and turned toward home. It was over. Joanne was gone. She breathed deep and leaned back to relax.

What a night. She needed noise, distraction, anything.

She switched on the radio and listened as the wipers kept tune with the beat.

For the first time in days, she felt all right.

CHAPTER SEVENTEEN

"There's a rumor going around about you," Tamara said as they entered the Student Union.

"Oh yeah?"

"Apparently, Joanne caught you peeping in on her while she was naked."

Adrian nodded, amused. "Is that so?"

"It sure is. She's telling everyone you're a pervert who liked to secretly stare at her in the buff."

Adrian hadn't heard from Joanne after the nude/yard/gnome incident and she'd been grateful. She would've had no idea what to say to her even if she had called.

"Guilty as charged, I guess."

Tamara led them to a nearby table. "That's what I figured."

"Thanks. I'm glad I could be of entertainment." She headed for the food court, leaving Tamara to save their table. She couldn't have cared less about the rumors, and that surprised her. But the past few days had been long and filled with a persistent mental anguish. She didn't know where it was coming from inside and she just wanted it to stop. It was like a faucet had been turned on within and the water just kept coming and coming.

"Excuse me," a young woman said as they accidently bumped while getting in line.

"No problem."

"Hi," she said, meeting Adrian's gaze. Adrian recognized her as the woman she'd seen around the Union before.

"Hi."

And she was still cute. With jeans, Doc Martens dark boots, and a thigh length leather jacket. Her hair was short and curly with blond tips. Her skin was dark and smooth with a moist sheen, like she'd used lotion frequently and recently. She didn't look as young as most of the other students. Adrian guessed she was in her late twenties.

"Nice day, isn't it?" She turned more toward Adrian, her posture open and friendly.

"I was just thinking the same thing." Minus the thoughts of Joanne, it was a nice day.

"Really? You looked sort of pissed off." Her lips eased into a smile to show she was either teasing or she was trying to cheer her up. "I'm Penny." She offered her hand.

"Adrian." Her hand was a bit rough but firm.

"You have class soon?"

"No, just got out."

"Hanging with the girl I saw you with?"

"Yes." She was quite a bit shorter than Adrian with a slight build. Adrian wondered how light she was. How easy it would be to pick her up—

"Oh. Well, tell her I said hi. And—" She dug in her jacket and retrieved a business card. "Call me sometime. If you should need anything or you just want to talk. Going for a drink might be nice too."

Adrian gave the card a glance. Saw her name and business address along with three different phone numbers.

She smiled fully this time, showing perfect teeth. "I'm into numbers," she said.

They moved forward in line and while Adrian grabbed two bagels and some juice, Penny only grabbed a Coke.

"So you're a student?" Adrian asked.

They paid the cashier. First Penny, then Adrian.

"You could say that," she said and touched Adrian's arm. "I'm taking some additional courses I'm interested in." They were standing by the tables and Adrian could see Tamara waving her over. Penny saw her too and waved herself. Then she gave Adrian one last smile.

"Have a nice day, Adrian."

She left her and walked toward the main doors, pushing through out into the sunshine.

That old familiar part of her began to race with excitement but she swallowed it down for Tamara.

"Who was that?" Tamara asked, taking her juice and bagel.

"Penny. She's a student."

Adrian sat and studied her business card.

"Oh really?"

Adrian slid the card in her back pocket. "Mmm-hmm. And don't worry. I won't call her." *Yet.*

"Don't even say it, Adrian. It's not me you're bullshitting. It's yourself."

"I'm not bullshitting."

"Yes, you are. But I don't want to talk about that."

"Okay." They both bit into their bagels.

Then, after several quiet moments, Tamara said, "Harriet's moving in."

Adrian knew she heard right but she couldn't believe it. She lowered her bagel and stared at her. "It's too soon."

"It's been nine months."

"That's too soon."

"Says who?"

"Says, I don't know, some rule book or something. You should wait at least a year."

"She's moving in. Tomorrow. Think you can help?"

"I don't know." She felt sick all of a sudden. Like she was losing her best friend. She gripped the table and felt the world fall away beneath her. What the fuck was happening?

"What? You have plans or something?"

"Maybe."

Tamara sighed. "Fine. Come help if you can."

"Well you're kind of springing this on me. Giving me a damn day's notice."

Tamara pushed away her food and folded her hands. She looked solemn. "Because I knew you'd be upset."

"I'm not upset."

"Yes, you are."

"I'm not upset for me. I'm upset for you. It's too soon."

They finished the meal in silence with Tamara staring out the windows while she sipped her juice. Adrian had also pushed away her food, unable to think about anything but Harriet. Her things would now be all over Tamara's place. And she'd be there from here on out when Adrian stopped by. She and Tamara would do everything together now and Adrian would never be able to enjoy time alone with her best friend. She wouldn't even be able to talk to her on the phone without Harriet muttering in the background and catching every other word.

Damn it.

They didn't speak on the way out to the parking lot, just walked quietly with Tamara slightly in front of her.

"I thought you liked her," she finally said as they reached her car.

"I do. I just think—" But she caught sight of Morresay and decided to stop. She was heading their way, waving.

"Great." Adrian took a step back. She'd again tried to avoid her during class but it was starting to become noticeably rude. She looked at Tamara and felt doubly asinine. But she couldn't help it. Tamara was everything to her. Sighing, she kicked an imaginary pebble and said, "What time tomorrow?"

Tamara opened her door and glanced up at her with hope in her eyes. "We're starting at eight."

Adrian mulled it over some more. Morresay was approaching quickly. "I'll be there."

Tamara wrapped an arm around her and squeezed. "I love you."

"Yeah, yeah. I love you too." But she still felt sick. Worse than sick. She felt numb and lost. Bobbing all alone on that stormy sea again.

"I'm glad I caught you," Morresay said breathlessly as she reached them. She swung her book bag back over her shoulder and smiled. Her whole being seemed to sparkle in the sunlight.

"Adrian, I was wondering if you would be interested in attending a life art class I'm helping out with?"

"You should, A. You're good." Tamara and Morresay both were watching her, waiting.

Did she have to ask right now? When her entire universe was beginning to collapse upon itself. "I don't think so."

Morresay's face fell but she tried to recover quickly. "Oh. Okay."

"Adrian," Tamara started, looking at her like she was a rude child. "You should—"

"I can't," she said quickly. "But thanks for the offer." She turned and searched for her car.

"Adrian!" Tamara was calling after her, but Adrian felt no need or responsibility to answer. Tamara was gone now. Slowly disappearing beyond the horizon. And all Adrian wanted to do was curl up in a ball and disappear herself.

She drove home with the window down, inhaling the cold air, letting it fill her soul and wishing it would freeze it for good. But the hurt was still there. The loss still a continuous slap in the face. She wanted to cry but couldn't. She wanted to shout and yell and scream, but her chest was hollow and her throat useless. When she got home she ran straight to the phone and dialed a number she hadn't dialed in a long while. She needed to hear her voice even though she knew it would only sprinkle on the fire of her emotions rather than soak them completely.

When the female voice answered, Adrian said, "Hi, Mom. Can I come to dinner sometime soon?"

CHAPTER EIGHTEEN

A drian sat in her car for a while trying to regain her bearings before finally heading up the walkway to knock on Tamara's door. Even though she'd been out all night, trying not to think about it, moving day had arrived nonetheless.

Harriet answered wearing a gray sweatshirt and a pair of paint-splattered old jeans. She looked cute in her eyeglasses. Still, it sent a jolt of weirdness through Adrian to see her there, knowing she would be there from here on out.

"Hi, Adrian." Her friendly gaze skimmed her and then fell with concern. "Are you okay? You look like—"

"Death warmed over. I know."

"I was going to say you looked like you just got the shock of your life."

Adrian laughed, short and clipped. "You're not far off." *I can't believe this is happening.*

"Come in, come in." She waved her inside and closed the door. She called for Tamara, who appeared at once, hair pushed back in a tight ponytail. She immediately checked out Adrian and saw her apparently shocked look and then put on an uneasy smile. She stared at Adrian curiously, probably wanting details, wondering what in the hell she'd gotten into.

"Thanks for coming," Harriet said, breaking the long silence. "Have you eaten?"

"No, but I'm not hungry, thanks."

Harriet looked at Tamara as if she didn't know what to say. Then she excused herself, claiming she was going to go work on unpacking boxes in the study.

Tamara watched her go and then raised an eyebrow at Adrian. "What's with you? Did you run over somebody or something?"

She shook her head. "No, I just had a bad night."

"Don't even tell me you went out with someone."

"Okay, I won't." She moved toward the kitchen. She'd gone out to drink at Core, unable to deal with all the thoughts running through her head. But Core had almost been worse than staying home. There was the laughter, the same old songs, the new couples making out in the corners. Alcohol had seemed to be the only thing that had helped her remain. And she'd had a little too much of that.

"Got any Coke? I feel like shit."

"You look like it."

"Thanks."

"My pleasure." She fished a red can from the fridge and tossed it to her. "So who is she?"

Adrian popped the top and slurped with greed. She hadn't realized how thirsty she was.

"No one."

"Uh-huh."

She collapsed into a kitchen chair.

"There wasn't anyone special." There hadn't been. Just a lanky tomboy she'd danced with for a little while. She couldn't even remember her name. Nor did she want to. Not after she saw her snorting something off the back of her hand in the bathroom.

Tamara waited for more, but Adrian had nothing more to say. Sighing, she pulled on some winter gloves and slipped into her red jacket. She opened the front door. "Let's talk while we work."

Adrian followed and they stood on the freshly shoveled driveway. As if on cue, a black Chevy truck eased by, slowed, and backed in. The bed was full of boxes held secure with bungee cords.

"Who's this?" Adrian asked.

"Harriet's brother Henry."

A stout man with a plaid hunter's cap emerged from the truck. Adrian could see through the small gaps of the hat flaps that he also had red hair.

"How are ya?" He removed a glove to pump her hand vigorously. "Henry." Freckles seemed to dance along his face.

"I'm Adrian."

"Nice to know ya, Adrian." He pushed on his eyeglasses in a manner that suggested he did it often. "Any friend of my sister's is a friend of mine." His smile was a lot like Harriet's. It reached his eyes and she knew he was sincere.

"Have you guys already gotten started?" Adrian asked as Henry lowered the tailgate.

"We finished packing last night, so Henry said he'd start with the boxes this morning."

"We got about three more loads of these," he said releasing the cords to heave a box. "Then it's the furniture."

Adrian hefted a big one and followed Tamara. They set them down in the garage where Henry said he'd begin to organize and carry them to the appropriate room inside.

"So do you like her?" Tamara asked as they returned to the truck.

"Who?"

"Whoever you met last night."

"I told you there was no one special."

"But you did go out?"

"Yes."

"Where to?"

"Core."

Adrian quickly slid out another box, avoiding her penetrating gaze. She took it to where the others sat. Harriet was there, too, helping her brother carry them inside. She gave Adrian a polite smile, and when Tamara joined them with another box Adrian suddenly wished she'd stayed home.

"How are things out here?" Harriet asked. There was a knowing silence. Everyone could feel the tension.

"Fine," Tamara finally said.

Harriet nodded but didn't say anything more. She seemed to know what Tamara was implying.

"I should've stayed home." Adrian walked back to the truck.

Tamara shifted another box forward. "Don't be ridiculous. You're welcome here. You know that."

"I don't feel so welcome at the moment."

"Why's that?"

"I feel judged."

"Really? Can't imagine why."

Adrian felt her chest tighten as she followed her with a smaller box. "Honestly, T I can't handle any more at the moment. I feel sick enough as it is."

"Well, you can't ignore it."

"Ignore what?"

"Your behavior. The way you run from yourself, always looking and needing a woman."

Adrian set the box down and sighed. "I'm not."

"Okay," Henry said, emerging from the house. "I'm ready to get these boxes inside." He began piling them according to the labels. "Then it's off to make another run. Who wants to help?" He was smiling that friendly smile again.

Adrian held up her hand, eager to get away for a while. "I will."

Tamara patted her on the shoulder and headed inside. "We'll talk later."

Adrian dreaded that and considered bailing so she wouldn't have to come back at all. But she couldn't do that. Maybe she'd be too tired later to care. She shrugged and followed Henry to his truck and whispered in response to Tamara's last statement, "I was afraid you were going to say that."

Chapter Nineteen

I had hoped to have you over for more of a formal dinner," Harriet said, easing onto a kitchen chair, a paper plate in her hands. Tamara passed her a slice of pizza.

"That's okay. This is just fine," Adrian said and then took a bite. It was after six and she was exhausted. She could barely keep her eyes open enough to eat. They'd worked for hours, first unloading the boxes, then moving furniture, then unpacking the boxes.

"You look beat," Tamara said.

"I am."

"Are you okay?" Henry asked. The steam from his pizza fogged up his glasses.

"I think so."

Tamara stared at her, knowing there was more.

"But to be honest, I don't really care how I am at the moment."

Henry coughed but Adrian was too tired to worry about manners and speaking frankly in front of him.

"What do you mean?" Harriet asked softly.

"I just don't care. I'm too tired, too fed up."

"What happened?" Henry asked.

"Nothing. Just had a little too much to drink is all."

"You should've stayed at home," Tamara said.

They grew quiet again. Adrian stiffened. Then, after seeing the hard glint in Tamara's eyes, she pushed her plate aside and rested her head in her arms. "I give up."

"Finally!" Tamara said. "From your lips to God's ears. I never thought I'd hear you say it."

"You're funny," Adrian said with her eyes narrowed. She didn't need this. Especially not right now.

"And you're not. You're so self-righteous." Tamara licked her lips in anger. "You know what the definition of insanity is, Adrian? It's doing the same thing over and over while expecting a different outcome."

"So now I'm insane. Lovely."

Harriet cleared her throat, obviously uncomfortable. She patted Tamara's hand as if encouraging her to lay off.

"Insane doesn't even come close. You're on the highway to hell, Adrian, and you've got to stop."

"How about a little credit?" Adrian said, voice raised. "I didn't sleep with anyone, I didn't ask anyone to come over. In fact, I walked away when I saw her snorting something in the bathroom."

A heavy silence fell over them and Adrian cursed herself for saying too much.

"So there was someone?" Tamara asked in a low tone.

"No. I just danced with her. That was it."

"You shouldn't have been out in the first place. Much less danced with some stranger. Some druggie. You know how I feel about that. A little weed on occasion, yes. But anything else is dangerous territory."

"Yeah, well, I'm not you."

"No, you're not. And it's plainly obvious. But what it really boils down to, Adrian, is that you just don't care about you. You even said it yourself."

Adrian shoved away from the table and stood. "I'm going to go. I'm beat and I don't need this shit."

"It was nice to meet you, Adrian," Henry said, rising along with her, like a true gentleman.

"Likewise. Harriet, thanks for dinner."

"We'll see you again soon. For a real dinner," she said with a smile.

Adrian nodded. "Sure." She left without another word and crawled in behind the wheel of her car. She peeled away in anger humming "Highway to Hell."

❖

Monday was slow and dreary. Adrian felt like she was moving in slow motion, edging through waist-high sludge, caught in one of those bad dreams where you knew you needed to move but couldn't. She downed numerous Diet Pepsis, hoping for a caffeine kick, but not much happened.

She was fed up with her life. Fed up with her mundane job and her lonely, unappealing existence. Why couldn't she find someone like Harriet? Why couldn't she settle down in a nice little house and cuddle up every Wednesday night to watch *Jade* or *The Last Seduction*?

She stood from the couch and stepped into her shoes. It was early evening and most of the damn day was gone and she had nothing to show for it. Nothing but eight hours given over to Uncle Jake. Her laptop called to her from the table but she didn't budge. A woman would take her mind off things, yes. But the hunt wasn't what she needed or wanted. Not today. She wanted something—she couldn't think of the right words. Frustrated, she ran her hands through her hair and grabbed her car keys. After locking the door behind her, she climbed in her car and took off.

Forty minutes later she was sitting in front of her mother's house, unsure how she'd even got there. She stared at the old but well-maintained mailbox, at the snow-covered lawn, at the neatly cleared driveway. The Oldsmobile was in the open garage.

What am I doing here?

But she knew she needed to face the demon head-on. It was beating beneath her skin and churning in her belly, demanding she do so. She crawled from her car and walked slowly to the front door. She imagined little voices coming from behind the shrubs.

"Don't go in. You know you shouldn't. Go back home."

But she kept on. Her intent driving her. She knocked hard and fast and heard Louis call out for her mother. The door opened a tiny bit and she saw an eye that resembled hers.

"Adrian." The door opened farther, revealing her future image. Her mother rubbed her hands on a dish towel and backed up to let her in. She was wearing pressed brown pants and a caramel-colored sweater over a blouse. The top few buttons of the blouse resembled pearls. Her face was made up nicely but lightly, her lipstick long worn off. The wrinkles around her eyes creased as she smiled.

"I wasn't expecting you so soon," she said as she hugged her quickly. They were standing in the kitchen, the setting sunlight coming in through the large window over the sink. The old yellow linoleum floor was clean and homey. Cozy.

"I know. I'm sorry for not calling."

"Who is it? Who's there?" Louis boomed from the living room.

Adrian shrugged out of her coat and hung it in the small sitting room off the kitchen.

"It's Adrian," her mother called back.

"Adrian?"

They heard the recliner buckle and groan. Soon he was in the doorway.

"Well, well, well." His mud colored eyes twinkled in the kitchen light. He clicked his tongue as he stared her down. His trademark "son of a bitch" sound. "Look at what crawled out from a hole to come see its mother."

"Oh, stop it."

"Shut up, Marge. I'm talking to Adrian."

"It has been a while," Adrian said.

"I'll say. All she ever does is yap about you. Adrian this and Adrian that."

"Why don't you go watch the football game and I'll start dinner?" her mother asked. "How does chili sound? Or vegetable soup?"

Louis didn't look away from Adrian nor she him. Amusement passed over his face as if he could tell something was different in her today.

"Why don't you ask your dear beloved daughter what she would like to have?"

"Adrian?" Her voice had gone up in pitch. Her trademark "I've got to keep the peace" sound.

"Whatever is easiest for you, Mom."

At this Louis cackled, throwing his bald head back, showing his yellowing teeth. His massive chest shook under his Chicago Bears sweatshirt.

"Whatever is easiest on you, Mommy," he mimicked. Then he turned and walked back into the living room.

Her mother let out a long sigh and smiled. "Vegetables sound good, don't they?"

Adrian nodded and sat at the kitchen table. Commercials played loudly from the living room.

"I'm sorry it's been so long, Mom."

Her mother turned from the freezer, frozen bag of vegetables in her hand. "Oh, that's okay, honey. We understand. You have your own life."

"Do you need any help?"

"No, no. You just sit right there." Her mother loved to cook and insisted on always doing it herself. Adrian supposed it gave her peace of mind to have total control over something.

"How have you been?" her mother asked. "Have you found that special girl yet?"

Her mother had always been very accepting and supportive of her lifestyle, which had always surprised her. Even Tamara's folks still struggled with her sexuality.

"Not yet."

"Well, why not?" She smiled. "No nice girls?"

"It doesn't seem like it."

"Oh, there has to be some somewhere. Maybe you're not looking in the right place."

"You sound like Tamara." She'd done nothing but mull over her words ever since she'd left her house. They just kept replaying over and over. Insanity. Insanity. Was she insane? Yes, maybe she was. Why else would she be sitting here in the lion's den?

Her mother cut open the vegetable bag after putting a large pot on the stove.

"How is Tamara?"

"She's just fine and dandy." She was surprised to hear one of Louis's phrases come from her mouth. All smart-ass and sarcasm. Maybe he always felt this angry and lost. Maybe she'd never really understood him at all. "Her girlfriend just moved in."

"I never understood why you two didn't ever get involved."

"Ha! Right. I don't think so. We're too different, that's why."

Louis walked back in, scratching the seat of his sweatpants. "She's colored. That's why. Adrian doesn't want no colored girl."

Adrian clenched her jaw just as she'd done for years, every single time he made a comment about Tamara's race. *Keep talking, old man. Keep talking.*

"Louis, hush."

"What?" He opened the fridge and fished out a near beer and cracked it open. He slurped loudly.

Louis wasn't a drunk. He used to be, back when Adrian was young. Those had been the good times.

Now Louis was sober and had been for years. And he was a mean sober.

"Don't tell me what to do," he said, wiping his chin. "I'm talking to Adrian." He sauntered over to her. "So how's work?"

"The same."

"Jake hasn't wised up and fired your lazy ass?" He laughed, amused at himself. "He always was a stupid son of a bitch."

"He's your friend," she said quickly.

He cackled again.

"I think he's rubbing off on you. You're getting a smart mouth."

"Louis, I think your game's back on," her mother said, pouring in the vegetables.

He stared at Adrian some more, made a clicking sound, and walked away.

"I see things haven't changed much," Adrian said. This was exactly why she'd come. To feel alive again. To feel that gut-tightening, stomach-churning, blood-beating feeling of hate again.

"Oh, he's just tired. Work's been hard this year."

"It's hard every year."

"Well, it must be harder this year." She dropped a cube of vegetable flavoring into the pot and got busy dicing potatoes and onions. "You know it's not easy for a man this day and age. Jobs are scarce and the ones available are physically demanding, and they don't pay like they used to."

"It's the same for everyone."

"Men especially. And you know, they don't get to come home and whine and have the wife just go out and work. They have to do it. They don't get to cry about it."

Adrian rubbed her temples. "I take it you still aren't working?" Her mother hadn't had a job since Louis's first day of sobriety. He wouldn't allow it.

"I've got work to do around here."

"If times are so tough, you could go back to work at the library and help out financially."

"No, no." She looked quickly toward the living room. "I'm fine here."

"I'm just saying, Mom."

"I know, honey. We're fine. Work is just hard on Louis."

Adrian swallowed, knowing what she must ask. She had to ask it each visit. "He's not hitting you, is he?"

"Don't start that again," she said, scooting the onions off the cutting board and into the pot with the knife.

"I have to make sure."

"You know it makes me very uncomfortable."

"I know, Mom, but I have to be sure. With his temper—"

"If he does it's our business, not yours or anyone else's."

"So you're saying he does."

"I'm saying no such thing."

"Then what are you saying? He pushes you? Shoves you around like he used to?"

"Adrian."

"I need to know, Mom."

"Why?"

"So I can—"

"So you can what? There's nothing you can do."

"I could kick his ass." Oh yes, please. How she wanted to. Now more than ever.

Her mother looked quickly again to the living room. She hurried over to her and sat. She wrung her tired-looking hands.

"You always do this. I don't know why you even come. You know I'm just going to ask you to leave."

"Which is why I don't come!"

"Adrian, my darling girl, just stop this, okay? I'm married to Louis and this is our life. You must not come in here and rile things up. It isn't healthy."

Adrian scoffed. "You don't have to live like this, Mom."

"I want to."

"No, you don't."

"He doesn't hit me."

"He's mean."

"He's stressed. And frankly, do you know how hard it is for him not to drink? He battles that addiction every day. Every day." She tapped the table with her index finger to emphasize her point. "I think he deserves some credit for that."

"He shouldn't be drinking near beer. That only adds to his frustration, I'm sure."

Her mother sighed. "Why won't you give him a break, Adrian?"

"Honestly, Mom? I don't know. I mean, I think I know, but I'm not sure."

Her mother looked uncomfortable and rose to stir the soup.

"There's the fact that he's mean, yes. But it's more than that. It's the control, the violence, the lying."

"The lying." She chuckled. "Louis doesn't lie."

"Okay, Mom."

Her mother shook her head and tapped the wooden spoon on the pot. "Let's stop this, Adrian. I never get to see you. Can't we enjoy a nice dinner?"

Adrian knew she could stop but she knew Louis wouldn't be able to. So she nodded, made her mother smile, and sat biding her time. Her mother spoke of family and friends and what she wanted to do to her garden come spring. The kitchen came alive with smells of the cooking soup as the sun began to dip in front of the house.

Soon Adrian rose to wash her hands. She went down the hall into the bathroom she used to share with her sister. Each time she visited her mother she marveled at how small the rooms now seemed. She paused in the doorway as the memories came. She shook them away, they were too powerful. She stared at her reflection for a long while as she ran her hands under the running faucet. She wasn't the same kid, the same Adrian. But somehow the words didn't resonate. She didn't feel totally in control. She didn't feel grown and safe and secure. She turned off the water and dried her hands on her jeans as she continued down the hall to her old bedroom. Her mother had kept her twin bed and small chest of drawers. But she'd added a table and a chair where she sat at her sewing machine. A quilt Adrian had never seen before hung on the wall. The blue carpet was the same, just a little more worn, and she wondered if it still smelled the same. How many times had she hidden under her bed and cried, burying her face in the carpet so her mother wouldn't hear? How many times had she held her breath and stifled her cries as her mother came looking for her?

She closed her eyes. It was okay to cry now. She didn't have to worry about her mother's feelings. But she wouldn't allow herself. She still felt like she had to be strong. Had to be tough. It had nothing to do with being in her mother's house.

She left the room slowly, heading back to the kitchen. The three of them scooted in at the small table and passed a loaf of French bread around. Adrian tore herself off a piece and dunked it in her soup. Louis was watching her, eyeing the bread as she brought it to her mouth. He wouldn't say anything about it. He hadn't since she moved out. But she knew he was thinking about it. Could see it in the cool but callous way he stared at her as she ate. Her mother, as usual, beamed at them both, obviously pleased to have them there together.

Louis chewed loudly and spoke before his mouth was completely empty. "So how you been, Adrian? You afraid to bring your lady friends around?" He chewed heartily on some more bread.

"Haven't had anyone to bring," she replied.

"That's a shame. You know your mother and I don't have any problems with that."

"I know that, Louis, and I'm grateful. Truly."

He nodded and stirred his soup with his spoon.

"Old man Lewinski down at work, he bitches all the time about his faggoty son. Drives me bananas. I'm always telling him, you gotta live and let live. If your boy wants to take it up the chute that's his business. Just be glad it ain't you."

Adrian forced herself to swallow. Her mother was watching her, her brow furrowed with concern.

"Louis, maybe we shouldn't talk about that at the dinner table."

"Why the hell not? Adrian's a dyke. She doesn't have a problem with being a dyke, do you, Adrian?"

"No, Louis, I don't."

"See? We should be able to talk about it."

"Adrian, tell us about you. What are you doing for fun these days?"

"Maybe she's quilting," Louis said, slurping more soup. "Like her mother. I swear to God that's all she does all damn day long. We got quilts up the ying yang, hanging in the bedroom, hanging in the office. She even hung one in your old room. Ugly as sin too."

Her mother ate quietly, staring at her bowl. Adrian felt the thrumming within grow stronger.

"Guess that's why she has to hang 'em. They're too ugly to sell or give away."

"Will you make me one, Mom?" Adrian asked, shushing Louis.

"Of course."

He laughed. "Go ahead. Act like I'm not here."

"We're not acting like you're not here," her mother said softly.

"Go ahead, I don't care. You're both useless. Good for nothing."

"Louis," her mother said.

He drank from his can, eyes trained on her. When he lowered it he began to make his clicking noise.

Adrian saw her mother physically harden at the noise. She was grounding herself, ready for an assault.

"You make her an ugly-ass quilt for her to hang in her ugly-ass apartment. I'm sure an ugly quilt will bring the dykes running right in."

"Adrian, you never did tell us what it is you're doing for fun."

"Because she doesn't want to."

"I'm taking an art class."

Her mother brightened. "That's wonderful."

Louis scoffed. "Figures."

"Sorry?" Adrian said, looking at him.

"I said it figures. All that artsy shit is for queers."

"I am queer, Louis."

"I know."

"I thought you didn't have a problem with it."

"I don't. You are what you are. Your mother coddled y take you off her tit, and now you're queer. Queers do the a

Adrian stared at him and smiled. This was what she abuse. It had been a while, a long while. And she had dead inside.

"It's really neat," she said. "You would like it, M

"Like hell. Don't even say it. She's not taking n

"Why not?"

"Adrian, Louis is right. I have plenty to do here."

"I ain't having her down there with a bunch of queers. Bunch of hippie dykes—"

"Actually, there are all kinds of women taking the class."

"I said no."

"And our instructor is really nice—"

"I said no!" He pounded his fist, knocking some soup from his bowl.

Adrian stared at him, fists clenched. *Bring it, you bastard.*

"No one asked you, Louis."

His eyes darkened and he pushed himself away from the table. Sweat glistened on his bald head.

"You know you don't talk to me like that."

"Or what?"

He angled his head and clicked his tongue. "You got old-timer's or something?"

She laughed softly even though she was trembling.

"It looks like you do."

"Adrian, why don't you come back another time?" Her mother tried.

"I wanted to see your quilts," she said, holding Louis's stare.

"Another time. Why don't you call me this week?"

His thin lips crept into a sinister smile, challenging her.

"Adrian, please." Her mother was frightened, pleading. Just as she'd always done. *Adrian, please. Just shut up. Just be quiet. Don't get him started. Don't set him off.* And Adrian had always listened because it wasn't her that paid the price. It was her mother.

Her hammering heart was filling her body with what she needed. What she'd come for. She had it now and she grinned in return, grateful.

"As always, it was wonderful to see you both." She stood, wiping the corners of her mouth with her napkin. "Mom, thanks for the dinner. Louis, thanks for having me."

He rose with her. "You're not going to finish eating?"

"I'm not feeling so well."

"Well, that's too bad. Your mother worked hard on that soup."

"I know. I'm sorry, Mom."

She stood, too, but didn't move. Adrian hugged her and kissed her. "I love you," she whispered in her ear.

"Guess we'll see you in another year," Louis said.

Her mother rested a hand at the base of her throat, watching as Adrian retrieved her coat and slid into it.

"Louis." Adrian gave him a nod, which he returned.

He followed her outside and she wasn't surprised. He lit a cigarette and flicked the ash in the snow.

"Gotta new snow blower," he said as she walked to her car.

"Yeah, the driveway looks good."

"It does, don't it?" He took a deep drag. "How's that Jap car of yours?"

"Good."

"Well, you know where to bring it if it gives you any trouble."

"Yeah, I do, Louis. Thanks."

"Any time."

He waved as she pulled away, cigarette glowing as it hung from his lips.

Every time she thought of him she pictured him like that, watching her drive away, cigarette in his mouth, eyes glinting, making sure she knew who was boss and just whose house it was.

"Whose house indeed, Louis. Whose house indeed."

When she got home she went directly to the stereo, switched on "Cold" and reached for her large sketch pad. She shrugged out of her coat, tossed it aside, and rolled up her sleeves. She fished her charcoals out of her supply box and began scratching firm line after line, creating a stark, angular face and a smaller sharper body. She drew with harsh movements, each trail of dark charcoal a slash across Louis in her mind's eye. She cursed and mumbled and held the pad close as she sank into the chair and started smearing with her fingertips.

"This for Mom," she said as she drew. "This is for me. This is for making me feel like a worthless piece of shit. This is for calling me fat when I was perfectly fine. This is for your words, your looks, your goddamned controlling ways. This is for all of it."

She worked diligently for what felt like a few short minutes. When she finished and checked the clock it was after midnight. "Jesus." She wiped the sweat from her brow and tossed the sketch pad. She watched as it slid along the table. She left it there as she powered off the stereo and headed for her bedroom. The image she'd drawn was still in her head, flashing behind her eyes. It was a face with angry eyes and a wide open shouting mouth. This time there was no *X* on the face. It was on the chest, where a heart should be.

CHAPTER TWENTY

The sun had already set by the time Adrian reached the community college on Wednesday. She eased into a parking space and walked through the snow-salted parking lot. She hadn't spoken to Tamara since Sunday and she wasn't looking forward to seeing her in class. She could've skipped today's session and probably should have, but she dreaded going home to be alone. The restlessness was getting worse, along with the mental torture of her mind. When she wasn't thinking about the past she was thinking about the present and how she'd lost her best friend and never had anyone special and never would. Her life felt like a massive mess and she just didn't like sitting at home in the middle of the pile.

She entered the building, and even though she was a bit early she headed for the classroom. She breezed into the room and inhaled the pleasant smells. She hung her coat and was about to sit on her stool when Morresay entered. She halted her movement for a split second when she saw Adrian.

"Hi," she said as she crossed to her desk. "I wasn't expecting anyone to be in here quite yet." She brushed back the loose strands of her hair and Adrian found herself wishing she wouldn't. She liked seeing them hang loose around her face.

"I can leave if you want." She heated at her thoughts and words.

"Of course not. I didn't mean you weren't welcome. You're always welcome." She seemed to be fumbling for words and she was arranging the things on her desk even though they didn't appear to need arranging. When Adrian sat at her stool she stopped and ran her fingertips lightly across the desktop as if in deep thought.

"I'm actually glad you're here. I wanted to talk to you about the other night and my e-mail invitation to attend the life art class."

Embarrassment came like a cloud of mist and settled over Adrian. It made it difficult to breathe. "I'm sorry about that—"

But Morresay stopped her. "Please, let me finish. I'm the one who should apologize. I didn't mean to pressure you or make you uncomfortable."

"You didn't." Adrian searched for what to say. "It was me. It was a bad time."

"Regardless." She held up her hand. "I should've approached it differently. I just think with your talent and your potential...I wanted to talk to you about it. But if you're not interested, you're not interested."

"I didn't say I wasn't interested."

"I shouldn't have pushed it."

"I'm...having a hard time..."

Morresay began fidgeting with her desktop belongings again. "Just please know that I care and that I know how emotional art can be sometimes." She paused and when Adrian didn't speak she seemed to struggle again for words. "And about the invitation for coffee—"

Adrian stopped her, nearly coming out of her skin at seeing how embarrassed she was. "It was to talk about art, right?"

Morresay visibly flushed. "Yes."

"Okay, then. No need to explain or apologize."

Voices came from the hallway as students headed for the classroom. Morresay hurried and continued talking, going on about emotions and surfacing feelings and how she understood and how she would leave her alone, but that if she ever needed her she would be there and—

Oh God, it was too much and Adrian felt so responsible and so embarrassed and Morresay was so kind and so beautiful, standing there apologizing, trying to make her feel better. What could Adrian do? What could she say other than I'm sorry? She had to say something. People were coming. And Morresay was struggling, blushing profusely.

Adrian stood and racked her brain but nothing was there. Nothing but... "You're beautiful."

Morresay closed her mouth and looked up at her, blinking her soulful eyes. "Pardon?"

Adrian forced herself to swallow. Her heart was in her throat. "You're beautiful."

Morresay appeared completely shocked and the red in her face darkened at the delicate curve of her cheekbones. Two other students walked in at that moment, laughing and carrying on, oblivious to anything around them.

Morresay sat behind her desk and looked to be trying to compose herself. Adrian sat on her stool and looked away, unable to bear the sight. She'd just embarrassed them both further.

"Fuck." She rubbed her temples, wanting to dart from the room. And when Tamara entered looking hard and stubborn, she really wanted to run.

But where would she go? What would she do? Go drinking? Go hunting? She wasn't like that. And she'd prove it by staying and finishing out class.

Morresay called attention to the front, but Adrian didn't follow her form. She couldn't deal with the rejection she knew she'd see in her face. She'd just told a straight woman she was beautiful, and that was a death sentence. Now she'd be lucky if Morresay spoke to her at all. Maybe it was for the best. Maybe now her mind would let her rest when it came to her.

She hoped so. Because she truly couldn't take much more. She rose and got her supplies as Morresay instructed them on how to bring in more detail with pastels. Adrian didn't want to use Tamara's chalk and she knew she was being an ass, but Tamara was too, having said nothing to her so far. They'd argued like this before a long time ago and the silence would last for days until one of them caved. Adrian would be damned if it was her this time. She had enough issues to deal with, and if Tamara couldn't understand that then she deserved the silent treatment. She was the one who had someone to go home to. Not Adrian. She returned to her seat and started in on drawing the assigned object. She kept quiet and worked quickly, making sure to add every single speck of detail and then some. She made the drawing pop, made it look like it could float right off the page and slap someone senseless. She did that for Morresay. For all the kind words and compliments. For the embarrassment and rudeness on her part. For the "you're beautiful" comment, even though she'd meant it. She worked hard to make up for all of that, but Morresay didn't seem to notice or care. She didn't touch her shoulder when she came by and she didn't comment on her work. So when Adrian finished before everyone else, she rose, put away her supplies, grabbed her jacket, and left her drawing on her table.

She headed into the night and hurried to her car, so drained from the effort she'd put into the drawing she almost didn't make it home.

❖

Adrian still couldn't get Morresay from her mind. She'd tossed and turned and dreamt about her for two nights straight. Images of her standing there against that desk, green eyes stirring her, touching her soul. The way she'd said the words "apologize" and "uncomfortable." The way her hands had seemed restless, the way her hair fell. And then there was her scent. Chai.

What did it all mean? She didn't know. A part of her, when she'd awoken on Thursday morning, was convinced the whole incident had been a dream. And she'd relaxed and gone about her day thinking just that until she received an e-mail from Morresay at noon. She'd apologized for not getting a chance to finish their conversation. And she asked for a chance to do just that.

The real world had come rushing back then, crushing her. She'd really blurted out "you're beautiful" to a woman she didn't know. Her teacher. Instructor. A straight woman who had looked scared to death afterward.

"You're mad. Absolutely mad," she said aloud as she logged off. "Tamara's right. You're fucking insane."

"What are you mad about?" Benny asked, peeling off shipping labels to stick on some smaller boxes they had waiting to ship.

"I'm not mad upset. I'm mad crazy."

"Oh." He slapped on a sticker and slid the box along the floor toward the door. "Why?"

She ran her hands through her hair wishing she could meet Tamara for lunch. But that wouldn't be happening. They still weren't speaking.

Her despondence, she decided, would have to be worked off by running a flat-out sprint for a mile or by talking to Benny. Neither sounded appealing.

She groaned. "Have you ever blurted out something stupid to a woman before?"

He seemed surprised she was actually asking him. She almost waited for him to look behind himself to make sure she wasn't speaking to someone else.

He peeled off another label and side stepped to locate the appropriate box. "How do you mean? What exactly did you say?"

She plucked up a pencil and put it to her nose and inhaled. The scent soothed her and sent her blood racing. Her fingers actually tingled, eager to create.

"I told a woman she was beautiful."

He groaned as he bent to slap on the sticker. "That's it?" He laughed a little as he straightened. "Christ, I thought you were going to say you had said you'd wanted to fuck her, or hey, your tits are huge or something like that."

"I'm not a man, Benny."

"Yeah, but you're close."

She fired the pencil at him but he ducked, his reflexes improving. She'd have to move quicker. Ninja like. "Are you going to help me or not?"

"What do you want to know? As far as I'm concerned you gave her a compliment. What's wrong with that?"

She winced and leaned back in her squeaky chair. "No, Benny, you don't get it. She was talking to me, this nice woman, my art teacher, and I just blurted out 'you're beautiful.'"

"Your art teacher?" He made a face like what she'd said tasted sour. "Since when do you go to art class?"

"Since—I don't know—that's not the point. I sounded like an idiot. I feel like an idiot. I *was* an idiot."

"Still are."

"Benny," she groaned. Why was she telling him this? Was it because she'd had no one to talk to but One and Two for days on end? It sort of felt nice actually hearing someone respond.

"Okay, okay." He sank heavily into his chair and it protested loudly when he placed his feet on the desk and bit off a hangnail as he thought. "What did she say?"

"She just paused and said 'pardon.'"

"Hmm. Did she seem mad?"

"No. But I think she was flustered. Embarrassed."

"What did you do?"

"Nothing. I just did my assignment and I left."

"You didn't say anything else?"

"What the hell was I supposed to say in a classroom full of people? I was freaked out and embarrassed too."

He shook his head. "And you're supposed to get women better than me? Even I wouldn't have left."

"Why not?"

He folded his hands on his beer belly. "It's a rule. Like a well-known fact."

"What is?"

"If you give a woman a compliment and she doesn't slap you, make a face, or run away…you're in."

"Get outta here," she said sounding like him.

"I'm dead serious."

"So I should've stayed? And said what?"

"Anything. She obviously liked what she'd heard. You should've asked her out."

"She's straight. You forgot that part. And she had a class to teach, so she couldn't leave."

"Says who? Look, all I know is, in the world of women, if you want to get one, you gotta follow the rules."

"These are rules men use?"

"Yep. They're sacred, so you owe me."

"She's my teacher."

"Well, you obviously like her if you blurted out what you did. And since when do you care? The shit you've told me—I figured anything with the right parts would do."

She chose to ignore that comment but she knew it would stab at her mind later, just like everything else did these days. "What about her man? She's got a picture of him on her desk and I saw her hugging him in the parking lot."

"Adrian, you told the woman she was beautiful. You didn't grab her ass. Relax a little. And if you like her, ask her if she's married. If she's interested, she'll find an excuse to meet you somewhere for drinks."

She sat in silence, a little amazed at his knowledge. Everything he was saying was making sense.

"Actually, she asked me out for coffee. Before all this, though."

He planted his feet firmly on the ground. "Get outta here."

"She did. That's what we were talking about when I blurted."

"Now the question is, does she still want to go?"

Adrian chewed on her lip for moment, flushing. "I think she does. She just sent me an e-mail."

"Then you're home free, girl."

"I don't think it's like that, though. I think she just wants to talk about art."

He laughed, obviously disbelieving.

"For someone who loves and knows women so well, you sure are clueless sometimes." He headed into the back office, on his way to the break room.

Adrian stared at her computer screen. Clueless. It seemed more than appropriate for the way she'd been feeling lately. Tamara's words came to her as she considered her reply to Morresay. *She's off-limits. Probably married. Focus on yourself.*

She stared at Morresay's words until they blurred and bulged from the page. She wanted to call her. More than anything.

Maybe she should call her. She was offering to listen, after all, and she'd offered more than once. But she was only being polite. A teacher going above and beyond to help a promising student. She in no way knew of Adrian's true feelings or attraction. If she did, she'd clam up and run for the hills just like any other straight woman would.

She buried her head in her hands, frustrated. The phone number seemed larger than the words, and it was growing bigger by the second.

"Fuck it." She grabbed the phone and punched in the number. She bit her nail, nervous as hell. What would she say? The line rang once and she ended the call. She lightly slapped the receiver against her forehead. "Shit, shit, shit."

A loud ring caused her to nearly drop it. The caller ID scared her even more. It was Morresay.

"Goddamnit." Why had she called her? What the hell had she planned on saying to her anyway? She couldn't talk to her. Every single bit of emotion she felt in regard to her and everything else would surely tumble out.

She hurriedly looked around, panicked. How would she explain herself? *Oh, I just accidently dialed your number and hung up?*

She forced herself to calm down and rid her mind of Morresay. But there was nothing safe to switch to. There just didn't seem to be any peace. Anywhere. Not in her mind, not in her apartment, not in her best friend. She paced, needing to escape. Benny returned and eyed her.

"What's with you?"

She swallowed down the ball in her throat. "I need to get out of here."

"Me too."

It was close to quitting time, but that wasn't what she meant. "No, I mean I really need to go somewhere. Anywhere. You up for it?"

He seemed surprised. "You serious?"

"Yes."

"My place, barbecue?"

Adrian nodded and the phone rang again. When Benny went for it her heart leapt.

"I got it," she said and stretched for the receiver. "Jake's."

There was a pause and then a woman's voice. It shot right into her ear and went straight to her heart, where it gently squeezed. "I'm sorry, I must have the wrong number."

Adrian inhaled sharply and when she heard the click she thought for a second she was going to lose her balance.

Thankfully, her chair was right behind her, and as she sank down into it she thought how wonderful it would be to hear that voice over the line time and time again.

CHAPTER TWENTY-ONE

"Did everyone get a chance to finish their pastel drawings at home?" Morresay asked on Saturday.

The class mumbled various replies, all of the women retrieving the drawings they'd been working on for a while, the ones where they'd drawn an object they'd brought from home. Adrian was wide awake and on edge, every nerve still attuned to Morresay. She'd done her best at finding distractions, even gone to Benny's house on Thursday evening, but nothing seemed to help.

Morresay moved closer and Adrian focused, watching her as she took a look at some of the drawings, touched shoulders and wove slowly through tables. She seemed quieter today, a little withdrawn, as Adrian felt herself. Her cable knit sweater was simple and beige, her pants a faded navy. Her slender hands had the telltale marks of charcoal and Adrian knew she'd been working recently. The image was strikingly familiar, reminding Adrian of the fantasy she'd had while at the party at Bobbie's.

"Would anyone like to share?" Morresay asked, returning to the front of the class. Adrian sat very still, convinced Morresay could feel her heating and read her thoughts. But when Morresay's eyes passed hers there was no pause or sign of recognition. It relieved her yet upset her a little. She didn't want to be called on for many reasons, but she also didn't want Morresay to hate her.

Her eyes continued across the room before settling on Tamara, who had risen her hand.

"Tamara. Tell us a little bit about yours."

Tamara held up her drawing and Adrian was surprised to see that it wasn't the drawing she'd originally seen her work on. This one was a rose. A single beautiful large rose. The detail was breathtaking. Tamara had really worked hard on it.

"What do we think, ladies? Very nicely done, isn't it? It looks almost real. Like you can pluck it right off the page and put it to your nose to inhale."

There were mumbles and agreements.

"But what's most important is why Tamara chose this to draw. Don't you think? What drew her to this rose? The color? The soft velvety texture? Or some other reason? Tamara?"

"All of those reasons. I knew I had to go relatively simple because frankly, I'm terrible at all of this." A few understanding chuckles came from nearby. "The colors were beautiful so I was hoping they would really pop. But as I drew it the real reason I chose it came to the surface." Silence fell over the classroom as everyone waited. Tamara's eyes glazed over as she stared at her rose. "I bought this for my girlfriend on my way home from work one day. I didn't buy a dozen and I didn't choose red. At the time I wasn't sure why. I just thought it was beautiful." She paused a moment as if gathering her thoughts and emotions. "I know now that I didn't need to get her the full dozen or the rich red. I just needed this one. This one was enough. This one was perfect."

"Tell us why," Morresay whispered, captivated.

"Because this rose represents us. We are simple. A single unit. And we are bright and yellow and full of radiant happiness. Yet we are burning with desire and passion as we open and bloom together, offering ourselves together to the world." She looked at the rose as if it were real and speaking to her. Her fingers skimmed over the paper. "I'm going to frame it and hang it in our bedroom. Because this rose, on this page, will never wilt. It is us at this moment, frozen in time."

There was a collective hush over the room. Morresay's eyes were sparkling. She was touched, her feelings causing her cheeks to redden. She had a hand over her heart as if it was helping it to beat, like maybe if she took it away her heart would stop. Adrian stared at her with her own heart lodged in her throat. Tamara had reached them all.

"And I just want to say," Tamara added, "that I hope all of us can find this in our lives." She sat then and eased her drawing back onto the table. Adrian wanted to tell her she loved her, that she was truly happy for her, but she couldn't. She couldn't say anything she was so overcome with raw emotion.

"Thank you, Tamara," Morresay said softly. She seemed to be having trouble speaking herself. "Does everyone understand the symbolism Tamara spoke of? How what we choose to create can represent just about anything in our lives?"

Women nodded and Morresay breathed deeply. "Good. Would everyone please turn in their work now? And when you return to your tables I want you all to unwrap the canvases you brought."

Adrian had turned in her drawing long ago, so she busied herself unwrapping her canvas and placing it in the standing easel. Morresay began weaving through the tables again, talking.

"Today we are going to shift gears and paint. I want to turn your brains on end and go from realism to free, raw, uninhibited expression. I want you to paint without thinking about creating anything tangible. Just grab your brush, choose your color, and fling, tap, or smear on your paint. Get wild. Go crazy. Have fun."

Adrian felt herself gearing up, like a race car sitting idle at the starting line.

"Whenever you're ready, you may begin."

There was rustling and talking and excited laughter. Adrian reached for the paint at the center of the table. She left her brushes lying there and used the bottle alone, squirting deep navy paint onto her canvas. It shot out like mustard from a bottle, spraying at first and then shooting across the canvas in a jagged lightning line. Quickly, she stripped off her sweatshirt, stood from her stool, and began to smear the paint with her hands. She used the bottle to squirt on some more, smearing that as well. Then she left some fresh lines, angling them this way and that. Then it was on to a new color. Bright yellow and bright green. She crisscrossed and stabbed the bottle at the painting like a madman wielding a knife. Which gave her an idea. Not caring about the fresh paint on her hands, she dug in her pocket for her keys and opened the small Swiss Army knife she had attached. Without missing a beat, she took it to the painting, turned it flat on its side and spread some of the green and yellow lines into crescent smears. She even pressed into the canvas with the side of the dull blade, making slight indentions and cuts. Then she used the tip of the knife to scratch across the canvas in random strides.

Women were starting to approach, curious, watching her closely. But she was in her own world already, caught up by that invisible magnet, the one pulling her and holding her to the canvas. It wouldn't release her until she finished.

She flung the knife and keys on the table and reached again for the paint. She squirted on more lines, flinging the paint from the bottles in quick jerky gestures. Then she added long, deliberate lines and used the knife again to layer on more of the navy mixed with a deep violet.

When she finally stepped away at the end of class, the painting was mesmerizing and looked like dark skeletal trees and wild streaks of lightning in a neon chaos. She even stepped up to add a few more scratch marks, bringing the trunks of the trees alive with veiny bark.

She stood staring at it for a long while, unmoving while women trickled through, looking for themselves. Tamara was speechless, staring at it with watery eyes.

The class started filtering out, a few of the women still in back cleaning up their brushes. Morresay was helping students find their graded work on their way out. She spoke to a few, giving lots of praise and encouragement. Adrian headed for the sink, her hands a complete but satisfying mess. As she scrubbed she heard Tamara and Morresay talking, going over Tamara's work. From the way they related so easily to each other, Adrian could tell Morresay had spent quite a bit of time helping her.

She returned to her canvas and set it along the wall to dry in a space between some of the others. She wiped her wet hands on her already dirty jeans. Paint had crusted dry on the waist and thighs, some of it in swipes, some in handprints. She was starting to regret wiping paint on them, but she'd been so caught up in her work she hadn't cared.

She grabbed her car keys and walked slowly toward the door, not wanting to interrupt Tamara and Morresay. They were the only remaining people in the class.

"Hey, Adrian, wait up," Tamara said, readying some of her work to take home. She began to roll them up, using her leg for support as she did so.

"Actually, I have some of Adrian's work here too," Morresay said. She opened the large art binder and pulled out both the pencil drawing and the charcoal drawing. "As I was telling Tamara, I wrote some brief notes on the Post-it on the back."

Adrian took them and glanced at the notes quietly. Morresay voiced them aloud.

"Have you given any thought to what I mentioned before? About maybe going to school for your art?"

Adrian had read her e-mails. Several times, in fact. But she didn't know what to tell her. Art school was the last thing on her mind. She had a job and wasn't really thrilled at the thought of starting over.

"Adrian, I think that's a great idea," Tamara said. "I mean, if you really think she's got a future in it." She looked at Morresay.

"I do. She has a lot of raw talent."

Adrian still didn't speak. She had the feeling they'd talked about this before, on their own. And she was still clawing her way out of the dark, twisted forest with neon chaos. Her insides were churning and she felt worked up and restless, yet dark and distant. She couldn't bring herself to look at Morresay. There were too many things spinning out of her control right now and she knew she'd be drawn into her wistful eyes and her mysterious spicy scent. She'd want to touch her, feel her under her swollen fingertips and kiss her slender fingers one at a time.

"Are you okay?" Tamara asked.

Adrian closed her eyes and nodded. "I need to go," she said, swallowing her desire.

"Okay."

Morresay wished them a good night and left them to walk to her desk. Tamara followed Adrian out of the building, where the wind pushed at Adrian's drawings hanging from her hand.

"You better roll those up," Tamara said.

"I've got a better idea," Adrian said, hurrying over to the trash bin just outside the building. She held the papers up and dropped them inside the open barrel.

"What are you doing!" Tamara went to grab them but Adrian gripped her arm.

"Don't."

"What's wrong with you?"

"I don't want them."

"Well, I do."

"No." She wouldn't release her.

"Why the hell not?"

"Because." She shook her head in frustration. "I don't want to look at them. It makes me—" She dropped her arm and headed farther into the dark wind. Hands shoved in her pockets, she hurried to her car. Tamara was breathless when she caught up to her.

"Adrian."

"Don't, T. I can't take it."

"Please tell me what's wrong."

Adrian stopped. "I don't know!"

"Has something happened?"

"You mean other than you and me fighting? No. Nothing has happened. But yet everything. And I'm feeling lost and confused."

Tamara's face washed over with hurt. She was hurting for her and Adrian knew it. It only made her feel worse.

"Come over. Harriet and I—"

"No. I need to go."

"I don't want you to be alone."

Adrian unlocked her car. "I don't plan on being alone."

Tamara caught her meaning. "Don't do that, Adrian. Please. Just give yourself some time."

"I gotta go." She climbed in her car and shut the door. Rolling down her window she said, "I'll call you later," and drove off into the night.

CHAPTER TWENTY-TWO

L ater that evening Adrian was freshly showered standing in front of Penny's door. It pulled open slowly.

"I was surprised to hear from you," she said just before she broke into a wicked smile.

"Is it too soon? We can still go out for coffee or something." They'd briefly discussed meeting for coffee on the phone but Penny had invited her over instead. Adrian had readily agreed.

"Or...something."

"Yeah."

She took a step back and opened the door farther. "Come on in."

Adrian didn't hesitate. She knew why she was there and Penny seemed to know as well, wearing a black satin bathrobe, walking in her bare feet. Her house was a lot like her. Confident and a bit bold. Huge canvases of abstract art hung in her living room over black leather couches with bright throw pillows. Deep-barreled candles burned on the coffee table.

"Nice place," Adrian said.

"Thanks." She smiled slowly, with barely hidden intent. "Forgive my appearance," she said, crossing the plush carpet to sit. "But I was already in for the night."

Adrian sat across from her, watching as the candlelight played off her face and hair. She crossed legs that shimmered, looking as supple as her lips.

"You're different tonight," she said. "Your energy has changed. You're not upset or uneasy like you were in the Union."

"No."

"Why?"

"I don't know."

Penny seemed to think for a moment. "You're telling the truth, aren't you?"

"Yes."

"You want to stay the night with me."

"Yes."

"You need something."

Adrian felt a shudder run through her. It was dangerous, birthed from that same somewhere where anger resided and brewed, waiting to be called forth. It was the fire she always sought after, only it wasn't. The flames weren't licking up her insides like they usually did.

"Yes, I can see it in your eyes. They're flashing tonight." She stood. "I know that look."

Adrian stood as well, her heart thumping, forcing heavy, leaden blood through her. She felt bold. Fierce. "Are you analyzing me?"

The corner of her mouth lifted. "Yes. Does that bother you?"

"I don't think anything can bother me tonight."

"Be careful. I'm listening, you know. And I'll hold you to that."

"I look forward to it."

Penny curled her index finger. "Come on, then. Follow me."

They walked down a dark hallway to the last room on the end. Double doors led into a dimly lit master bedroom with dark carpet, heavy black lacquer furniture, and a large flat bed covered in black satin sheets. Blue bulbs burned in several wall sconces, sending fins of eerie light onto the walls.

Penny crossed to the bedside and lit two candles, then shook out the match. Adrian breathed in the spent sulfur and approached. Penny welcomed her by pressing her hands to her chest to ease her out of the leather jacket. It fell to the floor in a heap but Penny wasn't concerned.

"Let's get you out of these clothes." She worked her T-shirt out of her jeans and pulled it over her head. Her eyes flickered when she saw Adrian's bare breasts.

"Very nice." She took a nipple between her finger and thumb. She tugged roughly.

"Ah—ah," Adrian let out.

"Do you like that?" She did it again, pinching first.

Adrian hissed again and clenched her jaw. The pain was fierce and fast, followed closely by a rush of heat. Her nipple bunched so hard it ached, and a hot pressure pushed behind her clit. Penny narrowed her eyes with desire, tugging hard on her jeans, tearing the buttons open easily. She shoved them down firmly and Adrian stepped out of them and kicked them aside, completely nude.

A warm hand trailed across her face as Penny angled her lips up toward hers. Just as they were about to kiss, the heel of her hand pushed against Adrian's sternum, sending her sprawling back onto the bed. Strong legs straddled her as Penny pinned her arms above her head, binding them quickly around the wrists. Adrian tugged, unable to move, and watched as Penny lowered herself to do the same to her ankles.

"If you want free, you better say so now," she said, standing next to the bed.

Adrian clenched her jaw again, her flesh throbbing between her legs.

She had only one concern. "You aren't going to hurt me, are you?"

Penny stripped off her robe. "Pain is guaranteed. Coupled with pleasure. But rest assured, pain alone will not be experienced here."

Adrian blinked at her shiny black corset. It fit her contours like a second skin, curving just under her breasts to push them upward and out. Her soft, large nipples had a purple tint to them and they puckered as she moved, breezing across the room to retrieve something from a large walk-in closet. When she emerged she carried it at her side, dragging what looked like thick strings along the carpet. She moved quickly, coming up to the side of the bed with a hard look in her eyes.

"What—" Adrian tried to speak but Penny surprised her by raising her arm and bringing down the tails of the whip. It lightly stung all across Adrian's torso, causing her to call out and jerk.

"Here's my touch," Penny said. "This is all me. You feel it?" She raised the whip again and again, using the flat leather flails on Adrian's breasts, then trailing them slowly down to her belly.

Adrian watched, breathing heavily. The whip was actually a flogger with rainbow-colored flails. Each was knotted at the end with fur extending beyond that.

"I asked you a question," Penny said sternly. "Do you like my touch?"

"Yes," Adrian said, surprisingly strong.

"Oh you do, do you?" She moved the flogger along her body, down to her hips. Then she brought it down again, stinging her waist and hips and just above her pubis.

Adrian gasped, the pain sharp for a split second, then burning blissfully. And as Penny moved down her body, she began to anticipate each biting snap, clenching her teeth and tugging at her bindings. By the time Penny turned her attention back to her breasts, Adrian was covered in a thin sheen of sweat. Her skin burned and tingled, alive and yearning.

"Do you like my touch?" Penny asked again.

"Yes," Adrian said, her voice threatening to give out.

Penny pulled the flogger away, and the flails retreated like the ocean before a large wave. She brought it down harder than before, stinging her breasts in a dozen different places at once.

"Do you like it?" Penny called out again and again.

Adrian flexed her ass, pushing her back up off the bed, arching her herself into each blow.

"Yes!" she cried. "Yes, yes!"

Penny stopped and dug at the braided leather handle of the flogger. She pinched something between her fingers and crowded over Adrian.

"What are you doing?" Adrian asked, watching helplessly. Penny set the whip on Adrian's stomach and grabbed her nipple with one hand while sliding something on it with the other.

"Ah!" It was a bobby pin. A small bobby pin, pinching her nipple. Penny moved quickly to the other breast and did the same thing, leaving Adrian tight with sweet pain. The pins were so small and tight, her nipples looked pale. Then the flogger came down again. One, two, three times, right across her breasts.

Breath caught in her throat as the knots brushed the pins, tugging on her nipples. She cried out louder as the stinging intensified.

"Do you like my touch?" Penny asked, bending to quickly flick her tongue at her nipples.

Adrian groaned, a hiss escaping her as she threw her head back when Penny resumed her actions.

And she stopped again. Adrian's eyes widened as Penny raised the burning candle over her.

"How about now?" she said, dribbling the hot wax down onto her nipples.

Adrian winced and cried out, and for two white-hot seconds she thought she was going to come out of her skin. But then the pain dissipated, like smoke from a match, and she licked her lips and tried to catch her breath.

Penny didn't give her long. She laughed wickedly as she poured the rest of the wax, covering first one breast and then the other.

Adrian thrashed, almost unable to take the exquisite torture.

"Yes, that's a girl," Penny said from the foot of the bed. The flogger snapped and Adrian opened her clenched eyes and watched. Several more light blows followed, and even as the wax still gripped her nipples in heat, Penny crawled between Adrian's legs and forced them farther apart, pushing her knees up and out. The leg binds had given a bit and as Adrian was wondering how, Penny once again started with the flogger, trailing the tails across her swollen flesh.

The sensation was overwhelming, almost incomprehensible. Another teasing touch of the flogger had Adrian starting to close her legs, but Penny dipped her head farther and buried her face in her, hot wet tongue bathing her. This time a scream did come and Adrian tensed and pulled as hard as she could at her binds, wanting desperately to hold Penny's head to her and fuck her madly.

But all she could do was watch and feel and take. And oh, it was so fucking insanely good. She moaned and held her breath repeatedly as she held her head up off the bed, watching. Penny's head shook from side to side, sucking her so hard it made tight slurping sounds.

"You're going to come now," she said, tearing her mouth from her for a second.

Adrian nodded, desperate.

"Because I'm letting you," she added. "You understand?"

She nodded again.

Then Penny re-attached herself and shook her head, pulsing at Adrian's clit with her tongue as she sucked her.

Adrian bit her lower lip and pumped into her and Penny grabbed her hips and pressed herself into her harder.

"Oh God, yes," Adrian said as the pleasure came. "Oh fucking God, yes."

She pumped again, unable not to. Penny held fast to her, sucking her hard, bobbing at her with her tongue as she held her in her mouth.

"Oh fucking God, yes!" And she came, screaming at the top of her lungs, thrashing like a madwoman, a prisoner breaking free from a deep, dark cell. Her body arched up off the bed, slick with sweat, strained with burning need. Penny stayed on her, holding tightly to her flesh, forcing her to take it all, all, all and then more, more, more until Adrian was begging for mercy with nerves so sensitive she couldn't bear another pinprick of touch.

"Please. Please." She kept moving her hips but now it was to escape the hot, sucking mouth. At last Penny released her and there was a smacking sound. Adrian drew her legs together, panting.

Penny looked like a sated vampire with Adrian running down her chin.

"Did you like my touch?" she asked, deadly serious.

"Yes."

"Good." She crawled up Adrian's body and sank her knees down on either side of her head, resting her shins on her shoulders and her ass on Adrian's upper chest. "Now you're going to like my touch in another way." She lifted herself and maneuvered over Adrian's face. "You're going to feel me with your mouth. And you're going to feel me real good, aren't you?"

She lowered herself farther and Adrian felt her bare flesh and the edges of the black corset. Her panties were slit down the center. *Crotchless.*

Penny made a small noise as she came down on her. Adrian tasted her at once and felt the heat of her arousal. She was wet and swollen, her clit easy to take hold of. She sucked her lightly at first and watched as she jerked and drew into a steady rhythm.

"Oh yeah, girl. Suck that. You know you like it." She moved quicker and Adrian began to use her tongue, slipping it just inside her opening, rubbing it against the ridged skin. Penny stopped speaking then. Just made deep guttural noises. And then right before she came she started again.

"Oh yeah. You're going to do what I tell you to do, aren't you? Like a good girl. Like a bad girl. Uh."

She rocked faster. She let out a long hiss and then came, smashing herself down on Adrian full force, rubbing herself furiously. Her thighs cinched around Adrian's head and she could no longer hear. Everything was muffled and muted and heavy and forceful. She couldn't breathe and started to squirm.

Penny rode her out long and hard, her flesh pulsing and pushing. Adrian kicked and moaned. And just as she was about pass out, freedom.

She gasped for air and blinked for focus. Penny was nowhere to be seen.

She called out for her but there was no response. The room flickered menacingly in the candlelight.

"Hello?"

Silence. Her nipples ached, so badly she imagined them chained to hooks hanging from the ceiling. Each breath felt like the chain tightened, stretching her upward.

"Hello?" she shouted.

"Shh, shh." Penny drifted into the room once again wearing the silk robe. She came quickly to the bed and worked the wax with her fingers, peeling it from her skin. Once the nipples were exposed she slid off the bobby pins and Adrian felt her eyes widen with great relief.

"Ah, ah God. Thank you," she groaned. And then her throat tightened as she caught sight of Penny's dark, deadened eyes. The hunger and curiosity Adrian had originally seen in them was gone. Adrian caught her own scent coating Penny's lips. It was strong now, and suddenly unappealing. This wasn't what she wanted. Wasn't *who* she wanted. The room became strange and threatening. This wasn't home. This was a stranger's home. Anxiety filled her soul and pushed into her mind. She had to go. Now.

"Untie me," she whispered urgently.

Penny stopped moving. "Are you sure? We're not finished yet."

"I can't do this."

"You just did."

"It was a mistake." Oh God, she just wanted to go. She tugged at her bindings. "Let me go. Please."

Penny stared at her some more, as if she didn't want to believe her. Then she unbound her wrists. Adrian sat up and loosened the binds on her ankles and bolted from the bed.

"What's wrong?" Penny asked, watching her dress.

Adrian didn't answer, knowing if she did she'd lose it completely.

"Adrian?"

"I can't." She tugged on her shirt, not bothering to smooth it out. "So please stop asking." Her voice shook. "I just can't." She stepped into her shoes and patted her jacket to find her keys.

"Why not?"

Adrian headed out the bedroom door and down the hallway. When she reached the front door, she felt Penny's hand close around her arm.

"Adrian, stop."

"No."

"Tell me what's wrong. What's the problem?"

"I need more than this." *I need*— She thought of those sparkling green eyes, sun and sand–colored hair. The gentle voice, the kind words. The slender fingers. Morresay. It came like a whisper in her mind.

"More? More what? You don't think this was more than just a scene, do you?" She shook her head. "Adrian, come on. Don't tell me you're like all those other women. Don't tell me you want all that commitment bullshit."

"No, I—I don't want those things—not with you."

"Well, good. Because I don't want them either." She dropped her hands and Adrian noticed again the vacant look in her eyes. She'd shut off. Adrian might as well have completely vanished. She knew exactly what it felt like to *give* that look. And for the first time ever, it made her sick.

"Listen, it's been real. But you need to go now. I don't want any drama up in here. I'm drama free, baby."

Adrian trembled and swallowed painfully. She was hearing what many of her former lovers had heard from her. Realizing that only made it harder. She felt so frail and slit wide open. She would've given anything for an embrace, for a calm pat of understanding. Someone just to say it was all going to be okay. But she knew she wouldn't get it. And she didn't deserve it.

Penny must've seen the tears forming in her eyes because she straightened with a determined expression and sighed. "Look, it's not you, it's me."

Adrian could only blink. And then a strange laughter came up from her chest. How many times had she said that, never truly grasping the meaning?

"No, Penny. You're wrong. This time it's all me."

Leaving her with a look of bewilderment, Adrian stepped out the door.

With the car started she took off, peeling down the street. She drove until she was out of the neighborhood and then pulled over at an abandoned gas station. The ground was slick with patches of ice and she almost fell a few times after she exited the car. Leaving the door open, she ran to the back of the station and faced the woods.

Grabbing her head, she screamed as loud as she could and then fell to her knees, broken up with sobs. Her chest tightened and burned and then burst forth with powerful sobs. Hot tears streamed down her face. She cried for herself, for her life, for her loneliness and inability to find love. She cried for her mother, for her life, for the constant abuse she took. She cried for all of it until there were no more tears to come.

CHAPTER TWENTY-THREE

I'm really worried about you," Tamara said for the third time. "Won't you please come to lunch with us or something?"

Adrian blinked, her eyelids heavy. "Not today. I don't feel like it." She was still in bed, a heap of covers on top of her. The clock read two p.m. It was Sunday. Or was it?

"What's today? Sunday?"

"Yes. Adrian, I'm really worried. You don't talk at lunch, and when we speak on the phone you hardly say two words."

"I need time alone. That's what you've always said."

"Yes, but not like this. This isolation. It's not good."

"I'm fine. Just tired." She was, indeed, incredibly tired. She just felt drained and completely devoid of life.

Tamara sighed. "Will you call me tomorrow?"

"Yes."

"I mean it. Call me."

"Okay."

They rang off and Adrian tossed the phone aside and turned over. Her bed felt cool and comfortable, tempting her to remain. But her eyes were no longer heavy. She rose and crossed to the bathroom. Her reflection told her tale.

A pale, drawn face with deep blue eyes stared back at her. Her hair had grown a bit over her ears and long on her neck. It stood up on one side. Her fingers trailed along the dips in her collarbones and the white plains of her flat stomach. Her nipples had recovered slowly from the night with Penny but she no longer touched them, uninterested in anything that reminded of her sex or intimacy.

The shower came to life as she turned the knob. She waited for it to steam before stepping inside. At once she sighed and relaxed, the water a blessing, a kind, caring friend she always seemed to forget about until she was under its touch once again.

It was the only time of day her face softened enough to almost smile. She let it come now, let it spread across her face. Today it remained a little longer but it still felt foreign, stinging her cheeks as if they were cracking and made of stone.

She let it ease from her face and turned the water a bit hotter, wishing it could somehow massage her bones. When she finally emerged, she dressed in soft jeans and a gray flannel shirt. Pages of artwork hung limply along the edge of her dresser and she had to weave through canvases as she made her way to the living room. She'd done nothing but sleep and create, and her apartment was overflowing with finished canvases and rolled papers. She still hadn't figured out what she was going to do with them all, if anything.

She assumed her position on the couch and stared through the television. Nothing interested her, not even the Discovery Channel. Empty soda cans stared at her from the coffee table, along with paper plates and old issues of the newspaper, still unopened. A stack of mail sat below the papers. She didn't feel like cleaning but she didn't feel like staring through the television, either. She rose and pulled open the blinds, sending sunlight streaming in. Dust particles danced and floated down onto Two, who was sitting in the light, squinting.

She knelt and scratched his head, warming at the sight of his huge golden eyes. One immediately came trotting over, eager for attention. As she petted them she realized she'd been neglecting them as far as physical attention.

"Poor guys." They both rolled to their backs, happy to lounge in the large square of sunlight. She left them and gathered the trash off the coffee table and dumped it in the garbage bin. She slid in some CDs she hadn't heard in a long while and hummed as she worked, dusting and then vacuuming. She found herself smiling as some of the old songs came on. They brought with them old memories, fun memories. And when she finished cleaning, she put in a load of laundry, cracked open the front window for a fresh cold breeze, and created some new playlists on her iPod.

She was downloading some new songs and considering snacking for dinner when someone knocked at her door.

Surprised, she rose and looked out her peephole.

"It's Harriet!"

Adrian opened the door. "Harriet, hi." She stepped aside. "Come on in."

"Thanks," she huffed, carrying a good-sized box.

"Here, let me get that." Adrian eased it from her arms and set it down.

"This is nice," Harriet said, looking around.

"You should've seen it this morning." She closed the cracked window, the room taking in a chill. One and Two scampered at the loud noise.

"Aw, I didn't mean to scare them." Harriet tried to woo them back with soft kitten calls.

"You didn't. They'll come back." Adrian glanced at the box and rocked on her feet, hands in pockets. Then she pointed to the couch. "Have a seat."

Harriet did, crossing her legs with a smile. She nodded at the box. "Those are for you."

Adrian took a peek. "Books?"

"Not just books. Lesbian books."

Adrian raised an eyebrow.

"Tamara said you'd probably never read any. There's all kinds in there. Romance, mystery, sci-fi."

"Lesbian characters?"

"Uh-huh."

She leafed through a few, intrigued. It had been ages since she'd last read. But as she thought about it, she couldn't recall why.

"Thank you."

"You're very welcome. I thought they might cheer you up."

Adrian joined her on the couch. "So Tamara sent you." She shook her head. "I told her I was okay."

"She's worried. In fact," she looked around, "I'm worried too. You don't look well, Adrian."

"I'm okay. I'm coming around."

"Truly?"

"Yes, truly."

"What have you been doing? Have you been okay?"

Adrian stood and walked to the kitchen table. She switched on the light as Harriet rose and joined her.

"This," Adrian said pointing to the canvases stacked and leaning against the wall. A neat pile of her drawings sat on the table with tissue paper edged between each one. It had taken her a while, but she'd put everything together in the dining area.

Harriet gasped and moved to tug on the leaning canvases. She riffled through them all like someone searching for their favorite album. "These are incredible," she said. "You must've spent hours and hours on these."

"One a night. Two on the weekends."

"Good heavens."

"Probably explains why I look like shit. I've done nothing else other than go to work."

"Yeah, Tamara had said you'd even missed some classes."

Adrian shrugged and walked back to the couch. Morresay was off-limits. But she couldn't explain that to Harriet or anyone else.

Harriet returned to the couch and sat. Her posture was perfect but not in a snobbish way. She crossed her denim clad legs again and Adrian noted her Nike runners and a soft-looking jacket. Her hair was down and nearly shimmering.

"Tamara shouldn't have sent you. I'm fine."

"Are you?"

"I wasn't." She pushed out a long breath. "But I think I'm going to be okay. I feel different. Like I don't need to do the same things I've always done."

"You mean like dating?"

"Yes." She laughed a little. "I don't think Tamara believes me, but I haven't seen anyone. I don't even log onto the chat room anymore."

Harriet seemed to consider what she said. "She believes you, Adrian. But she's still worried about your well-being."

"Well, I don't know what she wants from me. I'm doing the best I can."

Harriet shifted, pressing her lips together as if what she was about to say was difficult. "Adrian, I came over here because I wanted to talk to you about that."

Adrian grew nervous.

"I know we don't know each other very well, but I'm hoping we can change that."

Adrian agreed. "I'd like to."

Harriet smiled and folded her hands in her lap. "I am worried though. About Tamara."

"Why?"

Harriet blinked a few times and searched the room. When her gaze finally fell back on Adrian, she spoke. "It's you, Adrian."

"Me?"

"Tamara's a wreck. She's worried sick. It's not just about today. Or last week. Or even last month. Tamara has been looking out for you, taking care of you, and worrying about you for a long, long time."

Adrian felt like she'd just been slapped. "What are you saying?"

"I'm saying I'm worried about her. I'm worried your friendship is too codependent."

"You want me out of her life? Is that what you're saying?" Her mind raced and her insides knotted painfully.

"No! No, of course not. I'm not saying that at all." She looked alarmed. "Maybe I'm saying this wrong. Please, it's not like that. I like you, Adrian, and Tamara loves you."

Adrian struggled to breathe. Her throat had tightened and threatened to close off with anger and tears.

Harriet touched her hand. "Oh God, I'm sorry. I didn't mean to— I'm just so bad at this." She rose and brought Adrian a tissue from the end table. She sat and gave Adrian a few moments before she continued. "We're worried about you. And I think it would help Tamara a great deal if you started caring about yourself as much as she does."

The words sent Adrian over into tears. She cried into the heels of her hands, her body shaking. Harriet slid over to her and wrapped her arms around her. She didn't tell her to stop, she just held her and soothed her. Adrian turned into her and allowed herself to be fully embraced. She couldn't control herself and she couldn't stop. It just came and came like it had that night after Penny's. It didn't hurt her chest as badly this time, and when she finally managed to stop she felt clearer.

Harriet brought her the tissue box and helped her wipe her face.

"I'm sorry," Adrian said when she was able to speak. "I know things need to change. I'm ready for them to change."

"Are you sure? Because you seem really depressed."

"I have been. The past couple of weeks especially. I just gave up. On women, on love."

"On yourself?"

She sucked in a sharp breath. "Yes. God, it hurts to say that."

"What are you going to do about it?"

Adrian laughed and it burned her throat. "I don't really know. I know I don't want to date. I don't want to even think about women. But I don't really want to think about me, either."

"It's okay to think about women," Harriet said lightly. "Just don't go out with a different one every night."

"No, I'm not. Not at all. Not anymore. I just can't do it anymore."

"But you know you can't sit in here and waste away, right?"

"Yeah."

"What do you like to do? What floats your boat? Flips your switch?"

"Art."

Harriet patted her leg. "Art's a start. What else?"

"Music."

"Go on."

"Movies. Reading."

"Do you like to work out?"

"I used to."

"You should check it out. And look into the other things that you like too. I have an idea." She patted her leg again. "Grab your jacket and put on your shoes."

"Where are we going?"

"You'll see."

❖

Harriet made small talk as she drove. Her car smelled like vanilla, and Adrian was amused at the lazy piles of paperbacks on her backseat.

"I cleaned out my bookshelves today," she said. "Those are going to charity."

"You love to read, don't you?" Adrian asked.

"You have no idea." She pulled into a large shopping plaza and parked in front of a popular local bookstore. She killed the engine. "I'm not the only one."

Adrian followed her inside and was at once hit with the strong smell of coffee and books. It made her smile and she wanted to look around.

"Not yet." Harriet tugged on her hand, forcing her to focus. "Back here." They wove through the store, through dozens of packed shelves, small, trendy sitting chairs, and several people standing about, leafing through their next read.

Harriet turned one last corner and Adrian stepped into the children's area. Colorful rugs and short tables covered the floor. Yellow bookcases lined the walls. About a dozen children were sitting near the corner on one of the rugs. They stirred with excitement when they saw Harriet.

"Hi, guys," she said. She tugged on Adrian's jacket, pulling her next to her.

"What's going on?" Adrian asked, feeling all the little eyes on her.

"It's reading time."

"Okay."

"So how about it? Wanna read to them?"

"Me?"

"It'll be fun."

Harriet addressed the children. "What do you think, guys? Should my friend Adrian read the first book?"

"Yes!" Little hands shot up in the air as they cried out.

Harriet gave Adrian a wink and helped her out of her jacket. Then she handed over a book. "Go get 'em, tiger."

Adrian's skin burned. She was nervous, but not with fear. It was shyness and insecurity.

"Okay, everybody, let's quiet down so we can hear Adrian. This is her first time reading, so let's encourage her to be loud and clear." She gave Adrian a nod and stood in the back.

Adrian settled down on the stool and opened the book. She cleared her throat and breathed deep, then started reading. She paused at the end of every page and showed them the pictures. The kids oohed and ahhed and laughed and giggled. Adrian laughed along with them at some points and as she reached the end of the story she found herself totally relaxed and...moved.

The kids clapped as Harriet came over. To Adrian's surprise, she hugged her.

"That's the first time I've ever seen you truly lit up from the inside, Adrian." She pulled away and held her face. "Hold on to that."

Adrian nodded, unable to speak. Tears threatened again.

"You up for another one?"

Adrian wiped her cheeks. "Yes!"

She took the next book and the kids cheered as she settled down on the stool.

She read with more emphasis and even lightened her voice as she read the characters' dialogue. The kids ate it up and as she caught their smiles and contagious giggles she felt it deep inside and knew Harriet was right.

And she wasn't going to let it go.

CHAPTER TWENTY-FOUR

The coffee shop was strong-smelling, warm, and thankfully, not very crowded. Adrian sipped her mocha and ran her fingers across the smooth page of her paperback. She'd started the book the day before and she'd hardly been able to put it down. It was one Harriet had given her. Lesbian fiction. A mystery.

She'd tried the romances but she hadn't quite been ready for those yet. The idealism was still too far-fetched for her and she'd found herself feeling cynical. So she'd left the box of books alone for a few more days before returning to it and deciding to try a mystery. She was glad she did, very much liking the way she could relate to the main character.

A small beep sounded as the door to the coffee shop opened. Adrian set her book aside and stood.

"Mom." She rounded the table and hugged her, kissing her briefly on the cheek. "Thanks for coming."

"Thanks for calling. I really didn't think you would."

They sat and Adrian watched as her mother hung her heavy-looking purse on the back of the chair. Then she eased out of her dark wool coat. The same coat she'd worn for the past ten years. It had large round black buttons and it scratched Adrian's cheek every time she hugged her. It also smelled like her mother's perfume, which she found soothing.

A short, young waitress came and asked for her mother's order. She scribbled it furiously on a thick pad and hurried behind the counter.

"You know, you should really try something different," Adrian said.

"I like what I like," her mother said, spreading her palms flat on the table top. She was nicely dressed as always in a lavender silk blouse and cream-colored cardigan. This time the pearls were in her earlobes.

"Coffee, black, one sugar?"

"You're making fun of me." She laughed.

"Not at all. It's you. I like that."

Adrian sipped her mocha. It was after seven on a weeknight and she was a little surprised her mother had agreed to come.

"How's Louis?"

"Why?" Her fingers curled, intertwining.

Adrian set down her mug. "Just asking."

"You never ask about Louis."

"You aren't going to tell me?"

"He's fine."

Adrian nodded once. "Anything wrong?"

Her mother tensed. "Why does something have to be wrong?"

"I don't know. You're out with me after five. He demands his dinner at six thirty with you sitting directly across from him."

Her mother looked away.

"Mom?"

"Can't we just enjoy this time?"

Adrian cupped her warm mug, studying her. Something was going on. Quickly she scanned her mother's face and neck for signs of injury. As far as she knew, he'd never struck her mother before, but he did manhandle her and push her around. To Adrian's relief she saw nothing but smooth, pale skin as her mother turned to meet her gaze again.

"Okay, Mom. Let's enjoy our time. It is why I asked you here, you know. So we'd have some time without him."

Her mother seemed to relax a little. "I see you've been reading."

"Yes. Just started back up." She slid it across the table. "It's really interesting. It's about a detective. A lesbian detective."

"Really?"

"Yes. And it's really good."

"I didn't know they had books like that."

"Me neither. The world's changing."

"I guess it is." She lifted the book and skimmed through the pages, then returned it to the table.

"I remembered the other day, while I was reading, how much you used to like to read."

"Oh, I used to love it."

"Then why aren't you doing it anymore?" She'd stopped years ago. Adrian knew because her books had suddenly been boxed up and stacked in the garage.

"I just lost interest." Her eyes were soulful. They always had been. Which was why she always looked away. She knew Adrian could read her.

"Maybe you should start back up."

To Adrian's continued surprise, she didn't argue.

"Maybe." A single finger lifted, then fell.

Usually, she was wringing her hands, holding to them fiercely. She smiled at the waitress when she arrived with her coffee. She sipped it right away. What was up?

"You look well, Adrian. What's changed?"

Adrian drank from her own mug. "A lot."

"Oh?"

"Where should I start?"

"Wherever you like I suppose."

"You act like you have all the time in the world." She chuckled.

Her mother simply looked at her.

"Seriously, what time do you need to be home?" The whole point of their meeting outside the house was so it wouldn't upset Louis. She wanted the least amount of confrontation possible. For herself and for her mother.

"Not too late." She didn't seem concerned.

"Louis didn't give you a time?" He always gave a time. For when she shopped, when she shit, for everything.

"No."

Adrian pushed her mug away and looked around quickly. "You didn't kill him, did you, Mom?" She was half kidding but when her mother looked like she might crumple, she grew very concerned. "What is it?" She gripped her hand. "Are you okay? Did he—" She looked around again making sure no one was listening. "Did he hurt you?"

Her mother shook and cried.

"I'll kill him," Adrian whispered. She'd worked through a lot of her issues with Louis recently through her art, but the thought of him physically hurting her mother still sent her over the edge.

"No." She covered her mouth, trying to get control of herself. "He didn't touch me."

"What did he say?"

"He didn't do anything." She sobbed. "He left."

Adrian wasn't sure she heard right. "He what?"

"He left." She cried some more and wiped her eyes with a paper napkin.

Adrian blinked and sat back in her chair. "Well, where did he go?"

"To her house."

"Her?"

"Yes, that woman he's been seeing. That Claire Ann."

Adrian wasn't following. She'd suspected Louis for years, having caught him in several lies. But actually hearing it was another thing. "How did you find out?"

"Oh, the whole town knows. It's been going on for over a year."

"Did you…know the whole time?" It seemed incredible, but nothing was out of the question when it came to her mother and Louis.

"Yes. I knew soon enough. When he started wearing that god-awful cologne, I knew he was at it again."

"Again?"

Her mother blew her nose with a tissue she fished out of her purse.

Adrian wasn't sure what to say. She watched her mother fidget for a while, hands digging in her purse. She eventually came up with some TicTacs, popping one in her mouth.

"So he's gone?"

She nodded. "He moved out last week."

Adrian's eyes grew wide. "He moved out?"

"Yes."

"Holy shit, Mom. Why didn't you call me?"

"Because I wasn't yet sure he meant it. I—"

"What? What aren't you telling me?"

"I almost killed him, Adrian." She swallowed the last word and gripped the table.

"What?"

"It was either him or me. I just couldn't take it anymore. He had come home and found me quilting and he ripped it from my hands and took a knife to it. It was the one I was making for you, and I—he ran with it to the cellar door and threatened to go put it in the furnace." She stopped, swallowing back more sobs. "And I just lost it, Adrian. I wanted to push him down the stairs. I wanted to kill him."

Adrian squeezed her hand. "But you didn't, Mom."

"I wanted to. More than anything. And I told him so."

"What happened?"

"He laughed and came at me. Blew his breath in my face. I didn't back down. I looked him straight in the eye and told him I would do it. If not the stairs, then while he slept. I'd had enough."

"Mom—"

"I think he knew I meant it. He tossed the quilt aside and said good riddance. He had somewhere he'd rather be anyway. But he made it clear he was leaving me. Not the other way around."

"That's fine. Anyway he goes, we'll take it." She patted her hand. "Why didn't you call me, Mom?"

"You just would've told me you told me so."

"Like hell!" She laughed. "I would've thrown a fucking party is what I would've done."

"Shh! Adrian."

"I don't think you understand how good this is, Mom. You're free."

"I nearly killed my husband and he left me for a tramp."

"I don't care if he left you for the devil himself. He left. And will you stop saying that? You didn't do anything wrong."

"I thought about it and that's bad enough."

"Jesus, Mom, I've been fantasizing about it for years. And so has every other human being in Louis's life. Give yourself a break." She palmed her mug again, thinking. "You don't think he'll come back do you?"

"He took his things. His tools. Everything. He's gone for good."

Adrian suddenly imagined him coming back after fighting with the new woman. She also imagined him changing his mind as soon as he got wind her mother was moving on.

"Maybe you should come stay with me. In case he tries to come back. Or what if he starts drinking again and shows up in his underwear?"

"He moved to California."

"Cali—"

"And I have to sell the house. It's part of the divorce agreement."

Adrian sat dumbfounded. "Where are you going to go?"

Her mother shrugged, chewing on the mint. "I'll get a little apartment somewhere. Someplace nice."

"Maybe near me?"

Her mother focused on her again. "I'd like that."

"Me too."

CHAPTER TWENTY-FIVE

The class was buzzing with excitement, dozens of pairs of hands molding and massaging clay. It was the last session, and most were talking about how they wanted to continue on with Morresay's next class, where they would focus more on each medium. Adrian was considering taking the class, too, already having passed up Morresay's offer on the life art class. It had already started, and even though Tamara had continued to try to get her to go, she'd said no, still unsure of herself around Morresay.

But still, she enjoyed art more than she ever could've imagined. It was like being in her own world with the sounds muted and reality smeared. Only this world was completely under her control and she had full function of her mind and body. And this connection she had between her mind and hand…it was almost magic, and she was unsure where it came from. Her mind just somehow knew exactly what to do, where color needed to go, what finger would smudge just right, and what to try when the answer wasn't there.

It was a miracle. Her miracle.

At least she thought. Until now.

While everyone else chatted and created little dogs or human figures, she sat playing with a lump.

"Nothing's coming to me," she finally said to Tamara, who was molding what looked like a rose.

"How come?"

"I don't know."

"Are you feeling okay?"

That was just it. She'd been feeling great. Better than she'd ever felt. "Yeah."

"Maybe you're tap's dry today. It happens to the best you know."

"Maybe I'm just not going to be able to use clay."

She watched Tamara, moved by her precision. She was rolling out thin, delicate pieces then cutting them and wrapping them carefully to the layer before.

"Why another rose?" Adrian asked.

"Harriet bought me one yesterday. A small white one. Said it represented…" She stopped suddenly and pretended to concentrate. It was obviously a private thing. She changed the subject. "Harriet said you're doing great with the kids. I'll have to come watch next time."

"It's fun." She'd been three times to Harriet's bookstore to read for the children. She'd also signed up to be a reading mentor on Fridays. It was a program at the local elementary schools where volunteers came to help children read one-on-one. Harriet suggested it and did it herself.

"She said you're in the store quite a bit too."

"I was. But all those books started killing my bank account. I had to get a library card."

"She's got more she's ready to give you."

"Really?" She smiled. "I need to get her something nice. For all that she's done for me."

"You already have." Tamara winked. "Me."

Adrian groaned. "Ugh, God. Was I really that bad? So bad that she was worried about you worrying about me?"

"It was pretty bad. I just…I didn't think you cared about yourself or your future."

"I was trying to find what you had found. What everyone else had seemed to find."

"But you're doing fine without a woman. That's what I wanted you to see. You only need you."

"I know." She pressed her thumb into her wad of clay. "I understand now exactly what you meant." She'd been spending a lot of time on her own the past few weeks, not purposely leaving Tamara alone, but really just discovering herself and doing things she was interested in doing.

"You're doing great, Adrian. I've never seen you more content and…at ease with yourself. Really."

She gave her that "you know I mean it so you better accept it" look. "So now if and when love calls, you'll stand a really good chance at a healthy relationship."

"I'm not even thinking about love." The statement wasn't entirely true. The concept of love and lifelong companionship had eked its way back into her mind.

Her gaze drifted once again to Morresay. She had moved from her desk and she stood at a nearby table. She had on worn-looking black jeans tucked into fur lined boots. Her sweater looked soft and it matched her eyes. A gold ring dangled from a chain on her neck as she bent to examine a woman's work. Adrian hadn't seen her wear it before and she didn't want to think what it might represent or to whom it belonged.

"Are you giving up?" Tamara asked.

"I did a long time ago," she said softly, thinking of Morresay.

"Huh?"

Adrian focused back on her piece of clay. "I mean, no." She trimmed around the thumb print and held it up for Tamara's inspection.

"Your fingerprint?"

Adrian nodded. She now knew exactly who she was and what she needed in life. "Not just my print…my identity."

CHAPTER TWENTY-SIX

Her grandmother's hands. Adrian had always been fascinated by them. She sat huddled at a corner table in the coffee shop, sketching the hands from memory. She'd loved everything about them, from the deep grooves in the pads of her fingers to the soft slippery skin on the back of her hand. She didn't know why she'd thought of her, but she guessed it probably had something to do with her nieces, whom she'd spoken to earlier in the day. It had been wonderful and energizing to hear their voices. It filled a part of her she hadn't even realized was empty and she'd promised to call again real soon. It wasn't as good as seeing them, but it would do.

"You should've molded those with the clay."

Adrian looked up, startled. Morresay was smiling softly.

"May I?"

Adrian stood a little and gestured toward the chair. "Please."

Morresay settled in and Adrian blinked a few times, having trouble believing it was actually her. She looked beautiful in a loose peasant blouse and tight jeans. The necklace was no longer around her neck. She pointed at Adrian's sketch.

"Someone you know?"

"My grandmother." She closed the sketch book, suddenly modest.

"The clay," she said. "That's a good idea. I was going to ask you what was going on the other night. I noticed you were having trouble. Was everything okay?"

"I just wasn't feeling it at first. And when I did come up with something it felt way too easy."

"I've been there. I think it's a form of writer's block."

"Feels like it."

"Everything else you've done has been really good. And I see you're still working even though class is over."

Adrian caught a quick flash of pain in her eyes. It was gone so quickly she stared at her, wondering if she'd seen it at all.

"I meant to thank you the other day," Adrian said. "For all your help and everything. But you were swamped with people."

Morresay smiled. "Yes, everyone was saying good-bye."

"Everyone really liked you," Adrian added and then felt a flicker of embarrassment.

"I don't know about everyone," she said softly. "In any case, you're very welcome. Although I'm not sure I helped you all that much."

"You did."

Morresay glanced down at the table and Adrian searched for something to say in the heavy silence.

"I've been drawing quite a bit. Mostly with charcoal."

It seemed to do the trick because Morresay looked back up with hopeful eyes. "Are you enjoying it?"

"Oh, yes." She cleared her throat, feeling a bit exposed by her eager answer.

Morresay chuckled and then stared at Adrian's hand for a moment. Then, slowly, she pressed her hand over hers. "You don't have to hide your feelings for art, Adrian. It's okay to let me know you're liking it."

"I do like it," she said, hoping Morresay couldn't feel the tremble rushing through her. She stared into her eyes, her skin burning so sweetly she almost teared. She opened her mouth to tell her, to ask her if she was married, to ask her if she felt the same. But she halted, remembering that life wasn't fiction. Even if it set your heart aflame and caused everything you were made of to combust and come alive.

Quickly and oh so gently, she pulled her hand away. Morresay moved hers as well and appeared flustered and even embarrassed. Adrian struggled to make her feel better. She wanted her to know she did indeed like her. She just couldn't...touch her.

"You've been drawing as well." Adrian pointed to her hand.

She studied her fingertips. "I should've washed them. I'm sure I look filthy."

"I like it," Adrian said. Morresay's eyes darted to hers and she hurried to explain. "I like to leave it on. I like the way it smells."

Adrian could feel the heat from her gaze. It was as if she were opening Adrian up and touching her with liquid hot hands. Examining her insides like the pieces of a long lost treasure.

"What can I get you?" the waitress asked. It was the same one Adrian saw each visit. Her name was Brittney, and today she didn't seem too keen on being at the shop.

Morresay smiled at her and then thought for a moment. "Tea. With skim milk please."

Brittney didn't bother to write it down before she walked away.

"She's usually friendlier," Adrian said.

"You come here a lot?"

"Only recently."

Morresay took in their surroundings. "I got tired of Starbucks and decided to try something different today."

"On a quest for tea?"

"No. I'd actually wanted a Frappuccino."

"Why didn't you get one?"

"I don't know. I guess I got cold."

Adrian felt her mouth go dry. She pretended to sip her coffee, though it was long gone.

"So what do you do, Adrian? Aside from drawing? God, I can't believe I just asked that. Don't you hate the way our identities consist solely of what job we do?"

"Yes, I guess I do. But then again, my job isn't exactly impressive. I think if it were I'd mention it more often." She grimaced. "What does that say about me?"

Morresay laughed. "I guess it says you're normal. And not very secure about your job. Do you enjoy it?"

"Not really." She fidgeted with a sugar packet. "I was always taught you had to grow up and work hard. I was never told I had to like it."

"I know what you mean. My grandparents were that way. Worked their fingers to the bone at back-breaking jobs for next to nothing for years. They never understood the idea of college or actually doing something you enjoyed. I think they were right in many ways, but I learned from their mistakes too."

"What about your parents?"

"Are you kidding? They'd rather die than work like that, scrubbing someone else's floor for pennies. They were of free mind and spirit and did just about everything they could to not emulate their parents." She paused as Brittney arrived with her tea. She thanked her and dipped the bag in the hot water, bobbing it. "In other words…they were hippies."

"Really?"

"Uh-huh. And I'm not talking the weekend hippies either. I'm talking full-blown. How do you think I got my name?" She chuckled. "I think my dad said he saw it on a street sign one day and decided he liked it as a name."

Adrian laughed. "So what was it like? Growing up like that?" Louis had hated the whole hippie movement and its leftovers. He'd bitched about it for years.

"It was quite nice." She poured in her milk and stirred. "They moved away from the commune before I was born, so I grew up in a small house out in the country. I had a very good childhood. Got to see a lot of places, meet a lot of people. We always had friends, and there was always someone over. We grew our own food and gave back to the community. My father rescued animals and I got to help him a lot. And then of course there was art."

Adrian almost sighed. It sounded so wonderful and free. She would've given anything to grow up like that.

"What about you? You look almost dreamy."

Adrian was leaning on her hand, imagining a childhood different than her own. "Sorry?"

"Where did you go?" She laughed and clinked her spoon on her mug to shake off the excess tea. When she brought the mug to her mouth, Adrian had to look away.

"I got caught up in your story."

"It wasn't really a story." She looked at her expectantly over the rim of the mug.

"It was to me." She sat back and pushed out a long breath. "Do you want the nice version or the not-so-nice version?"

"I want all the gory details."

"Oh God."

"It's that bad?" She set down her mug and her smile fell. "I'm sorry. You don't have to tell me anything."

"I can tell you. It really wasn't all that terrible. Not at first. My mother raised my sister and me after our father died suddenly of an aneurism. We did okay for a while but then the bills became too much and Mom couldn't do it anymore. She started dating, saying she needed help and companionship. I swear she must've married the first one she met. His name is Louis."

"I'm so sorry. That must've been hard to lose your dad like that."

"It was. It was really hard. But luckily I had my mother and my older sister."

"Until Louis?"

Adrian nodded, a little surprised that she was sharing all this. A tiny part of her still felt like her mother. Like she had to hide things and make it all look nice and normal. Ugh. She hated that part of her. Wanted to scream at it. "Louis was a harmless drunk at first. If a drunk can be considered harmless. Life wasn't horrible. Crazy and a little sloppy maybe, but not horrible."

Morresay nodded, listening intently.

"And then he got sober." She studied her hand, unable to keep looking at Morresay.

"And things got bad?"

"Yeah."

"How bad?"

"He became a monster. One hell-bent on control and cruelty."

To Adrian's relief, Brittney refilled her mug. Adrian held it to her lip and blew some air across the surface. As she did so, her gaze fell into Morresay's. It was warm and kind and encouraging, asking Adrian to push the door to her heart open just a little bit further. Adrian took a brave sip of hot coffee and continued.

"Our lives became totally and completely his. He was God in any and all ways. Mother never stood up to him. Ever. And we weren't allowed to. If we did we were verbally and mentally tortured by him and then ignored by my mother." She paused. "Needless to say, I got out as soon as I could."

"And your mother?"

"She's…she's okay now. They just recently split."

"Are you okay?"

"I wasn't, no. But I am now."

"Things like that have a way of hanging on to us."

"Yes, they do."

"That's why art is so important to me. It's helped me through a lot. I can see it's helped you too."

She sipped her tea, watching Adrian closely.

"That's why you started the class?"

"Mmm." She nodded, keeping her hands warm with her cup. "I teach art at the middle school. But I wanted something different. Something less restrained. Something you can't really teach." Her eyes danced. "So I thought on it a while and decided to offer a class for women. One based on art and pure expression. I didn't want to follow the standard teaching methods. I wanted my students to learn themselves as they went. To not worry about whether they were doing it correctly or not. Of course, I'd be there to help and guide, but I wanted it to be freeing and therapeutic."

"I think you've succeeded."

"You think so?"

"I know so."

Morresay drank some more tea. "Are you going to tell me what you do for a living? Or am I being too nosy."

Adrian smiled. She felt like she could tell her anything. "There's not much to tell. I work at an auto parts shop. I do a bit of everything, but mainly I work behind the scenes on the computer or in the warehouse."

"How long have you been doing that?"

"Since high school."

"Wow. And you don't enjoy it?"

"I did at first. I liked having the freedom from Louis and the ability to make my own money. But it got old fast. Every day is the same. In some ways, that's comforting. In others, it's boring."

"Ever think about changing? Doing something different?"

Adrian almost said "like what?" but stopped herself. "Not until recently."

Morresay smiled. "Don't worry. I won't bother you about art anymore."

"You didn't bother me. I've heard everything you've said."

She nodded. "Okay, that's good to know."

"I didn't mean to be weird about it. I just...I've been going through some stuff...life-changing stuff and—"

She held up a hand. "Adrian, you don't have to explain. Just knowing you heard me and considered it is enough."

She took another sip of her tea and glanced at her watch. "I'm sorry. I have to go. I'm late." She stood and dug money out of her jeans pocket. She looked at Adrian suddenly as if something had just come to mind. "You're not going to that art class I was telling you about, are you?"

"The life art?"

"Yes."

"No."

"Didn't think so." She counted out some ones and left them next to her cup. "It was nice seeing you."

"You too."

She made a move like she was going to hug Adrian but then thought better of it and stuck out her hand.

Adrian shook it and felt that instant rush of heat and knowing and understanding again. She clenched her jaw, forcing away her rising blush. Morresay must've seen her expression change because she released her hand, gave a nervous wave, and hurried away.

Adrian watched her go, more shook up and moved by her than ever.

CHAPTER TWENTY-SEVEN

Friday evening Adrian found herself at her kitchen table working the clay into the form of her grandmother's hand. She had a bowl of water, the tabletop covered in newspaper and a loose pile of toothpicks. She'd been at it for over an hour when Tamara called.

Adrian put the call on speaker and turned down her stereo. She was listening to Norah Jones and thoroughly enjoying it. She no longer felt the need for "Cold" although she still loved the song.

"Hey, A. Wanted to see what you were up to."

"Same old, same old."

"Drawing?"

"Nah, I'm working with the clay tonight."

"I don't know how you have any creative energy left. You're at it all the time."

"It's not always there. This clay thing has been bugging me, but someone gave me a new idea to try out."

"Listen, Harriet wanted to know if you'd come to dinner next Saturday."

Really? She was going to paint. Start in on a canvas for Benny.

"I'm not sure."

"Harriet's starting to think you'll never come."

"I see Harriet all the time. She knows I love her."

"So come over."

"I'll try."

"You still need to make sure you have a social life."

"I do. Sort of."

"Some adult lesbian time will do you good."

"Sounds kinky."

"Just come."

"That sounds kinky too." She laughed at herself.

"You're reading too many of those damn books."

They both laughed.

"Are you going to play with clay all night?" Tamara asked.

Adrian started to answer her but then remembered. A quick glance at the clock sent her panicking. She'd been thinking about it since her run in with Morresay at the coffee shop.

"Oh shit, T, I have to go."

"Why? I thought you were going to stay home."

"Not tonight."

There was a pause.

"I'll explain later. Bye."

Ten minutes later she was showered, dressed and out the door. She made it to the college in the nick of time, trotting inside the large classroom with five minutes to spare. She folded the printed-out e-mail with the class information Morresay had sent a while back and shoved it into her jacket pocket.

The room was a good-sized lecture hall with a stage up front. Easels were arranged in a half-circle in front of it. A few students were sitting at them, touching up drawings and talking quietly.

Adrian felt a little uneasy and glanced around quickly for Morresay. To her dismay she didn't see her and she hoped she'd come tonight. Adrian had wanted to surprise her, feeling guilty about not showing any interest in anything she'd suggested. She'd learned recently that sometimes even doing just the little things made those around you feel cared about and heard. Morresay deserved to be heard. And she needed to know that Adrian did appreciate her effort.

She walked slowly down the steps toward the front. A man in a sweater vest and eyeglasses saw her and approached. He whispered like they were in a library.

"Can I help you?"

"I…Morresay asked me to come?"

He nodded like she'd just relayed something to him in secret code.

"We don't have any extra easels, I'm afraid. Unless Morresay brings hers. Would you like to sit and observe?" He gestured toward a seat in the front row.

She agreed softly and slid into the desk. The man moved about and brought out a tripod. He placed it in the center of the room, up on the first step. Then he attached a small video camera and turned it on. A large screen lowered from the ceiling and an image of the stage came to life.

Adrian grew a little uneasy, staring at the nude figures on the students' easels. She realized what the class was and the words "Life Art" sang throughout her head. She wiped her palms on her jeans and looked again for Morresay. Would she sit next to her? Would she draw? Would the model be a woman?

The main doors leading onto the stage opened and Morresay hurried in. Adrian shifted in her seat and almost waved. But Morresay disappeared quickly behind a folding dressing screen.

And suddenly it hit her and her heart nearly jumped from her chest. She half stood, wanting to flee, but the lights came on, illuminating the stage, causing the few wandering students to hustle to their easels and get seated. A hush fell over the class and the quiet man smiled at her and nodded. "I don't believe she brought her easel. Did you want some paper?"

She shook her head and sank back into her seat, feeling trapped and helpless. He slid into the seat next to her and opened a leather briefcase. He began mindlessly flipping through papers.

Adrian tried to control her breathing, but when Morresay emerged wearing a white satin robe she nearly choked. She felt the man look at her and she coughed a little and covered her mouth. Her flesh burned so bad she thought for sure the man could feel it. It nearly caught fire when Morresay spotted her and hesitated. Adrian looked down at the desk, hand on her forehead.

This was why Morresay had asked if she was coming the other night.

Oh God.

Or wait? Had she wanted her to come? Was this why she had recommended it? She looked up as a student rustled with his paper. He was flipping through his pad and Adrian saw drawings of a nude male as well as a female. Morresay hadn't been modeling all along. They'd had others modeling.

Meaning Morresay probably wanted to make sure Adrian wasn't here on the nights she did model.

Oh God. She didn't want me here. Holy fuck.

Morresay kept her eyes toward the left side of the room. She disrobed and stepped into the brighter light. Adrian's heart surged in her ears. She tried to look away, to stare at the desk, but the man would see her and wonder why. She allowed herself to look at Morresay's face. Her cheeks were scarlet. Adrian looked up and caught sight of her on the huge screen. She could see the pulse jumping in her neck.

She buried her head in her hand again and prayed. She prayed for the class to be over. For the fire alarm to go off. For something, anything.

The man next to her rose and for a second she thought maybe her prayers had been answered. But he only moved to the video camera, zooming it in farther. Adrian sank lower in her seat but the image was there, right in front of her, bright and clear.

She swallowed hard as her gaze traveled up Morresay's beautifully long legs to her pale, delicate hips, up the slight curves of her torso to her taut breasts, which moved ever so slightly with her rapid breathing. The bright pink areolas tightened suddenly, and her nipples hardened.

Adrian's breath shook in her chest. Blood rushed madly to every last nerve ending, and suddenly she couldn't bear to look away. She moved her hand slightly and stared openly at the screen, like a long-suffering soul viewing heaven for the first time. She stared, insatiable. Morresay kept her gaze away, allowing Adrian free rein. And free rein she took.

A timer sounded and Adrian tensed. The students all flipped to a new page and Morresay moved. Adrian's heart hammered as she turned, this time facing Adrian. She pulled her hair back and tied it off, then arched her back a little and placed her hand slightly over her breast. Adrian looked away for a moment, and when she looked back, Morresay was staring right at her.

Adrian squeezed the desk and looked away again, embarrassed and ashamed of herself. Morresay would surely understand. But when she looked back again Morresay was still watching her. Looking her dead in the eyes.

Adrian glanced up at the screen, hoping it would help, but it only made it worse. She could see clearly Morresay's racing pulse, her swollen lips, her crimson cheeks, her riveting gaze. She was watching Morresay stare at her.

Adrian shifted again, unable to get comfortable. Even though Morresay was naked and under the lights, she felt like the one under a microscope. She cleared her throat again and tensed as the man next to her continued to flip pages. She could hear every small noise in the room. A timer sounded again. Sooner this time.

Morresay moved. This time opening her legs a little more. Adrian stared at the small patch of golden hairs. Morresay's slender fingers slid down her hip to cover it. Adrian nearly groaned and she crossed her own legs, trying to stop the rushing of arousal pounding toward her center.

Morresay never looked away from her, and when Adrian glanced back up at the screen she saw her lick her lips.

Oh fuck.

The eyes flashed. And did her hand move? Just ever so slightly against her patch of hair?

Adrian kept telling herself she was imagining it. Kept telling herself Morresay was just doing what she was supposed to be doing.

But as Adrian looked directly at her again, there was no denying the heat coming from Morresay. It hit her like an invisible wave, pressing her to her seat, insisting she melt down into it while she sat there and watched, forced to stare into the most dangerous eclipse she could ever imagine.

The timer sounded again and Morresay stood. The students stood as well, and stretched and chatted. Morresay slipped on her robe and disappeared once again behind the screen. Adrian rose, feeling like she had to peel herself from the seat. The man was with the students, going over their work. Quickly, she hustled up the stairs and exited the classroom.

The cold air jammed into her and she huddled against it, hurrying to her car. Her skin still burned despite the frigid cold and it wasn't until she actually went for her car keys that she realized she'd left her jacket behind.

"You forgot this," Morresay said.

Adrian stilled, hand on her door handle. "I didn't know you would be—" She turned.

Morresay moved closer, holding out her jacket. Her face still looked flushed and she still had that hungry, confrontational look about her.

"I know."

"I'm sorry." Adrian took her jacket but didn't feel the need to slip it on. She was still fevered and shook up.

The parking lot was dark and still around them. Eerie. Like the perfect stage for this long-awaited moment.

"Sorry for what?" She stepped closer.

"For…you know."

"For looking at me?" She took another step.

Adrian inched back, feeling the car against her. "Yes."

"Did you not like it?"

She didn't know what to say. "I—"

"Because I liked it. And I liked looking at you." She touched her face and Adrian surged with heat and life. It was a hundred times stronger than any fire she'd ever felt before, like the waves were solar and shooting out from the sun itself. Morresay felt her respond, Adrian could see it in her eyes and she stepped into her, kissing her quickly.

Adrian was completely still. The moment seemed surreal. But then Morresay moaned softly and Adrian lost it. She pulled her closer and returned the kiss, capturing her impossibly hot lips again and again with her own. Morresay pushed into her. When her tongue came, Adrian groaned as if it had touched her clit and she spun Morresay, pinning her to the car. She kissed her deeply then, and held her, wanting her so badly, every last inch of her. Wanting to touch her, taste her, devour her. Wanting to touch and taste all the parts she'd been captivated and stirred by in the classroom.

"Your hand," Adrian said, remembering. She brought it to her face, the hand warm and slender and nearly feather light in her palm. She rested it against her lips and kissed, recalling the way it had pushed against her golden patch of hair. She snuck out her tongue, desperate for a taste.

Morresay's breath hitched and she jerked her hand away and grabbed Adrian's.

"I'm losing control," she said, tugging Adrian to her. "I want you so bad." She pushed Adrian's hand into her loose jeans.

"Oh fuck." Adrian hissed as she felt her fervent, slick flesh. They collided in a fierce kiss, sucking and nibbling, holding lips captive with teeth.

Feeling her so wet and ready and gliding so easily beneath her fingertips, Adrian pushed herself up inside her, curling her two fingers snug against her walls.

The sound Morresay let out was primal and erotic. And suddenly Adrian realized what they were doing. And where. She slid her fingers out and pulled away, her head spinning.

Morresay made a small whimper of protest as their bodies came apart. She was breathless as she adjusted herself and picked up Adrian's fallen jacket.

"Are you okay?" she asked softly.

Adrian was pacing. "I can't do this."

"Why?"

Adrian felt the hurt rising, the disappointment right on its tail.

"The man. The man on your desk—the man I saw you with—"

"The man on my desk?"

"The photo. Who is he?" She stilled, waiting for an answer. The bitter cold started to seep into her skin.

Morresay's face fell. She crossed her arms. "Let's go somewhere and talk."

Adrian knew what it meant, and the hurt was more than she could've imagined.

"I don't want to." It was just better not to know. To just cut and run.

"I don't want to do this here."

"I don't want to do it at all." She opened her car door but Morresay stopped her, holding her arm.

"Please, Adrian. Come talk to me. I'm not going to let you get away this time."

"But you're—"

"Follow me. To my house. Please."

"No one is there?"

She looked confused by the question. "No."

"No one will show up while I'm there?"

"No." She gripped her harder. "I swear to you we will just talk. No one is going to hurt you."

She touched her face and Adrian felt that raging burning and stirring of life. No one had ever had that effect on her before. It scared the hell out of her just as much as it moved her.

"Okay."

"Thank you." She hurried toward her car and Adrian followed her closely, driving to near where Tamara lived.

The house was a little bigger than Tamara's with a garage, a steeped roof, and two front windows. A little courtyard protected the front door. Morresay closed the garage door behind Adrian and led her into the house.

It smelled of warmth and spice and Adrian stood in shock as she took in the sitting room with the great brick fireplace and high-backed reading chair. It was just like the room in her fantasy.

"Would you mind if I start a fire?" Morresay asked.

Adrian shook her head.

"Please have a seat."

Adrian sat on the brown leather love seat across from the chair. She took in the beautiful oriental rug, the brown glass shaded lamps, and the framed charcoal drawings on the wall. A radio was playing light rock softly from somewhere nearby.

"Are those yours?" she asked as Morresay stood, pointing to the drawings. She nearly caught her breath as the firelight framed her form.

"No."

"Where are yours?"

"In my studio."

"Why don't you hang them?"

Morresay laughed softly as she sat next to her. "I have. I have some in my room."

Adrian flushed and looked toward the fire. Her heart jumped to her throat as she saw another framed photo of the same man on the mantel.

"Is he your husband?" she finally asked.

There was a long silence and Adrian felt Morresay's hand rest on her thigh. She felt her move closer.

"Is that why you've been avoiding me? You thought I was married?"

Adrian got lost in her sparkling eyes. The flames from the fire danced in them.

"Are you?"

"No."

"Divorced?"

She smiled slightly. "No."

"Boyfriend? Ex-boyfriend?"

She laughed. "No and no."

"Then who is he? I saw you hugging him in the parking lot one day after class."

"He is Malachy. My brother." She squeezed her hand. "He doesn't live here, and the day you saw us he'd just arrived and he'd driven to the school to surprise me."

Adrian glanced back at the photo. His hair was a bit darker than Morresay's and the eyes were different. But as she looked closer she saw that the smile was the same.

"I feel really stupid."

"Don't."

Adrian stared into her once again. "I acted like a real ass."

"You had reason to. I can see why you suspected that."

"What about the ring you wore around your neck…"

"Ahh." She closed her eyes briefly. "That ring was my father's. I wear it every year on his birthday. He died five years ago."

"I—I'm sorry."

Morresay gripped her hand and squeezed. "Now you know my secret. Why don't you tell me yours?"

"I'm not sure how."

"Try. Please. I know there's more to why you avoided me. Tamara hinted at something but she never said."

Adrian thought for a moment, unsure how to say it. "I've never had a serious relationship." She swallowed. "Ever."

"Okay."

Adrian sighed. "I've gone from woman to woman. Serial dating, I guess you could call it. And lately it's been one nightmare after another."

"Did you enjoy dating like that?"

"I enjoyed the idea of meeting *the one*. The excitement of it. The anticipation. I didn't do it for mindless sex. Well…okay, it usually always led to that."

"What about now?"

"Things have changed. I've changed. I just couldn't do it anymore. I wanted more for my life and I had totally lost myself. So the past few weeks, I've been spending a lot of time with just me. Finding who I am and doing things I enjoy."

"Like art."

"Yes."

"I've also been dealing with my past and trying to let that go."

"Sounds like you're doing well."

"I am. I really think I am."

"And that's why you're scared of me."

Adrian blinked, surprised at her accuracy.

"Other than thinking I was married," Morresay added.

"Yes."

Morresay touched her face, lightly stroking her jaw. "We have a dilemma, then."

Adrian struggled for breath. She was a thousand burning suns, Morresay her energy.

"And I'm already breaking my word by touching you."

Adrian covered her hand, holding it to her face. "Don't stop."

"I have to. If I don't I'll lose control. And if you don't think you can do this or want to do this…"

"I want to do it. I want you—more than I've ever wanted anything. I'm just afraid."

"But what if it's just easy and wonderful and beautiful?"

"I don't know if I believe in beautiful. I mean, I know it exists. I'm just not sure it exists for me."

"I know you haven't seen or had it much in your lifetime, but I promise you it does exist. For you."

"Really?"

"Very much so. In your heart you know it's possible. It's the risk you have to take to get it that's scaring you."

They stared at one another for a long moment and Adrian heard "Cold" beginning to play on the radio. As the lyrics came, everything in her seemed to stir to life and beat in tune with her racing heart. How many times had she listened to this song, dreaming about love and passion and the fire she always craved? Countless times. And now it was playing for Morresay. For Adrian. For what she'd finally found.

Adrian leaned in and kissed her as if the journey she'd trekked to reach her had been fierce and long and had lasted decades.

Morresay responded right away, reaching up to thread her fingers through her hair as she moaned softly. Adrian had never tasted anyone so sweet, so warm, so seemingly made just for her. When Morresay pulled away it felt like a piece of her was missing. She reached for her…desperate.

"We can take it slow," she said, touching Adrian's lips. "If it will help."

"I don't think I can. I've already touched you and nothing will ever be the same for me again."

"Then let's go slow another way."

"How?"

"Tell me what it is you want at this very moment."

"You."

"How do you want me?" She trailed a finger down her neck. "Tell me how you've thought of us. What were you thinking about when you were watching me today?"

"So many things."

"Close your eyes."

Adrian did and leaned back against the couch.

"Now tell me what you see. What you want."

"I see you. You're naked and you're standing in front of me."

"Go on."

"You come to me and put my hands on you. We kiss."

"Then what?"

"You tell me you want me inside you and you crawl on top of me, taking my hand and putting it between your legs. I slip inside you…"

"Open your eyes, Adrian."

Adrian sighed and opened her eyes. Morresay was standing in front of her completely nude, firelight kissing her skin. She came toward her, took her hands softly and placed them on her hips. Adrian shuddered at the smooth, warm feel of them.

"Touch me," she whispered, cupping her face.

Trembling, Adrian pressed her lips to her stomach and ran her hands up and down her beautiful body. Morresay sighed and arched into her, running her fingers through Adrian's hair.

"Your fingertips feel just like I imagined. So talented and knowing. Bringing me to my knees."

She knelt and kissed Adrian passionately, her tongue pressing into her eagerly, swirling and claiming, growing hungrier and more demanding by the second. She pushed Adrian back and crawled atop her, straddling her lap.

Breathless, they separated and she took Adrian's hand and led it slowly down her bare skin to her center.

"I want you inside me," she said.

Adrian stared into her face as her fingers found her slick folds and slid deep inside. Morresay nearly crumpled, eyes closing, mouth falling open to suck in a quick, shaky breath.

"Oh God." She held tight to Adrian's shoulders and began to rock. "Oh God. Adrian!" Her eyes flew open and they looked wild and dangerous and so completely pure with raw beauty. Adrian cradled her jaw, wanting to capture the look on her face and remember it forever.

Morresay made small noises and turned her head to take Adrian's thumb in her mouth. She held it with her teeth and then sucked on it.

"You're beautiful," Adrian whispered. "So, so beautiful."

"Mmm." She lifted her chin, releasing Adrian's thumb. "You are, Adrian. And I've been thinking about you for so very long. Watching you. Wanting you, moved by you and your inner passion. Oh God!" She moved faster, eyes locked on Adrian's. "I can't believe you're here. I can't believe you're in me. Tell me, tell me how you feel."

Adrian could hardly speak so caught up in everything about her. "I—you—are so amazing. So beautiful. The most beautiful thing I've ever seen. Ever felt."

"And you've wanted me."

"Yes."

"Longed for me."

"Fuck yes. I've dreamt about you. Fucking ached. So deep down inside. I couldn't stop it. Not for the life of me."

"And—oh God—" She clenched her eyes closed, too worked up to finish her sentence. "Adrian. You feel so good. Oh! Oh God, you feel so damn good fucking me." She was writhing, quickening her hips.

Adrian pushed up with her fingers, loving the way she felt all hot and slippery, encasing her. She studied her smooth skin, the undulation of her beautiful muscles, those beautiful curls dangling next to her face. Adrian did what she'd longed to do since one of the very first times she'd seen her. She loosened Morresay's hair clip and gasped at the tendrils of sun and sand–colored hair as they tumbled down on her shoulders.

"This," Adrian whispered, running her hand through it while staring deep into her eyes. "You, me, my life, the way I feel about you. This is what I would call perpetual happiness."

Morresay's breath quickened and she made a noise like she might cry. "Kiss me, Adrian. Kiss me now. Kiss me while I—"

She took Adrian's mouth with a savage need, shoving her tongue deep inside again and again, emulating Adrian's fingers. Her cry was powerful, pushed into Adrian, eaten up by the kiss. Another cry escaped her as she tore her mouth away and bit into Adrian's neck and ear.

"Oh God, Adrian. Oh my dear God," she said, her body finally slowing. She held Adrian's face and kissed her several times as spasms shot through her. She laughed, deep and nearly hoarse when she finally stilled.

"That was…"

"The most incredible moment of my life," Adrian finished.

Morresay blinked slowly, as if she couldn't believe Adrian was real. "You're really here."

"Yes."

"Come here." She stood and tugged on Adrian's hand. They embraced in front of the fire and Adrian inhaled her chai scent and pressed her hands to her moist back. "I don't ever want to let you go," she said, holding Adrian tighter. "I want to stay just like this forever."

Adrian closed her eyes. "I've imagined this moment. Just like this. The room, the chair, the fireplace."

"Me too."

"It's you in my arms. It's been you all along." She held her tighter. "I think I'm starting to believe in beautiful."

Morresay laughed softly. "If you'll let me, I'll show you beautiful each and every day."

She pulled away and swayed with her, hands tangled in the back of her hair, arms resting on her shoulders.

"Would you like to stay the night?" Morresay asked.

"Yes."

"In my bed?"

"Yes."

"In my arms?"

Adrian kissed her. "Yes."

Morresay took her by the hand and led her to the bedroom. She flicked the light switch and a small lamp in the corner softly breathed upon the room. The shade was draped with a red sash, and a red Indian patterned bedspread covered the queen-sized bed. The room felt warm and welcoming, like Adrian had just stepped into a familiar place in her own heart. A place she knew was there but had never walked into before.

"This is nice," she said, taking in the small white dresser and a bountiful plant on a stand. A neat pile of underwear and flannel sleep pants sat on one side of the dresser. Morresay hurried to put them away.

"No, don't." Adrian caught her arm. "Leave them. It's you. How you are. I like it."

Morresay dropped her hands. "Okay," she whispered.

Adrian gently squeezed her hand and moved to the two drawings that hung on the walls.

"These are yours?" Adrian asked. They were of people, women in flowing dresses, staring into the sun. In the other a woman was kneeling in the forest, earth clenched in one hand. They were incredible, the detail breathtaking. Adrian touched the frame, wanting to stare at them for hours.

"That's how I feel about your work," Morresay said, standing next to her.

"Like you could look at it for hours?"

"More like days."

She led her to the bed. "And I could look at you for days." She began to undress her. "Is this okay?"

Adrian nodded.

She slipped her sweater over her head and touched her breasts, massaging them through the thin T-shirt. Then she slipped that too over her head.

She licked her lips as she stared into Adrian's eyes. And then, with slow deliberation, she dropped her gaze and took Adrian in. Adrian saw and heard her breath catch. Then she felt her tugging on her jeans, first unbuttoning them and then easing them down. She did the same with her panties, gliding them down slowly and helping Adrian step out of them.

Her lips and breath bathed Adrian all the way back up.

"Morresay," Adrian whispered, threading her fingers into Morresay's hair.

"Tell me, my love, tell me." She trailed her tongue up Adrian's thighs and skimmed the lips framing her throbbing flesh. "Tell me you want me to taste you."

"I—" Her tongue was already there, pressing inside, lightly touching her clit. "Ye-es."

Morresay groaned and gripped her hips, working her way all the way in, tongue lapping fully at her, saturating her clit again and again. Adrian hissed and clenched her eyes closed, hands now tangled in her hair.

"Oh my God," Morresay panted, working her long and slow. "You are—" She groaned again. "Unbelievable."

Legs weak with pleasure, Adrian stumbled backward and Morresay pushed her onto the bed. She crawled on with her and threw back the bedcovers, encouraging Adrian to burrow under them. Then she pulled the covers up and worked her way back down between Adrian's legs.

"Wait," Adrian said. "I want to look in your eyes the first time."

Morresay smiled and slid along her side. She kissed her breast and teased her nipple as she trailed her hand up Adrian's thigh to her wet flesh. There she sank her fingers alongside her clit and stroked, causing Adrian to move beneath her.

"Like this, my love?" Morresay asked, staring into her eyes.

"Yes," Adrian said, already tensing.

"That's it, Adrian. Look at me. I'm right here."

"Mm. Ah, Morre-say."

"Yes." She moved her hand faster, side to side.

Adrian couldn't speak. Could barely hold her head up. She stared into her eyes and...

"Wait."

Morresay stilled.

"I don't want to come yet."

"Why not?"

"I want it to last. This moment. This feeling. It's so good."

Morresay stroked her again, slowly. "Is it?"

"Oh yeah."

"It's good?"

"Really fucking good."

"What if I told you it doesn't have to end? We can go as long as you want. I can tease you as long as you want. Make your flesh pant and ache and beg for it…and then give it what it wants so fast and hard and thorough—"

Adrian gripped her wrist, the pleasure coming.

"Yeah?"

Morresay quickened her hand. "Oh yes." And then she stilled her hand and Adrian gasped. Morresay stroked her again, very slowly, very carefully, milking her. "If I could see this look on your face forever I'd never ask for another thing again."

"I know what you mean," Adrian said, the pleasure building again.

Morresay stopped again and smiled with intent as she made her way down to rest between Adrian's legs. Adrian lifted her head and stroked her face, her flesh already reacting to Morresay's breathing.

Then she watched as Morresay closed her eyes and lowered her mouth to kiss her flesh again, working her way quickly to the insides of her folds. She licked her long and slow, moving toward the center, finally reaching her clit with quick little flicks. Adrian tensed and gripped her hair at her temple, watching her tongue sneak out and press in long, drawn-out movements and then those quick little flicks again.

"Morresay," she whispered, throwing her head back against the pillows.

"Yes," she said and buried her mouth in farther. Her tongue worked harder, over and over her clit in an up-and-down motion and then around and around, teasing it from the sides. "You're so good," she said in between breaths. "Taste so good." She kissed her flesh firmer, longer. "Adrian." And then she pulled her clit into her lips and tugged, sucking it.

Adrian tensed again and lifted her head. It felt too good for words. And seeing that it was Morresay, loving her, making love to her, it made it so good she wanted to scream.

"I—you—" She tossed her head back, the pleasure drawing in and coming closer to that sweet place known only as orgasmic oblivion.

"Tell me, Adrian," she said, sucking her and licking her at the same time, holding her captive in her working mouth.

"I—" But no words would come. Adrian lifted her head again, knotted her hands in her hair, and when she met Morresay's eyes she burst into climax, her face collapsing with ecstasy.

"Yes, Adrian." And she kept on. "Oh God, sweet yes." She kept giving, releasing her clit to swirl around it again and again until Adrian was bucking madly and crying out with sweet prayers, pleading for it to never end. "You're the most beautiful thing I've ever seen."

Adrian clung to her, body shaking. She could feel her flesh flooding and pouring in around Morresay's mouth.

Morresay kept speaking to her, telling her again and again how beautiful she was until Adrian could no longer hold herself up and the pleasure evaporated, leaving her bones heavy and glowing with bliss under her spent muscles. She pulled Morresay up to her and kissed her long and soft, telling her all about the intense pleasure she'd experienced without saying a word.

When she finally finished, Morresay laughed and nuzzled her neck. "I thought it was great too."

Adrian groaned playfully. "Did you?"

"Yes." She hurried out of bed and flicked off the light. Adrian yelped and laughed as she jumped back in to bury with her under the covers.

"Are we going to sleep now?" Adrian asked.

"If we want to take it slow."

Adrian nestled farther into the pillows. "I'm ready to fall asleep in your arms."

"Are you?"

"Mmm-hmm. But you have to promise me something."

"Anything."

"Next time, you tell me what it is you've imagined. And we do it your way."

Morresay kissed her neck, nibbling a bit, causing gooseflesh to erupt along Adrian's skin.

"We better get some sleep, then," she said, laughing wickedly.

Adrian turned into her. "Not after that statement. There's no way we're getting sleep now."

Morresay cried out in laughter as Adrian headed farther under the covers.

CHAPTER TWENTY-EIGHT

I don't believe it," Tamara said as she opened the front door. "It's my best friend Adrian. And she's standing at my door holding a bottle of wine. And wait—it's dinnertime." She called to Harriet. "Honey, grab something. The earth's about to shake."

Adrian just smiled. "Are you going to invite me in?"

"Did you bring a good year?"

"Your favorite."

Tamara waved her in.

"Wait," Adrian said before stepping in. "I brought a guest."

"You brought a what?"

"A guest." Morresay stepped into view, wearing a flowing green blouse, jeans, and a long coat. She stood next to Adrian and held her hand.

Tamara's mouth fell open.

"I told you she'd be surprised," Adrian said.

"Hello, Tamara."

"Morresay." She shook her head in disbelief. "Come in, come in."

The entered the house and Adrian handed over the wine and took Morresay's coat and hung it along with hers. Tamara called to Harriet, who joined them quickly. She looked just as shocked as Tamara.

"Harriet, this is our art teacher, Morresay. Morresay, this is my partner, Harriet."

"Hi, Harriet, pleasure to meet you."

"You too," Harriet said, shaking her hand. "Please, have a seat."

Morresay did so and at once saw the frames on the wall. Adrian followed her gaze and took a second look.

"These are Adrian's, aren't they?'

Tamara had a guilty look. "Uh-huh."

"You went back and got them?" Adrian asked.

"Uh-huh."

"Why?" Oddly enough, she could stand to look at them now. They still made her feel, but it wasn't as sharp as before.

"Because I like them. And because you drew them."

"They're really good, Adrian," Harriet said. "I'm the one who insisted we hang them."

Morresay was obviously confused.

Tamara explained. "Adrian threw them away one night after class."

Morresay held Adrian's gaze. There was no shock or horror or judgment. Just a knowing calm. Adrian had told her just how difficult the feelings the art brought up had been to deal with. "I'm glad you got them," she said to Tamara. "You're a true friend."

Adrian smiled at her and Morresay returned it. They had such a quiet connection. A million words spoken in one long gaze.

"Do you want us to take them down?" Harriet asked Adrian. She was still so sincere and so caring.

"Nah."

"You're sure?"

"I'm okay with them now. You guys enjoy them."

"If you ever want them, they are yours, you know," Tamara said.

Adrian nodded. She never felt more loved than she did at that moment. She smiled, so eternally grateful for these three people.

"Can I get you a drink?" Harriet asked Morresay. "Adrian?"

Tamara spoke up. "I'll get the drinks, honey. Adrian? Would you help me?" She nearly dragged Adrian into the kitchen with her. "What the fuck-fuck? What is going on?"

"She's not married."

"She's not?"

"No. She's not straight either. And…she's crazy about me."

Tamara hopped up and down. "When did this happen? How did it happen?"

"She kept asking me out for coffee, remember?"

"Vaguely. Once."

"No, a couple of times. I kept putting her off, avoiding her. It was killing me because I liked her."

"You did?"

"Yes."

"Why didn't you tell me?"

"Because we agreed she was off-limits. And because I was trying to change. But honestly, Tamara, I was burning for her."

Tamara shook her head. "I can't believe this. She's—she's wonderful, Adrian."

"I know."

"So tell me more. Did she make the first move?"

"She kissed me, T. Told me how she felt. And I melted. When she touched me, it was like a million stars exploded to life inside of me. Every cell in me burned with life. It was amazing and it was crazy and it was…"

"Love," Tamara said simply.

Adrian hesitated and then exhaled long and slow. "Yeah."

"Oh my God. My best friend has finally found love." She enveloped her in a long hug, squeezing her tight.

"Don't get too carried away," Adrian teased. "We are taking it slow, you know."

"Good." But she was all grins.

"As slow as we can, anyway." She recalled the way they could hardly keep their hands to themselves whether they were alone or not. The way Morresay teased her some nights, kissing her long and slow and hot and then whispering good night and blowing a kiss as she slipped out the door, leaving Adrian trembling. The way they forced themselves to do nothing but talk, sitting on the ends of the couch staring into one another with compassion and understanding.

It was the sweetest torture she'd ever experienced, and she couldn't get enough.

"Are you happy?" Tamara asked, studying her closely.

Adrian blew out another breath. "I'm so happy I'm scared shitless."

"Yep." Tamara nodded. "It's love."

Adrian laughed. "You mean this is…how it is?"

"Oh yeah."

"The thinking about her every second? Wanting to stare at her for hours on end? Wishing I could crawl into her soul and feel her around me and in me forever?"

"Yep."

"I think it might kill me."

"It'll come close." She patted her back and set to opening the wine. "But every time you look at her and she looks at you—"

"I'll feel more alive than ever."

Tamara smiled. "You got it, A. You finally got it."

About the Author

Ronica Black spends her free time writing works that move her, with the hope that they will move others as well. She is a firm believer in "that which does not kill you makes you stronger." Each step she takes in life is a journey meant to be experienced, whether it be a smooth step paved with green grass or a rocky one marred with boulders. She keeps stepping, keeps writing, and keeps believing that women are far stronger than they think they are. She's an award-winning author with six books currently published by Bold Strokes Books. She also has several short stories published in the Bold Strokes Books Erotic Interludes series: *Stolen Moments*, *Lessons in Love*, and *Road Games*. Her work also appears in *Ultimate Lesbian Erotica 2005*.

Books Available From Bold Strokes Books

Chasing Love by Ronica Black. Adrian Edwards is looking for love—at girl bars, shady chat rooms, and women's sporting events—but love remains elusive until she looks closer to home. (978-1-60282-192-7)

Rum Spring by Yolanda Wallace. Rebecca Lapp is a devout follower of her Amish faith and a firm believer in the Ordnung, the set of rules that govern her life in the tiny Pennsylvania town she calls home. When she falls in love with a young "English" woman, however, the rules go out the window. (978-1-60282-193-4)

Indelible by Jove Belle. A single mother committed to shielding her son from the parade of transient relationships she endured as a child tries to resist the allure of a tattoo artist who already has a sometimes-girlfriend. (978-1-60282-194-1)

The Straight Shooter by Paul Faraday. With the help of his good pals Beso Tangelo and Jorge Ramirez, Nate Dainty tackles the Case of the Missing Porn Star, none other than his latest heartthrob—Myles Long! (978-1-60282-195-8)

Head Trip by D.L. Line. Shelby Hutchinson, a young computer professional, can't wait to take a virtual trip. She soon learns that chasing spies through Cold War Europe might be a great adventure, but nothing is ever as easy as it seems—especially love. (978-1-60282-187-3)

Desire by Starlight by Radclyffe. The only thing that might possibly save romance author Jenna Hardy from dying of boredom during a summer of forced R&R is a dalliance with Gardner Davis, the local vet—even if Gard is as unimpressed with Jenna's charms as she appears to be with Jenna's fame. (978-1-60282-188-0)

River Walker by Cate Culpepper. Grady Wrenn, a cultural anthropologist, and Elena Montalvo, a spiritual healer, must find a way to end the River Walker's murderous vendetta—and overcome a maze of cultural barriers to find each other. (978-1-60282-189-7)

Blood Sacraments, edited by Todd Gregory. In these tales of the gay vampire, some of today's top erotic writers explore the duality of blood lust coupled with passion and sensuality. (978-1-60282-190-3)

Mesmerized by David-Matthew Barnes. Through her close friendship with Brodie and Lance, Serena Albright learns about the many forms of love and finds comfort for the grief and guilt she feels over the brutal death of her older brother, the victim of a hate crime. (978-1-60282-191-0)

Whatever Gods May Be by Sophia Kell Hagin. Army sniper Jamie Gwynmorgan expects to fight hard for her country and her future. What she never expects is to find love. (978-1-60282-183-5)

nevermore by Nell Stark and Trinity Tam. In this sequel to *everafter*, Vampire Valentine Darrow and Were Alexa Newland confront a mysterious disease that ravages the shifter population of New York City. (978-1-60282-184-2)

Playing the Player by Lea Santos. Grace Obregon is beautiful, vulnerable, and exactly the kind of woman Madeira Pacias usually avoids, but when Madeira rescues Grace from a traffic accident, escape is impossible. (978-1-60282-185-9)

Midnight Whispers: The Blake Danzig Chronicles by Curtis Christopher Comer. Paranormal investigator Blake Danzig, star of the syndicated show *Haunted California* and owner of Danzig Paranormal Investigations, has been able to see and talk to the dead since he was a small boy, but when he gets too close to a psychotic spirit, all hell breaks loose. (978-1-60282-186-6)

The Long Way Home by Rachel Spangler. They say you can't go home again, but Raine St. James doesn't know why anyone would want to. When she is forced to accept a job in the town she's been publicly bashing for the last decade, she has to face down old hurts and the woman she left behind. (978-1-60282-178-1)

Water Mark by J.M. Redmann. PI Micky Knight's professional and personal lives are torn asunder by Katrina and its aftermath. She needs to solve a murder and recapture the woman she lost—while struggling to simply survive in a world gone mad. (978-1-60282-179-8)

Picture Imperfect by Lea Santos. Young love doesn't always stand the test of time, but Deanne is determined to get her marriage to childhood sweetheart Paloma back on the road to happily ever after, by way of Memory Lane—and Lover's Lane. (978-1-60282-180-4)

The Perfect Family by Kathryn Shay. A mother and her gay son stand hand in hand as the storms of change engulf their perfect family and the life they knew. (978-1-60282-181-1)

Raven Mask by Winter Pennington. Preternatural Private Investigator (and closeted werewolf) Kassandra Lyall needs to solve a murder and protect her Vampire lover Lenorre, Countess Vampire of Oklahoma—all while fending off the advances of the local werewolf alpha female. (978-1-60282-182-8)

The Devil be Damned by Ali Vali. The fourth book in the best-selling Cain Casey Devil series. (978-1-60282-159-0)

Descent by Julie Cannon. Shannon Roberts and Caroline Davis compete in the world of world-class bike racing and pretend that the fire between them is just professional rivalry, not desire. (978-1-60282-160-6)

Kiss of Noir by Clara Nipper. Nora Delaney is a hard-living, sweet-talking woman who can't say no to a beautiful babe or a friend in danger—a darkly humorous homage to a bygone era of tough broads and murder in steamy New Orleans. (978-1-60282-161-3)

Under Her Skin by Lea Santos Supermodel Lilly Lujan hasn't a care in the world, except life is lonely in the spotlight—until Mexican gardener Torien Pacias sees through Lilly's facade and offers gentle understanding and friendship when Lilly most needs it. (978-1-60282-162-0)